Bixby Timmons

And

The Dragonthorp Riddle

Bixby Timmons Book I

By

Dwight D. Karkan

TinyFox
PRESS

A Tiny Fox Press Book

ISBN: 978-1-946501-27-1

Library of Congress Control Number: 2020951247

Tiny Fox Press and the book fox logo are all registered trademarks of Tiny Fox Press LLC

Tiny Fox Press LLC
North Port, FL

"Bixby Timmons and the Dragonthorp Riddle is an exciting debut into a world of high-tech gadgets and futuristic technology...**this story is sure to exhilarate young readers.**"

- Jessica Renwick, author of the award-winning *Starfell* series

"**Chock full of original and well-formed characters,** this paced and engaging book, will keep the pages turning well after bedtime. Readers will glean hints of Roth and Dashner as the twists and turns of the vast Holo unfold. Bixby Timmons and the Dragonthorp Riddle is sure to satisfy readers of all ages and **a must have on your YA bookshelf.**"

- S.P. O'Farrell, author of the *Simone LaFray* series

"**Bixby Timmons is a super-smart girl launched into a brainy and original adventure.** Fans of mysteries and thrillers will love the mysterious messages, riddles, and high-tech gadgets in a world that's complex, fun, and **where not everything is what it appears to be.**"

- Russell Ginns, author of the *Samantha Spinner* series

To the moms and dads who parent with veracity, because the next generation deserves our best.

For those who believe in us, even when we have given up on ourselves: for me it is my beautiful wife Amber, my daughters Selah & Delaney, and my man Theo!

And for those in our lives who are there to lift us to heights never imagined. Thank you, Jessica and Galen, along with your teams, for believing in Bixby!

PROLOGUE

IT IS A rare occasion in one's life when the world stands still, and all of humanity pays attention. For Bixby Timmons, she was barely able to tie her own shoes when Daemon Dragonthorp took to the podium on every Holo-Channel in existence and spoke with tears in his eyes.

"Today is a scar on the face of a once noble and proud Dragonthorp, Inc. We don't know why or how, but sometime last night, my passionate, jovial, and genius brother Cody, the creator, brain, and heart behind the entire Holo world, went missing."

The man paused, took a deep breath to recompose himself, then carried on.

"I can promise you all that we will do everything we can to see Cody home safely, and in addition to all of those efforts, I am personally offering a reward of one hundred million dollars to whoever finds him first."

The plea rang across the globe in an instant that day, and it continues to echo throughout the Holo ten years later...

CHAPTER ONE

EXTRAORDINARY NEW BEGINNINGS

Ten years later.

"IT'S NOT FAIR," Bixby Timmons huffed to herself as her family van pulled out of the driveway of the cruddy shed that *used* to be her home.

It was an odd feeling to have everything and nothing at the same time.

To everyone but Bixby, today was the best day of her life. Her father had been given the keys to Pinnacle Manor as the newly appointed caretaker. His job was to make sure all of the digital inner workings of Pinnacle were updated and running in tip-top shape.

For those who didn't know, Bixby and her family were moving into the most glamourous and mysterious house in the world; nobody knew much about what was past the front gates besides a short documentary made right after it had been built. All of her friends were envious of her; after all, who wouldn't be? Bixby would have full access to the last place Cody Dragonthorp had ever been seen, and with the reward money still up for grabs, it was the perfect place for any future hero to get their start solving the mystery.

Thus, Bixby should have been excited. However, all she could think about was what she was losing. How was she supposed to be happy when she felt like she was being forced out of the home she loved?

Bixby slipped in her earbuds as she pulled her hoodie over her curly red hair, yanking the strings tight. She wanted to be bitter for a little while longer so that her dad would feel extra guilty about it all. There was something satisfying about keeping her dad far enough away to make him uneasy; it gave her a sense of control, something she desperately needed right now. From the poorly packed second row of back seats, she watched his sad eyes in the rearview mirror. Her silent protest was being heard loud and clear.

In the rear-facing car seats in front of her sat her twin brothers Darby and Wyatt. For the next eight hours, Bixby would watch them cover everything they touched in the slobber and boogers that slid down their snot-covered faces. Bixby pondered what it would be like to be oblivious to the magnitude of the day as they were.

"Must be nice," Bixby mumbled as she flicked cereal at them. She'd hoped the piece might stick on their booger-soaked skin out of amusement, but it simply bounced off. Even the snacks, apparently, didn't want her to have a good time.

The next eight hours would test the limits of her sanity.

"Coming down the homestretch!" Mr. Timmons announced. A grin peeked from the corner of his normally stagnant face as he made the final turn onto Buckbird Place.

In the rearview mirror, Bixby watched her dad's joy morph from a grin to a full set of teeth, finally ending in jaw-dropping shock as the van began to slow.

"Oh, Cooper!" Mrs. Timmons exclaimed, clicking her makeup case closed and pointing to the spectacle ahead. "Is that it?"

"I'll be an uncle's monkey," Mr. Timmons replied in disbelief.

Up until then, they had not passed another house for what had felt like hours. Through the brush of trees on a hill stood a massive, wrought iron gate with the letters *PM* emblazoned on each barricade. This was most certainly the entrance to their new home. Bixby set aside her grandfather's old lock puzzle she was working and gawked at the lavish entrance. Sadly, the view was quickly obstructed by a sea of onlookers, news reporters, and cameramen who clamored outside the towering gates.

"Welcome to the house Cody built, Timmons family," Mr. Timmons said. "Not to mention our new home! Isn't it great?"

Bixby forgot to breathe for a moment as the reality that they were at *the* coolest house in the world, complete with a mob of people outside dying to see her and her family. Yesterday, nobody in the world knew who they were. Now, everyone thought that they did. Bixby wasn't sure how she felt about it other than that she had knots in her stomach.

She quickly regained her composure, realizing that once she passed through those mysteriously secret gates, still no one would really know who they were. Sadly, it meant she would be without her friends.

The van approached the gates as the mob was being alerted to their arrival. Mr. Timmons reached down to his control board and made sure that all of the windows were up and tinted as dark as they could go. Normally, he only used this feature to keep the sun out of the twins' eyes. However, with hundreds of onlookers trying to get the front page shot for their respective news agencies, he decided to keep his family's faces out of the media for as long as he could, even if it was ultimately futile.

"How do we get in the gates?" Mrs. Timmons asked. "They told you, right?"

"Yeah. They said that the security system will read the ID chip on the van's license plate and let us in," he replied, gently easing the van through the ever-growing crowd.

"Well, how long does that take?" Mrs. Timmons asked.

"I bet people try and sneak in all the time," he replied. "The scanners are probably checking the van to make sure there aren't any stowaways."

At that point, the van reached the still-closed gates, and Mr. Timmons brought the vehicle to a complete stop. A soothing voice then rang out over the dashboard navigation system: "Welcome, Timmons family. We're so glad you're all here.

Please enter your passcode and proceed through the gate to your new home. Have a lovely day."

Mr. Timmons reached down to type his passcode into the dash console and then turned to his wife. "This is it, Mary. This is it!" he exclaimed with a huge puff of pride as he entered in the last digit.

With pure jubilation, Mrs. Timmons leaned over and gave her husband a gentle kiss. Bixby could tell she was fighting back a few tears of joy. Her mom then spun around, and, overlooking the twins who were still focused on putting new things in their mouths, she shouted, "Bixby, you must see all of these people and this gigantic gate! It's just like they show it on the Holo-TV! Bixby? Bixby, are you listening to me?"

Bixby could hear her mother but had grown accustomed to acting otherwise from time to time. She'd learned to drown out her mom's high-pitched voice by raising the volume of her music. So, with a flick of her thumb, her mother was gone. Bixby had reserved interest in a new house, new room, new friends, and her same old family. Her dad would still be working all the time, just like he always had, and her mother would still be tied up with chasing the twins around. Manor or no Manor, after the first week, she'd be forgotten by her family all over again.

Mr. Timmons reached his hand over to his wife's. "She'll see it soon enough," he said. "Give her some time."

"I know. I just hope she sees that all of this is for her, too," Mary said, her voice full of concern.

For Bixby, their conversation was confirmation that, even though she was secretly taking the vastness of Pinnacle Manor in, her protest was still the only thing her parents could see.

A sharp, metallic creak rang out through the crowd as the great gates swung open. Mr. Timmons put the van back into drive, and they rolled forward.

"Everything and nothing," was all Bixby could think about.

"Whoopee," she muttered sarcastically, just loud enough for all to hear.

CHAPTER TWO

A LOT SMALLER THAN EXPECTED

A S THE FAMILY van left the front gate behind, Bixby was slightly intrigued about what was to come next.

"If the gates were that huge, what is Pinnacle Manor going to look like?" she pondered as she started catching glimpses of endless fields and tree lines. In the distance, she could make out marshlands running down to the tip of a lake that stretched to the horizon.

A sharp voice rang out over the van's Holo-Dash System, surprising everyone: "Hello, Timmons family, and welcome to Pinnacle Manor!" A tiny, well-dressed man with a chiseled, stern face appeared on the dashboard and every headrest. His hair was slicked-back and black, and he had a carved chin with a dimple at the end of it.

"Mr. Foreman, thank you so much for letti—" Cooper Timmons stopped talking, realizing that the message was a recording.

"Nice butt-chin," Bixby snickered. She wasn't fond of Mr. Foreman, the guy who was responsible for running her dad ragged throughout her entire childhood. Even having him in the car as a digital message gave her the heebie-jeebies. While the man rattled on about how ginormous and glamourous Pinnacle Manor was and how it was nestled into almost ten thousand acres, Bixby flicked the miniature holographic man in the head over and over again while she scanned the horizon for her new home.

"*Blah blah blah.* I'm wearing a cool Pedrodian suit that changes colors with an app on my phone. I'm so cool. Get to the good part where you're done talking," Bixby whispered. Even the boys were getting bored of his endless chatter as they tried to grab his holographic body and stuff it in their mouths.

Eventually, the flashy, yellow-tied Foreman said the magic words.

"...and don't forget to see if you can figure out the mystery of where Cody Dragonthorp disappeared to. Oh, and if you didn't know, Mr. Dragonthorp always loved puzzles. I'm sure there are several of his still there that you could test your wits on."

While Foreman continued to ramble on about Pinnacle Manor's features, Bixby knew that he was simply saying how fast and amazing everything was going to be for them. All she heard over and over in her head, though, was, "Mr. Dragonthorp always loved puzzles."

"Well, if we could hurry up and get to this house, maybe I could get started on one," she grumbled.

Foreman droned on for a bit before talking about the passcode they would have to enter. Apparently, they had to go over a high-security bridge because Pinnacle Manor sat on an island.

"How's that for timing?" Mr. Timmons asked. Everyone who was staring at the Holo-Man looked up through the front window to see what they were about to cross.

"It looks...safe," Mr. Timmons continued. The bridge was no more than a small, two-lane cattle bridge with wooden guard rails along the sides.

"I thought it would be a little more...grand," Mrs. Timmons said, her words in tune with everyone else's thoughts.

"Before I forget, you don't have to slow down for a second scan on the bridge. This is simply one last safety check before you arrive at Pinnacle Manor. We don't want any extra stragglers entering the property trying to steal a glimpse at the Manor's vast enigmas," Foreman said.

"I guess that makes sense," Mr. Timmons said, despite the fact that he ignored the instructions and brought the van to a stop.

"Good luck, enjoy being the caretakers of this fabulous estate, and remember: we are counting on you to help us keep Cody's manor in tiptop shape for when he finally comes home!" Foreman concluded with a salute.

With that, the hologram disappeared, and it was again just the five Timmons family members alone in the vehicle, taking it all in.

"What do you guys think?" Mr. Timmons asked.

He'd barely finished getting the words out of his mouth when Mrs. Timmons leapt across the center console and bear-hugged him.

"You big man muffin! Thank you for all your hard work!" she said.

Bixby rolled her eyes at her mother's fulsome doting, which seemed nonstop as of late. It was even worse when her parents used mushy names for each other.

Bixby wasn't going to join in on the celebration but instead affixed a scowl on her face as she focused her attention directly ahead.

Mr. Timmons' gaze traveled over his wife's shoulder and to the back seat. Bixby made sure he was looking deep into her eyes before giving an unenthusiastic nod and mouthing two words. *One chance.*

And with that, Mr. Timmons settled back into his seat, put the van in drive, and set out across the bridge.

The van rumbled onto the stone, two-lane path that hung a few feet above the breeze-kissed lake that stirred below. The bridge seemed to take an eternity to cross. Bixby couldn't tell if it was the jitters of seeing the inside of Pinnacle Manor or simply the fact that the bridge was long. Either way, the other side couldn't come quickly enough. Though hidden behind a mask of indifference as a protest to moving, Bixby's excitement began to swell as she wished her father would step on the gas pedal. It wasn't like there were police officers anywhere around to stop them.

After getting off the bridge and onto a long, winding paved drive, they soon reached a clearing that revealed Pinnacle Manor.

"Wait, there must be some mistake," said Mr. Timmons.

The manor—a quaint, stone home—was no bigger than the house they'd left back in Snagelyville. Some might even say this one was smaller.

Mr. Timmons shook his head. "This must be the guest home. I didn't see any other roads off the bridge, though," he said. "Tell you what: let's check this place out. Maybe there's a map of the island and not to mention a bathroom."

"A quick pit stop wouldn't hurt," Mrs. Timmons replied. "We've been in this thing for eight hours."

Bixby watched her dad as he made his way to the front door while her mother climbed out of the front seat and slid open the van's side door to check on the twins. Her mother ignored her silent protest, focusing her attention on wiping down the slobber and crushed cereal that the twins had managed to cake all over themselves and everything around them. Little did her mom know, Bixby had added a few extra pieces to the mess in order to entertain herself.

"Nobody is answering, and the door seems to be locked. We must be at the wrong place," Mr. Timmons grumbled, returning to the van. "Let's double back and see where we took a wrong turn."

Bixby huffed in loud disapproval, earning the evil eye from her mom. "Bixby—" Mrs. Timmons started.

"You're at the right place, Timmons clan," interrupted an unseen and unfamiliar voice. "Now, why don't you step inside and get settled in?"

CHAPTER THREE

THE HELP

EVERYONE SPUN AROUND when the rear hatch of the van suddenly popped up. Someone began digging into their luggage.

"Hey, get out of there!" Mr. Timmons shouted as he quickly started towards the back of the van.

The rummaging stopped. A head peeked around the side of the hatch, followed by the body of a man standing no more than five and a half feet tall with dark brown hair and a glitchy Scottish accent. "Begging your pardon, sir," he said. "I'm Hucklebee. At your service."

"Hucklebee? I was told there wasn't anyone else on the island," said Mr. Timmons.

"No, sir. You would have been told that there weren't any other *humans* on the island. I am a Holographic Digitized Robot programmed by the Grand Master himself. If you choose to assign me a name, H-bot will work just fine, but I'd prefer Hucklebee; it's what the Grand Master called me. It's also a way to distinguish me from the others. Now, if I may, sir, I shall retrieve your belongings." With that, he bowed and jollily dove back into the luggage.

"How many...*H-bots* are on the island?" Mrs. Timmons asked.

"There are four of us, madam," he started. "There is myself; I take care of the property. Anything you need or want to do, just tell Harvey, and he will have me arrange it. I also do all the handy work and tinkering that Harvey wants done around the hou—"

"Who's Harvey?" Mrs. Timmons interrupted.

"He is the program that manages the ins and outs around the Manor. A word of advice, though," he said, then leaned over and started to whisper: "Stay on his good side, madam. He can be a cranky old Scotsman if you rub him the wrong way."

"Oh, I see. Who else is there?" Mr. Timmons asked.

"Miss Marmalade is also here. She handles the cooking, washing, and tidying up. Nicest robot you'll ever meet, she is. Unlike that Bulldog fellow. Rough chap, but he enforces the house rules like none other. He was delivered when the security systems were updated a few families ago," he said. "Now then, is there anything else I can help you with?"

Mrs. Timmons wasn't one for shyness when afforded the opportunity to ask direct questions.

"One thing, actually. I was wondering, why did the other families leave? It was never mentioned in any of the documentaries," Mrs. Timmons probed. She had made Bixby watch nearly all the documentaries online about people who lived in Pinnacle Manor, but there were never follow-ups about where they were now.

Hucklebee pondered on the question for a moment.

"Oy, now that you ask. I'm not quite sure. That information seems to have been removed from my database. Probably for legal matters. Privacy agreements and all. It is a shame that they left, though; Pinnacle Manor is a lovely home for anyone, and it is yours for now," he said, wrapping up the answer the best he could.

Bixby found his response suspicious, but before she could press him, he continued.

"I have unlocked the door for you so that you can head in and freshen up. Harvey will meet you all in the den and give you a tour of the house. After that, we will help you to start your set-up. In the meantime, I will get this luggage up to your rooms," Hucklebee said as he struggled with Mrs. Timmons' wardrobe chest.

"Wait, you're saying this little house is Pinnacle Manor? This is supposed to be the lap of luxury of the modern world," grumbled Mrs. Timmons.

Bixby chuckled to herself, knowing her mom had been expecting a mansion resembling something more like a Barbie DreamHouse. In all fairness, however, she had expected something more, too.

"It *is* the lap of luxury," said Hucklebee, taking a small breather.

"This is nothing like the house on the Holo-TV. In fact, this is no bigger than our old house," Mrs. Timmons argued.

"*Oh!*" Hucklebee exclaimed, then laughed. "Nobody has explained to you how this house works, have they? Pinnacle Manor is exactly the way he programmed it when he lived here. We call this the default setting. Now that you live here, you can configure the home anyway you'd like."

Mr. Timmons gave Hucklebee a confused look.

Hucklebee tried again. "Say your family has a shared computer. When Mrs. Timmons wants to use it, she would log in as Mrs. Timmons, and all her pre-adjusted settings would formulate. Then, she logs off, and Mr. Timmons logs in, and his different, but pre-adjusted, settings formulate. This house is the exact same concept. When the Grand Master lived here, the settings were 'The Grand Master's' adjusted house. When guests come to the Manor, the house automatically adjusts to this 'Guest' setting. When they filmed that documentary on the Manor, we called that the 'Movie Star' setting. And now that all of you, the Timmons, live here, it will adjust to the Timmons' regulated house settings. Once you set them, of course," he said, gesturing towards the shack in front of them.

Mrs. Timmons's facial expression had not changed still, and Bixby smirked at her.

"Go inside and allow me to demonstrate," he said with a smile.

Mr. and Mrs. Timmons each took one of the twins, dropped them into their baby fanny packs, and marched up to and through oddly oversized wooden doors that led into Pinnacle

Manor. Bixby slid out the side van door and around to where Hucklebee was working to stack the luggage onto the luggage cart.

"When you say Grand Master, do you mean Cody Dragonthorp?" Bixby asked in a quiet voice.

Hucklebee froze, and then without returning Bixby's gaze, he said, "A greater man never lived than the Grand Master. I hope maybe one of you can bring him back."

With that, Hucklebee shut the rear hatch to the van and pushed on with his work.

Standing alone, Bixby could tell from the change in demeanor that Hucklebee had deeper insight. She wanted to know more but decided not to press him on the topic until later. For now, she wanted to see why people made such a big fuss about this dinky little house.

With her foot, Bixby pushed open the oversized wooden door and wandered inside. Only two steps over the threshold, she stopped, pulled out her earbuds, pushed back the hood that covered her face, and, for a second, lost the ability to breathe. The inside of Pinnacle Manor was grander than any Holo-TV could have ever depicted.

The entrance opened into the central hub for the entire house. The ceiling reached up at least three stories above the stone floor of the Manor, but the outside of the house looked like a small, two-story bungalow. As she'd learned from the Holo-TV, she knew this room to be the Great Hall; but how did it fit inside the dinky shell of what she'd seen from the outside? It was easily two-hundred-feet from the entrance door to the opposite wall, which was home to a grandiose fireplace made of massive boulders. The rustic cherry mantle stood proudly above a hearth that a bonfire would appear small in. The stone walls reminded her of living in a castle. The peculiar part about this room was that it was circular in shape. From the outside, every part of this home was made up of right angles.

Under her breath, she whispered to herself, "Okay, Bixby. Now we're intrigued."

"Isn't this the most amazing thing you've ever seen, Bixby?" her mother screeched from across the Great Hall.

Bixby stood dumbfounded at what she was seeing and couldn't even come close to formulating a good response to her mother. Barely able to hold rational thoughts, all she could come up with was, "It's definitely something, Mom."

She then turned to her dad. "How is this possible? I mean, it's bigger on the inside!"

"I, uh...I don't know, Bixby. It must be one of the surprises the Foreman was talking about," he replied, just as awestruck as Bixby.

While Bixby stood in the doorway in utter shock, what could only be described as an outrageous laugh came from one end of the hall, followed by the most jovial and pleasant Southern voice Bixby had ever heard. "Oh, my heavens, it's the Timmons family! Let me see you all!"

A woman with an inexhaustible amount of joy rushed into the Great Hall dressed modestly in a long skirt, a button-up blouse, and a cardigan with an apron over it all pushing a dessert cart. Everything about her screamed teacher mixed with housekeeper, and Bixby knew she had to be the H-bot maid that Hucklebee had told them about—Miss Marmalade.

Miss Marmalade reached Mr. Timmons and Wyatt first. "My, my, what a handsome bundle of joy you are!" she gushed as she bent over to tickle Wyatt's face. Standing upright, she continued, "Mr. Cooper Timmons, I hope you are as smart as you look!"

Blushing, Mr. Timmons could only reply with a simple, "Thank you."

"You are going to be an amazing caretaker of the Manor! I just know it!" she said with confidence.

Making her way over to Mrs. Timmons and Darby, she leaned in for a hug. "Mary Timmons, you are stunning! Let me get a good look at you!" She then gave Mrs. Timmons a kiss on each cheek and said, "We are going to have the best time, Mrs. Mary Timmons. I have so many recipes to share and things I want to show you."

Leaving Mary at an uncharacteristic loss for words, Miss Marmalade moved on to the toddler that was in the harness strapped to her chest. "Sorry, Master Darby, I didn't forget you. Just as handsome as your brother, you are," she said, pinching his cheeks. "I'd steal you both if they wouldn't shut me down and send me to the scrap yard!"

Halting in her tracks, she realized there was one more Timmons she was missing.

"Where is she? Where is the one with the fiery red hair they told us about?" she asked, then followed the gaze of Mrs. Timmons.

The H-bot spotted Bixby, who was still standing inside the front door and headed straight for her.

"Bixby, you come here and let Miss Marmalade get a good look at you!" she bubbled.

As Miss Marmalade dashed across the Great Hall, Bixby extended her hand to shake hers. Without slowing down, the H-bot grabbed Bixby's outstretched hand and spun her completely around.

"Oh, child, I have not seen a more beautiful young woman in my life. I must say, to have you under this roof would make the Grand Master mighty excited. I know you will do well by him; that's for certain."

Not sure what Miss Marmalade meant, and a little dizzy from being spun around by such a strange robot, Bixby retained her apathetic front for her new home and replied with a dry and simple, "Right."

"Okay, I have some lemon tarts, gingerbread men, and double fudge cookies. I didn't know what you all liked, so I stocked the cart this morning. Come on over here by the fireplace, and we will get you all settled in. Harvey will teach you all you need to know about this house."

Placing Wyatt in one of the two baby swings, Mr. Timmons nestled into the large, brown leather recliner. Miss Marmalade snatched off his shoes and replaced them with a new pair of house slippers as she handed him a sample platter of pastries and a glass of milk.

"Thank you very much, Miss Marmalade. You are quite efficient," Mr. Timmons said graciously.

She simply replied with a curtsy and a grin.

Seconds after being placed in his baby swing, Darby fell fast asleep, allowing Mrs. Timmons to make her way to the dessert cart. Her fingers tiptoed about, taking only the lemon bars. Bixby knew that her mother was telling herself that the word lemon qualified it as just healthy enough to fit into her "diet." After pouring a glass of cucumber water to go with her treat, she retired to the davenport to wait for Harvey's presentation on how to work their new home.

Bixby, however, didn't go to the dessert cart; instead, she indulged the urge to explore the massive fireplace. Besides the odd trinkets and boxes above the fireplace mantle that would require a small ladder to reach, she found herself literally standing inside the fireplace. Reaching up, she could barely touch the stonework below the mantle.

"A big house needs a big fireplace," Hucklebee explained.

"I guess so, but how does it work? I mean, it would take three men to bring in logs big enough to fill this fireplace," said Bixby.

"You are extraordinarily perceptive, Bixby. The house was developed using a form of digital refraction. Basically, when you tell Harvey how you want to change the room, he makes the adjustments needed that not only distorts the room and its size but the objects in it as well, such as logs for the fireplace. You'll find that nearly everything in this house can be adjusted in such a manner."

"That doesn't make sense. How can a small log become a big log, or a small room become a big room?" Bixby asked.

"Excellent question, and one I wish I had a better answer for," Hucklebee said. "Nobody knows precisely how things work around here, only that they do. The Grand Master would be able to explain it, certainly. Maybe your father was hired to help figure out those very mysteries. He seems quite intelligent, after all."

Just then, the lights in the house dimmed, and a voice interrupted Hucklebee's next thought.

"All right, you blabbering idiot, let the Timmons alone! It's my turn to talk to 'em."

The voice seemed to come from all around them, despite there being no noticeable speakers in the walls. Bixby promptly took a seat on the large leather couch with Hucklebee.

"How I love seeing him teach a new family how to work the house," Hucklebee whispered as he leaned over to Bixby. "His presentation is awesome."

In the snarkiest tone Bixby had ever heard, the voice began his introductory monologue.

"As I'm sure you know by now, my name is Harvey, and I'm here to help you...*yada, yada, yada, and all that junk.* Let me make it simple: I am everywhere in the house at all times. You need something that I can change digitally. Just say the word, and I'll do it. Within reason, of course. None of this, 'I want a genie in a lamp and a thousand wishes,' nonsense. And do try not to bother me with things that these three motor minds are meant to do. I have a busy enough day as it is."

"Hey! Harvey!" Miss Marmalade said, putting her hands on her hips. "Simmer down or I'll take a hammer to your hard drives!"

"Oh, pipe down, you gummy bag of bolts!" Harvey barked back. "As for you, Timmons, do your pretending to live like royalty, then up and leave like the rest of them. But don't expect us to get all mushy when you decide to scram, too. With that, I will meet each of you in your estate rooms in ten minutes to set up your space. The H-Toys will show you each to your own oasis. I look forward to having you stay here at the beautiful Pinnacle Manor."

With that, the voice stopped, and the lights went back up.

Smiling, Bixby turned to Hucklebee and sarcastically agreed, "Yeah. Totally awesome."

Hucklebee gave a sheepish look and shrugged.

"I must apologize; Harvey has never acted that way before," Marmalade started. "He became very close with the last care-taker and his family, and he's been in a cranky mood ever since they left."

"Why did they leave?" Bixby asked. "I mean, they were here for like three years. Nobody just up and leaves the Pinnacle Manor without reason, right?"

"I'm afraid we are not privy to that information. We awoke from our nightly charge to find that all the settings were back to default, and they were gone," said Hucklebee.

"How peculiar," Mrs. Timmons said after several seconds of silence.

"Well, the house is ours now, and I don't know about you, but I'm ready to start decorating my room," Mr. Timmons said, clapping his hands to his thighs.

"You and Mom can have at that grump first. I'm going to nose around a bit before setting up my room," Bixby said.

"Let us know what you find," Mr. Timmons said.

"I'll watch the little ones if you don't mind. Hucklebee, can you take the Mr. and Mrs. to their room?" asked Marmalade.

Nodding in agreement, Hucklebee jumped up from his seated position. "Right this way," he said, gesturing towards a long corridor.

Mr. and Mrs. Timmons stood and followed Hucklebee to the bedroom wing of the house. Bixby, now free to roam alone, dashed off in the opposite direction towards another hallway of doors. She had never seen so many doors in one spot, and she was dying to know what was behind each one.

Chapter Four
An Interesting Find

BIXBY WAS DETERMINED to put Harvey to the test. She ducked into the first grand room that she could find, the lights automatically switching on as she entered.

"I like your style, Harvey. All about saving energy," Bixby said to the empty room. She found herself in a lavish dining room large enough to accommodate at least one hundred people. While that was impressive, she wanted to put this '*ask and you shall receive*' promise to a proper test. "Hey, Harvey. I need more room than this for my next party. Set one long table for five hundred people."

In an instant, the room dimmed, and the tables vanished. As the lights came back up, a single table was in the middle of the room, and it began to grow exponentially. Within a matter of moments, the other end of the table was nearly out of sight.

"Make the chair at the other end large enough that I can see it from here," she added.

Like magic, it appeared in the distance. Bixby tried hard to play it cool, but excitement got the better of her.

"Shut up! Nice show, Harvey!" Bixby blurted out. She laughed and then recomposed herself as best she could before going on. "But let's keep this room simple, Harvey, because I don't see us using this room for more than just the five of us."

At that point, Bixby began pointing and placing items in the room until it faithfully recreated her old dining room back in Snagelyville.

"Harvey, this is where some of my first memories were made. Maybe one day we will get back to that, huh?" Bixby said, admiring her creation.

When she was done, Bixby started to walk out but stopped at the fireplace near the exit. The only thing that sat on its mantle was a wooden box with the phrase "Open Me Without Breaking Me" carved into the side. To most people, this would look like a silly little box that would be easily overlooked and most likely lost in a quick décor shuffle by Harvey. For Bixby, though, that box was like a glowing beacon. Realizing in an instant it was a puzzle box like the ones Grandpa had all over his house, she reached up and grabbed it.

"I'll be taking you..." she said, shoving it in her pocket so that she could solve it later. She then ducked out of the dining room as her stomach let out a tremendous growl. Bixby had missed out on the treat cart and was now paying the price with an empty stomach.

"Turn on the kitchen lights so that I know where it is," Bixby directed.

A room lit up at the end of the hall.

"Ah, there you are," she whispered, breaking into a brisk walk.

Entering the kitchen, Bixby found it a little old fashioned for her taste.

"Okay, Harvey, this room definitely has to change. It looks like something out of an old farmhouse. I want this place to look even older. Make it resemble something out of an ancient English castle with modern appliances," she said.

Harvey silently began to work his digital prowess, and Bixby nodded mostly in agreement. The countertops were turned into stone inlay with wooden spaces for carving. The cabinets were rustic and handcrafted. The floor turned to stone, similar to that used in the fireplace. The refrigerator looked like a cabinet door, and the cooking surface popped up out of the stone countertops. Everything that was modern was hidden in plain sight amongst what she considered antique amenities. Bixby even added a wood-fired pizza oven.

"Now *that* is cool, Harvey."

Her brain could hardly keep up with all the ideas Bixby had for the house. Her heart raced with pure joy, but her stomach decided at that point to let loose a long, loud growl.

Needing to tend to her hunger, Bixby decided to make a request for food. "Can you make me a sandwich while you're at it?"

A few moments went by, and nothing happened. Suddenly, she was startled by a voice.

"I hear you're having a wee bit of trouble with a sandwich, Bixby," Hucklebee said.

Bixby spun around to find Hucklebee standing in the doorway. "How did you do that?"

"How did I do what?" he replied.

"How did you show up without making a sound?" she said while trying to slow her heart rate.

"By walking, Bixby," he said matter-of-factly. "If I may, I like what you've done with the place. It's Medieval fusion with a contemporary accent."

"Thanks. If I'm going to live here, I might as well have a little fun, right?" Bixby mused.

"Quite right, indeed. You should know, however, that the person who does the most work in a room is the person whose default setting the room reverts to when you are both present, which, in this case, would be your mother," Hucklebee said.

"Well, then, I will have to make it a point to be in here only when I'm alone," she replied. "Man, I can't believe you get to live in the coolest house in the world."

"As do you, Bixby," Hucklebee noted.

Bixby smiled brightly; this was the first time she'd let her guard down long enough to be excited that she was *actually* living in Pinnacle Manor.

"Question for you: do you ever get bored serving other people, Hucklebee? I mean, I asked for a sandwich, and you had to make it. Not sure I'd like that as a job, especially when the person can do it on their own."

"I do believe I've never been asked that before, Bixby," Hucklebee said before pausing to collect his thoughts on how to answer. "Most people see H-bots as servants. Many times, we are expected to do what is asked and then disappear. But to your question: no, I don't get bored of helping people and making new friends every chance I get. It is probably one of the things I think I do best."

"You mean besides being a ninja and scaring people?" Bixby quipped.

Hucklebee chuckled. "Yes, and that, too, I suppose."

"But what's the big deal about breaking the coding of this house? Why didn't Cody just leave the directions for Dragon-thorp to follow? And why did Cody just up and disappear?" Bixby hoped that maybe if she asked Hucklebee enough questions, she could get some sort of clue from him.

Hucklebee stood for a few moments in silence, and Bixby assumed that he was probably trying to figure out how to word his next thought properly. Was he hiding a secret, or did he simply not know? Bixby wasn't sure.

"The Grand Master built this house and everything in it. He barely got a chance to enjoy it...then *poof*, he was gone without a trace. If I went missing, I sure hope someone would come find me, wouldn't you?" Hucklebee replied.

Bixby sat and contemplated Hucklebee's answer. How long would it take for her family to notice if she were missing? Even if Cody's family did notice his disappearance right away, he'd been missing for almost ten years, and nobody was any closer to finding him than the day he'd vanished. Distress tightened Bixby's features as the thoughts rumbled through her mind. Chances were, Cody's disappearance would never be solved.

"Now, about that sandwich before you go on your way, Bixby. What would you like to have prepared?" Hucklebee asked.

"Actually, I think I will fix it myself. You go sneak up on somebody else, or whatever you H-bots do when you're not scaring the pants off of people," she said.

"Very good, Bixby. I will leave you to it," he said as he walked away.

Bixby was now certain that Hucklebee was telling the truth about not really knowing anything about how or why Cody Dragonthorp had disappeared. It was a puzzle, and luckily for Cody, puzzles were something Bixby enjoyed more than anything else in the world. The conversation reminded her of the small box that rested inside her hoodie pocket, and she patted it to make sure it was still there.

Bixby pushed open door after door as she strolled down the next hall with a turkey sandwich dripping with cheese and hot sauce. In all, she counted a den, a dining hall, eight guest bathrooms, a sunroom, a carport which had the van parked neatly in one of the ten parking bays, seven guest bedrooms, a movie room, a laundry room, a parlor, a library, an entire corridor of Launch Rooms where she would be going to attend school, a door that read "TO THE LIGHTHOUSE," and a million silly pictures that looked more like finger paintings of goofy looking people. Each painting had a plaque on the bottom that specified what the picture was supposed to be. Bixby was only able to identify two things before having to look at their plaques for the answer.

"Harvey, what was the last room Cody was in before he disappeared?" asked Bixby.

After a few moments with no reply, she asked again, "Harvey, the easiest way to find Cody is to work backwards from the last place he was seen. That's like detective one-oh-one. So, which room was he in last?" No matter how she phrased the question, Harvey didn't respond.

"Great. A puzzle with no apparent start. This should be fun," she said to herself.

The hallway was long and well-lit. Just as she grabbed the handle to open the "Light House" door, she heard footsteps approaching from the other end of the hall. Bixby turned to see who was joining her on her adventures. Hoping it was Huckle-bee again to show her where to begin her search for Cody, she realized it wasn't *anyone* she recognized. That meant it had to be the Bulldog that Hucklebee had warned her about.

The man walking toward her was dressed in all black, and his strides were long and purposeful. His hands were folded behind his back, and he closed the distance between the two of them rapidly. In an instant, he stood in front of Bixby with his dark brown eyes and bleached blonde hair, looking nothing like a bulldog.

"I was—" Bixby started.

"You may continue your snooping *after* Holo-School Prime and enrichment. It has been a long day, and it is time for you to set up your room and go to bed," he barked.

"Aaaand that's why they call you the Bulldog," she whispered under her breath.

"Hurry along, Miss Timmons; there is no time for dawdling," he retorted.

"I can see that we are going to be best friends, Bulldog," Bixby continued as they walked back towards the Great Hall and the bedroom wing.

Stopping abruptly and spinning around to face Bixby, the man in black said in a very stiff tone, "It seems that Hucklebee has already filled you with misinformation. Let's clear a few things up, shall we?" he said. "My name is *Arthur*, and it would do you good to call me by my given name, Miss Timmons. I am here for the sole purpose of making sure this building is safe and secure and that everyone is following the rules. Unlike the other H-bots here, I have no concern for making friends, having tea parties, or playing childish games. If you break a rule, I will deal with you accordingly. Are we crystal clear, Miss Timmons?"

"How do I know what's a rule and what's not?" Bixby asked, annoyed.

"Neither H-bots, nor any other programs in this house, can lie. As such, we will tell you what the house rules are. Also, I do not discriminate based on who breaks the rules. If I say it's a rule and that you are breaking it, you will get only one warning. Do you have any other questions, Miss Timmons?"

"No, I think that clears it up," she responded with a gulp.

An Interesting Find

"Good. Now, to your room," he said as he turned and began to lead her again.

After a hurried walk through the corridor and the Great Hall, they arrived at the family wing of the house. Bixby was shown to the last door on the left.

"You have fifteen minutes to adjust the settings, ten minutes to prep for bed, and then five minutes of free time. After that, Harvey will be instructed to turn your lights out," Arthur said.

"As you command, Arthur," Bixby mocked with a salute and a cynical smirk. She could see that Arthur hadn't found it as funny as she had.

Bixby placed her hand on the large brass doorknob. Her original inclination was to pull out her cell phone, bring up her photos, and have Harvey make an exact replica of her room back home. However, Bixby was far too curious to take the easy way out. She pushed open the large wooden door and walked into her newest room.

The bedroom was average in size, though much bigger than her room in Snagelyville. On the far wall sat a simple, full-sized bed. The head- and footboard were made of rich mahogany wood adorned with hand-carved patterns. Covering the bed was a handstitched quilt and a few feather pillows. The floor was hardwood to match the rustic décor, and it ran all the way to the opposite side of the room, where it abruptly transitioned into floor-to-ceiling windows framing the moon as it rose just over Worthy Lake. It was dark, so she would have to wait until morning to see the rest of the view in all of its wonder. The other walls had been turned into bookshelves like an old library.

Her luggage sat neatly in the corner next to the fireplace—a smaller replica of the one in the great hall, and a fire was already crackling in its hearth. What really drew her attention was the large painting over the mantle. She could tell that it was a picture of something or someone, but it was as if someone had cut the picture into fifty different squares and then jumbled all of the squares up. To most people, it would have just looked like a messed-up picture, but Bixby knew it was a gigantic slide puzzle from the ones her grandfather used to help her do when she was younger. Each piece could be slid along a track, and once all the pieces were un-jumbled, it would make a picture.

"That is the biggest slide puzzle I have ever seen," she said, admiring the riddle on the wall. "Awesome."

Though she wanted to work on the puzzle box and the slide puzzle, she knew that the time was rapidly approaching for lights out. As such, Bixby decided that they would have to wait until tomorrow. Being short on time didn't stop her from scanning the oddities left on the excessive amount of bedroom bookshelves, though. There were a handful of old detective books and records with private eyes and spy glasses on them. In the empty places where there should have been books, the shelves were adorned with gizmos and gadgets that reminded her of toys her grandfather used to have at his house.

She was amazed at how each one was a complex blend of sprockets, dials, cranks, and gears. Every trinket was more visually stunning than the next. It was the perfect shelf to store the tiny puzzle box. Knowing that she still had to finish unpacking and adjusting her room, she grabbed a toy from one of the shelves and turned it in her hand, making one simple request to Harvey: "Can you make the bed a king-size?"

With that said, the lights dimmed a little, and the bed frame and quilt stretched out to afford her extra sleeping space. As the lights went back up, Bixby found a pair of nightclothes folded neatly on the end of the bed. She placed the gizmo back on the shelf along with the puzzle box she had found earlier and slipped into some fuzzy pajamas before she began to unpack her luggage. From her second suitcase, she gently unwrapped hand puzzles, comic books, some old leather-bound books of great mystery capers, and cyphers her grandfather had written for her before he'd left to go to a better place. She found an empty space on a bookshelf and settled them into their new home. After completing her work, Bixby felt oddly at home and comfortable in this room.

She climbed into the center of her now gargantuan bed and closed her eyes. She knew deep down inside that tomorrow would be the start to a great adventure, but she had no idea quite how big it was going to be.

CHAPTER FIVE
FRIENDS AND FOES

BIXBY SLOWLY BLINKED her eyes open and sat up, letting out a monstrous stretch. The sun was starting to crest over the mountain view and was reflecting off of the lake. She had anticipated a beautiful sunrise, but this was by far the most gorgeous sight she had seen in her thirteen years on this Earth. Normally, her view consisted of either the brick wall belonging to a bankrupt parts factory or the other window in her old bedroom that faced the fire escape on Mr. Farley's house.

She sat on the edge of her bed and took it all in. After a brief pause, she remembered that in Pinnacle Manor she simply had to ask for something, and it would appear.

"Harvey, can I get some breakfast delivered to my room?"

"Not today, missy. Your mum wants you all in the kitchen for you and your dad's first day," Harvey chirped back. "On a side note, I wanted to apologize for my tantrum yesterday. There. I said it."

This was the first time Harvey and Bixby had had an actual conversation, and Bixby wanted to make sure that she made a good impression.

"I get it; I lost my friends yesterday and didn't feel much like making new ones, either. But I guess we have to make do with what we have, huh?" she said. "I can be hard to get along with, too," she admitted. "So, next time, tell me when you're going to have a bad day, and I'll steer clear of asking for any favors. Deal?"

"Aye, as long as you promise not to change things around the house every two seconds—it gets rather annoying—I think we have an accordance," he conceded.

"Excellent. Now...about that breakfast," she said as she popped up out of bed and went to her door. There, she briefly paused to look back at the shelf of interesting gadgets and gizmos before adding, "I'll be back for you guys later."

Bixby wandered through the Great Hall, following the smell of French toast and the candy of all meats: bacon. She made her way to the kitchen and immediately noticed that her mom had, of course, changed every setting that Bixby had created last night in the kitchen. It was now modern with all high-end appliances. The cabinets were cherry, the floor was Telarian glass, the fixtures were all Demencourse chrome, and the stove was big enough to start her own restaurant. Bixby supposed she could put up with such gaudiness for one meal, though, simply because it smelled so good.

"Bixby, you're up," her father said.

Bixby's eyes nearly popped out of her head when she saw him in his brand new Holo-Suit, ready for the office.

"Pretty sweet, right?" Mr. Timmons said as he saw her jaw nearly hit the floor.

Before Bixby could respond, Mrs. Timmons chimed in excitedly, "I hope you slept as well as we did, dear. Your father set up the room with an emperor-sized bed and plush pillows as deep as your head could sink into, and Harvey kept the temperature just right."

"And I showered on the moon this morning," her dad said proudly.

Bixby didn't know if her dad realized that sometimes when he spoke, he was probably the most awkward man on the planet. All she could do was shake her head in disbelief at how unaware he was of his level of nerdiness. She drove her fork through a stack of French toast and piled it onto her plate next to the mountain of bacon while trying to erase visions of her dad on the moon from her head.

"Hurry up and eat. I don't want you to be late logging into Holo-School Prime on your first day. I just sent Miss Marmalade with your Holo-Suit to your room. When you're done there, go put it on and meet Arthur in the Launch Room." Mrs. Timmons chuckled to herself as she rambled. "Does anyone else find it funny that her name is Miss Marmalade? It's kind of fun to say. In fact—"

"Wait! I have a Holo-Suit like Dad?" Bixby interrupted.

"Not until we finish eating as a family." Mrs. Timmons replied quickly.

Bixby soured her face, frustrated at not being allowed to go see her new toy. However, she quickly realized that maybe her family would actually spend some time together now, so she decided to focus on that and ate another bite of bacon.

It was nice to have breakfast with her family. Usually, her mom delivered a bowl of cold cereal to her room and left it on her nightstand, and her dad was normally logged on to his work system well before Bixby ever made it out of bed. Bixby wanted to enjoy every moment of this because she wasn't sure how long it would last.

After half an hour of pleasant conversation about what they wanted the outside of the house to look like, Mr. Timmons pushed back his chair and said proudly, "Well, family, it's time to go to work."

Mrs. Timmons clasped her hands together with pride, "Go get 'em, stud muffin."

Bixby rolled her eyes at her parents' continued gawkiness.

"You'll do great!" cheered her mother. "See you both for dinner," she added.

With that, Mrs. Timmons pulled the twins out of their seats and started cleanup while Mr. Timmons disappeared down the long hallway towards the Launch Room corridor. Bixby sat alone at the table.

"Holo-Suit!" Bixby whispered excitedly to herself as she remembered that she now owned one. Bixby scooped her dish from the table and quickly dumped it in the sink on her way out of the kitchen.

"Thanks, Mom!" she hollered as she left. She was now in a full sprint across the Great Hall.

Once in her room, she saw her very own Holo-Suit laid out on her bed. She slowly walked up to it and ran her fingers across the waffle design pressed into the slick black suit.

"This is really mine?" Bixby asked, hoping Harvey was there.

Nothing but silence bounded from the walls.

She pulled the suit from the box and sat at the end of the bed thinking about her friends back in Snagelyville as they woke up in their homes and started getting ready to launch into their rickety old systems that only worked most of the time. They would turn on their standard-issue Bucksberry 1500, a basic system consisting of a light generator, wireless digitally enhanced Abicore 3-D helmet, and a set of pressure sleeves.

Within moments, they were in the digital school now known as Holo-School Basic. The helmet gave one a sense of looking at the school through a camera taped to the top of someone's head. Next, they would slide on the pressure sleeves. Once on their arms, the sleeves gave a brief sense that someone was digitally touching their hand or arm. Other than those two features, it was like sitting at home and going to school through a series of webcams.

Having a Holo-Suit and Launch Room changed the game completely. However, she felt a sting of guilt come over her as she bit her lip in frustration. Her friends back home were, at this

48

moment, logging on to their crummy Bucksberry 1500, and Bixby was holding on to a piece of material that cost as much as a house in Snagelyville.

"Pull it together, Bixby. It's just on loan from Mr. Dragon-thorp," she said, spurring herself to unzip the suit and slide it on. It made her feel better to convince herself that the suit wasn't really hers but instead borrowed from Cody & Daemon.

The "Holo" concept had been created by the twin brothers, Cody and Daemon Dragonthorp, who'd wanted to save tax-payers billions of dollars worldwide by eliminating the cost of school buildings. Their idea was to have each child log onto a system in cyberspace from the comfort of their own homes. It would eliminate bills for heating, electricity, and even paper if it were all done digitally. In fact, the only cost to send your child to school was that the district had to pay the teachers. Teachers' salaries were pennies compared to what the district paid to run the building.

Cody had been the brains of the operation, and for good reason. Everything Dragonthorp, Inc. had developed had come from Cody's brilliant mind. He had been voted "Smartest Person Alive" ten years in a row until he disappeared. Many theorized that his genius stemmed from an obsession with computers and puzzles from a young age that helped develop his brain. Some people, however, attributed his extraordinary abilities to his mild case of Autism. Though he was on the "Highly Functional" end of the spectrum, he was still the polar opposite of his outgoing brother. Either way, he was a great creator, but not so good around people. In his stead, Daemon ran the business end of Dragonthorp, Inc. He was able to sell the product to private schools immediately because they had the finances to switch the classrooms over to virtual schools. It also didn't hurt that it was the rich schools that were going to save the most money in taxes by not having a facility. So, Daemon was able to convince them easily.

Within the first three years of starting, the company had released its first Bucksberry system. This system used refracted light to bounce images off a bent shield inside a helmet that created the first holographic images the world now knew as Holo. Soon there were Holo-TVs, Holo-Phones, and Holo-Shopping. By the fifth year in business, Daemon was able to grow Dragonthorp Inc. into a multi-trillion-dollar business. Every home had adopted a Holo ecosystem. Businesses were lining up for Bucksberry systems for their employees to save on the cost of buying office space, janitors, maintenance, and having to pay insurance on top of the everyday costs.

Cody's only stipulation on the launch date to the schools was that all students were to be able to access a basic model of the most recent Bucksberry System and attend Holo-School Basic for free. Once logged in, the students had to be engaged for the entire school period of six hours so that they could access enrichment, their daily allotted time for video games. With the vast fortune Dragonthorp, Inc., had obtained in such a short time, Daemon had no problem with a gesture of goodwill towards the youth of the nation.

Cody had believed that, if kids were active in their schoolwork, they should be able to have some video game time as well.

Two hours was the daily amount given for enrichment to make sure people had human interaction outside of the Holo-System.

Bixby stood up and gave herself a glance in the mirror. "I look like I stole Batman's little sister's super suit," she muttered in disapproval. The Holo-Suit didn't fit anywhere, and it looked ridiculous; it was at least three sizes too big for her.

"I believe the word you are looking for is, 'Retract,'" Harvey finally spoke up.

"Retract?" Bixby questioned. As soon as the word came out of her mouth, the suit snapped tight against Bixby's body. "Whoa, that's pretty legit! What else does it do?"

"It launches you into Holo-School Prime." Harvey chortled.

Bixby had been attending Holo-School Basic on her Bucksberry 1500 since her very first day of kindergarten. She now had her own Holo-Suit and Launch Room. Usually, only the elite was able to afford these and attend Holo-School Prime.

"It's only on loan," she reminded herself as to not let herself get too excited. "But it will probably be the coolest experience ever," Bixby whispered to herself as she slid out of her room.

She made her way to Arthur, who was standing in front of a Launch Room with her name above it.

"I see you barely made it on time, Miss Timmons," remarked Arthur.

"Yes, Arthur, I did, didn't I?" said Bixby with a little sass in her voice.

"Please step inside," Arthur instructed with a sour look on his face.

"When I launch your room, you will feel a brief puff of air and a quick flash of light. That is your Holo-Suit syncing with the launch room. From then on, you will feel everything in your environment as if you were actually there," he continued.

"Epic," was the only word Bixby could think of to describe what was happening.

"As I was saying," Arthur continued, unamused, "you will be greeted by Headmaster Gabhammer. Do be on your best behavior, Miss Timmons. This is not the run of the mill school that you are used to. People actually expect you to perform well in Holo-School Prime," Arthur instructed.

"Alright, alright. I got it, Gabhammer," Bixby said and followed with "Bulldog" under her breath.

"I heard that, young lady," Arthur replied as he closed the hatch behind her.

A small hum began around Bixby. She closed her eyes; she had read that the first light beam to enter the room was always the brightest. Other than a brief puff of air, she could barely tell that the system had turned on. For the first time in a very long time, she was excited to be attending school. Bixby knew something was happening because she could smell the stale stench of cheap cleaning supplies and hear rumblings of other students all around her. She kept her eyes closed for an extra second just to take in the feel of being in her new school.

"Ahem, Miss Bixby Timmons, I presume?" came the deep voice of a man through the darkness.

"Ye...Yes, sorry, first time experiencing a Launch Room. Sorry." She quickly opened her eyes. "Mr. Gabhammer?" she followed as she looked up at a man who towered over her.

"That is correct, Miss Timmons. Headmaster Gabhammer, to be precise. Now, you're going to be late for your first class if you don't pick up the pace," directed Gabhammer.

Besides the fact that he was six and a half feet tall, built like a Gorgemex player and quite a striking black man, he could probably be related to the Bulldog. They both possessed a certain aura of sternness, appreciation for time management, and walking with their hands clasped behind their backs. So, even if they weren't blood-related, they'd definitely hit it off as best friends.

"That sounds good to me. Where are we going?" Bixby said in her usual lackluster tone that she always took when presented to an authority figure.

"Your first class will be with Mrs. Gable. She will then escort you to your next class and so on and so forth throughout the day," instructed Gabhammer.

Noticing that they were alone, Headmaster Gabhammer abruptly stopped, whipped his body around, bent over, and looked Bixby directly in the eyes.

"Miss Timmons, I want to make perfectly clear one important detail: this school is for people who actually work hard and achieve at a high standard. Every one of my students has been selected in the first round of the Business Draft. Just because your father happened to fall into the position that belongs to one of higher breeding does not give you a free pass to muddle around my halls. I have seen your aptitude scores and, even more so, I know how you spend your enrichment. Games and puzzles have no place in a school that produces only the finest quality of leadership and the next generation of executive masterminds. Please nod if you understand me," he said in a low, powerful voice.

Bixby rocked back on her heels with her chin tucked as far back as she could get it from Gabhammer's disgusting digital breath and foul tone. She composed herself, squared her shoulders, and held her breath as she leaned in face-to-face with Headmaster Gabhammer. She gave him a slight nod to end the troubling standoff that she currently found herself in with her new Headmaster, but not in agreement with what he was saying.

Standing back up, Headmaster Gabhammer reached into his coat pocket and pulled out a piece of paper.

"Excellent. Here is your class schedule. Please hand it to Mrs. Gable when you enter, and remember that you are at Holo-School Prime; try not to disappoint everyone," he warned. With that, he whipped himself around and began to march away.

"Lovely fellow. Remind me to invite him to a tea party with Arthur the Bulldog," Bixby said to herself as she turned the knob to her classroom.

A quick headcount made Bixby lucky number seventeen in the classroom, not including her teacher who was at the Holo-Board, drawing up math problems. As Bixby closed the door behind her, a hush came over the students who had been mumbling amongst themselves. The quieted students drew the attention of Lucinda Gable, a short, stocky woman who was pushing well into her sixties, wearing a red blouse and a black skirt with a hefty belt around her waist. She turned and looked over her spectacles to see what had brought the room to a standstill.

"Bixby Timmons?" she said through a voice that matched her festive outfit.

"Yes, ma'am," Bixby replied.

"Hurry up, then, and grab a seat there next to Mr. Ellerby. I'm just finishing up today's lesson on the Holo-Board, and then we will get started," she said, pointing to an empty chair.

The rows were staggered almost vertically like nosebleed seats in a stadium. Even though she was sitting in the second row, she could see well over the person in front of her. It would be impossible for Bixby to drift off or work on her puzzles because the teacher could see what everyone was doing. As she walked down the aisle, Bixby could feel her classmates' eyes on her and heard whispers about her bright red hair. She took her seat at the end of the row next to what could only be described as a homely boy with a few extra pounds around his midsection and messy brown hair.

As she sat down, the banter from other classmates began immediately. From the row that seemed to be right above her shoulders, a sniveling undertone beckoned a typical cliché: "Hey, Tipton, don't get too close to her. I hear that gingers don't have souls, so they snatch those closest to them."

The comment received a few giggles from those who could hear.

"If you're lucky, she might make you her fat little leprechaun buddy," teased another voice from a female in the same general direction. Her comments received the same amount of applause from those around them.

As Bixby unpacked her Holo-Writer and turned it on, she realized she'd already been hacked because a message streamed across her screen.

"You don't belong here!" scrolled over and over in bright red letters. Little did they know, Bixby was good at mind games.

Slowly, she turned in her seat and looked directly at her aggressors.

"I'm sorry that you're so misinformed," she began. "It's actually from the blood of my most recent victims. Any of you jokers care to hang out after school?" she asked as she pulled a lock of hair to her mouth to nibble on it.

The banterers were rendered speechless by her gull. The only thing their leader mustered up in reply was, "Gross."

Bixby turned her gaze back to Tipton, who was noticeably trying to avoid eye contact with her.

"You okay? You must be Tipton?" she said, sticking out an open hand.

"Um, well, um, yes," he said, still shivering slightly. "And you must be the highly talked about, hopefully not a murderer, Bixby Timmons?" he replied as he gave her hand a weak shake.

"I get it all the time for my red hair, so I've learned to have thick skin," Bixby said.

"Well, at least you're not a fat nerd. You'll survive just fine here," replied Tipton.

"Tell you what, Tipton, I'm not really good at keeping friends on account of them-becoming-victims thing, and it seems like you could use one. How about this...you be my friend, and I won't wash my hair with your blood," she joked.

"When you say it like that, how could I refuse?" he said with a bit of a nervous smile.

Mrs. Gable raised her voice over the class, grabbing everyone's attention. "Alright class, settle down, settle down. Let's get to these problems on the board."

Bixby quickly reset her Holo-Writer in order to erase the hacked message on her screen and put a few locks of her own on it so that it wouldn't happen again. It was confirmation that no matter where she went, there would always be bullies.

For the rest of the day, Bixby hopped from class to class, still amazed that she was actually standing in a Pinnacle Manor Launch Room. Everything she saw, felt, smelled, and heard was as if she was standing on campus. For once, she didn't mind being seated in a classroom during a warm spring afternoon, far away from where she was. Her old system couldn't hold a candle to what she was experiencing today. She wished that she could share it with the few friends she had back home in Snagelyville. For now, she had to make do with finding new friends, and Tipton seemed to be as much of an outcast as she felt she was. He was like a scared mouse in a maze filled with traps, and, lucky for him, she liked mazes.

Bixby's last class before enrichment was study hall in the tremendously large cafeteria.

The concept of a cafeteria had her confused at first. In Holo-Basic, students would have to log out of Holo to eat each day. However, in Holo-Prime, Bixby's lunch was seamlessly introduced into the Launch Room by Arthur each day at lunchtime. Though Bixby was actually eating real food in her Launch Room, to her it seemed as if she were eating right there in Holo with her classmates.

Bixby quickly found Tipton seated by himself in the corner. "Hey, Tipton," Bixby said as she approached.

With a slightly startled jump, he replied, "Oh, hey. Hi, Bixby. Sorry, usually when someone says, 'Hey, Tipton,' it's followed by something being thrown in my general direction."

Realizing that she was surrounded by most of the seventeen kids that were in her first class of the day, Bixby pushed on. "Well, that isn't very nice of them to do, is it? Tell me more about those guys." She gestured towards this morning's agitators.

Without looking up from his Holo-Writer for fear of getting caught looking directly at their bullies, Tipton gave her the rundown.

"The guy with all of the muscles and freakishly chiseled face who said you would eat my soul—that's Wesley Dagger. He is the son of Richard Dagger. He's the foreman at your dad's company."

Bixby smiled to herself as she remembered his butt chin from her dad's Holo-Mail in the van before arriving at Pinnacle Manor. He wasn't overly large like the mountain of a man the foreman was, but she could be sure that he was a mini foreman in the making. Everyone flocked around him, and when he told someone to do something, they followed without hesitation.

"He lives in Black Rock Castle. It's like Pinnacle Manor, but it doesn't have all of the features. His dad was super mad when he found out that Mr. Dragonthorp gave your family Pinnacle and not his. That's probably why he hasn't taken a liking to you," Tipton said.

"Most definitely," said Bixby as she stuffed a delicious bite of her turkey, cheese, and hot sauce sandwich in her mouth. It made Bixby a little proud to know that she had such an effect on jerks like that without even having to try.

"Anyway, he's most likely to go number one overall in the Business Draft our senior year. Every company is drooling to add him to their executive teams. Not only is his dad well connected, but he's also actually pretty smart on top of it." Tipton continued.

Cutting Tipton short of his next thought, Bixby asked, "That's the second time someone has mentioned the Business Draft. What's the big deal about it?"

"What rock have you crawled out from under?" Tipton asked.

Bixby could see Tipton cower a little when he realized he'd been sarcastic to a fault. She could see his mouth catch up to his mind as he tried to level with her.

"Okay, I'm about to drop something pretty heavy on you right now, Bixby. You can't be mad at me for ruining your day," he said, squirming a little.

"Deal," Bixby replied.

"Less than a year after Cody Dragonthorp disappeared, every business out there started paying Dragonthorp, Inc., a ton of money to have access to our rankings during enrichment. Most students of the world who attend Holo-School Basic think that they're simply playing games as a reward for doing their homework and getting decent grades. Basics don't really care about applying themselves to beating what they think are video games, because they don't know any better. For that reason, Dragonthorp, Inc., rarely pays any attention to the scores of Basics and focuses solely on Primes that are from elite families, helping to place their elite children. The high-ranking jobs go to Prime kids, while Basics are the people most qualified to work in the office pools and low-end jobs. The actual truth is that enrichment data collecting through Dragonthorp, Inc., is how the world decides who gets a good job and who gets stuck churning their wheels at the bottom."

"You're saying that Daemon Dragonthorp is keeping track of what we like to do during enrichment and how well we do it?" Bixby interrupted.

"And he's making a ton of money doing it. Rumor has it that the Business Draft is how he's keeping Holo afloat since Cody's disappearance," he replied.

"But how is that fair, if..." Bixby had a hard time saying the next word, knowing she was one, "...if Basics don't know they're competing for their future?"

"You're not naive enough to believe the system has always been fair, are you?" Tipton started. "Companies pay a small price to see who the best overall person is statistically to fill a top position, they enter the draft lottery, and then draft them. If you ask me, it's a scheme to keep the haves in the position to have, and the rest of us are none the wiser."

"How can they legally get away with that? Isn't that unfair to the people who don't know they're being watched? Most people don't have the money to buy better equipment like a Launch Room or a Holo-Suit," Bixby remarked, appalled at the new info.

"That's why a lot of people are really upset at Dragonthorp for giving your dad Pinnacle Manor. If the draft had been around when he was a kid, his GPA would have landed him a job as an office pool flunky, which he sort of was before a few weeks ago," Tipton said. He then shrank, suddenly realizing how harsh his comment was.

"I'm not mad at you, Tipton," she said with a scowl. "That is a huge smack in the face."

"If it makes you feel any better, I heard that when your dad went from cubicle to caretaker, it made a whole lot of executives irate." Tipton encouraged.

Bixby was somewhat comforted by the fact that her family had leapfrogged over so many high-ranking officials, but it didn't answer *why*, nor did it make her feel any less looked down upon. The only difference now was that when they looked down at her, they knew her name. Knowing that she couldn't stew on it for long, she wanted to know more about the other people.

"Who's that girl next to Wesley, the one with the jet-black hair and dark makeup? She was the one who called you a Leprechaun, right?" she asked.

"Penelope Dagger...Wesley's sister. Everyone just calls her Penny. Charming one, she is. Every tech company in the world is grasping at the chance to land her on their team. Last year, she hacked the school's mainframe so that whenever someone logged on in their Launch Room, they ended up in a sewer pipe under the school. It took the programmers two days to reset the parameters of the school. Needless to say, there are much better security firewalls in place now to avoid a catastrophe like that from happening again," Tipton replied while doodling in his Holo-Writer.

One by one, Tipton told Bixby about each of her classmates. Most of them were already ranked rather high in the 250 students to be selected in the first round of the Business Draft. They each had a different skill set ranging from mechanics, law, analytics, medical practice, and even teaching. As Holo-Schools' Primes launch, the high demand for teachers made it very competitive in order to get into a well-paying Holo-School. Now, instead of districts paying millions of dollars to maintain buildings, they were paying Dragonthorp millions of dollars to have a chance at the premier teachers.

As Tipton continued around the room, there were two other students that piqued Bixby's curiosity. First, she was going to make it a point to make acquaintances with Pippatilly Richards; Tipton said everyone called her Pippa for short. She was short and mousey-looking with straight-cut bangs across her neatly plucked eyebrows. According to Tipton, Gabhammer had suspended her twice because she'd insisted on wearing overly bold anti-meat propaganda, which was weird because Bixby was positive she was currently eating a double bacon cheeseburger.

"Her dad is the guy who creates all of the puzzles that we work on during enrichment. Some say he's the last of the employees at Dragonthorp, Inc., to see Cody before he disappeared. Pippa's IQ is off the charts, but I think her dad does her homework for her. They project her to go quickly in the draft to a company for national defense contracts doing cyphers and whatnot. I also think she's a member of the Cody Club I'm in; most people are really good at being anonymous in it, so I can't be sure."

"The Cody Club?" Bixby asked, intrigued.

"Yeah. We're an online group dedicated to solving the disappearance of Cody Dragonthorp. It's mostly speculation and data sharing about the life and times of Cody, but it gives us something to do."

"Hmm...I see," Bixby said, making a mental note of the online pool of information that might help her.

Just as Tipton was finishing the bio of Pippa, a kid in a blazer with patches on his sleeves, an *I ROCK* T-shirt, jeans, and sandals slumped down next to the couple.

"And this," Tipton said, sliding down on the bench, giving himself some space between himself and the new occupant of the table, "would be Marshall Grove, projected to go in the top twenty in the Business Draft."

"Top eighteen, Big Guy," he corrected. "What's up, Ginger?" he asked in a slimy voice, turning his attention to Bixby. Without waiting for a reply, he started into his monologue.

"You know that guy in the old prison movies who goes around telling everyone, 'If you need anything, I'm your guy'?

Well, those guys are amateurs. I am all about discretion; that's why everyone comes back to me. Need a system hack? No problem. Having an issue with your grades? Instant upgrade. Want more time in Enrichment? I'll have you gaming all night. Want your PB and J lunch to be pizza every day? Cheese or the works? Payment can be received in cash, completed homework assignments, and cash. Get what I'm getting at, Red?"

"You can get anything?" she questioned.

"Anything," he closed with a wink. With that, Marshall stood up and was gone.

"That's very good to know," Bixby said softly.

"He's shady at times, but he's never failed to deliver," Tipton said as they watched him walk away.

"What about you, Tipton? Where in the draft are you going to be selected?"

With a bashful chuckle, he picked at his fingernails and replied, "Well, the Headmaster thinks he could get a tech company to pick me up towards the end of the first round as a favor to Dragonthorp, Inc., for the work my father did for them. Plus, it would help to keep the school's rankings up."

"Well, that's awfully nice of them. Where were you projected to go?"

Tipton's face flushed red, and Bixby could tell she'd upset him.

"Nevermind; it's not important, Tipton," she said, trying to cover up the awkwardness.

"You might as well hear it from me before you hear it from those jerks," he said, appearing to muster his courage back up.

"As part of my dad's contract to help make the Vixaterian 4000 units, Dragonthorp promised him that I would attend Holo-School Prime if anything were to happen to him. He was the guy who went in and tested the light capacitors in the units—which is highly volatile and dangerous. While working on the seventh unit, one of the reactors malfunctioned. Dragonthorp, Inc., had to follow the rules based on his contract. My scores are the highest in Tech, but nowhere near good enough to get drafted in any of the seven rounds," he said sheepishly.

"I'm terribly sorry, Tipton."

"It's okay. You didn't know," he said, raising his eyes to meet hers. Bixby might have found the only other outcast in Holo-School Prime. *Not bad for a first day*, she thought.

Then, it hit her like a ton of bricks. Slumping back in her seat, Bixby's anger turned to sorrow. Her father was in a Vixaterian 4000 Launch Room right next to hers going about his day. He probably had no clue that Tipton's dad wasn't around anymore because of a system like his.

The final bell rang.

"See you tomorrow, Bixby," she heard through the haze as the Holo-Room went dark. Bixby needed to clear her mind of all the craziness that had happened in the last twenty-four hours; she needed to keep from coming undone. There was only one thing that normally held her sanity in check.

"Puzzles," she blurted out as she quickly remembered the shelf full of new puzzles in a house full of secrets.

CHAPTER SIX

CODY'S SECRET

MIGHT I SUGGEST setting up your shower?" Miss Marmalade said as Bixby quickly rushed back to her room from the Launch Room. It was at that point that Bixby realized it had been a day and a half since her last one, and she was starting to stink. As such, Miss Marmalade's suggestion was definitely on point.

When Bixby reached her room, she politely asked, "Harvey, if you're not having a bad day, please set up just a basic shower. I'm not feeling too fancy right now."

"Long day, Miss Timmons?" Harvey inquired.

"You could say that. And call me Bixby."

"Anything you would like to talk about?"

"No, but after supper, you could help me solve some puzzles if you wanted," Bixby replied.

"I have completed your shower settings, Miss Tim...sorry, Bixby. As for the puzzle solving, there are a few things in this house that my programming will not allow me to do. Solving the puzzles in this room for you is one of those things. I would be happy to keep you company as you attempt to solve them, though," Harvey said with an unusual amount of eagerness in his voice.

Bixby's skin tingled. She wasn't sure why Harvey was being nice to her, but when her stomach started to growl, her priorities became very clear. Shower. Food. Puzzles. With that plan in mind, Bixby raced through her shower and headed back towards the kitchen for supper.

"Something smells good, Miss Marmalade," Bixby said as she walked in. "I thought Mom was cooking tonight."

"Oh, she is, dear. Right now, she is getting the little ones up from their naps," Marmalade said as she bustled from pan to pan.

"Then how come it looks like you're doing all the work?" Bixby asked.

"Can I be honest, Bixby...without being tattled on?"

Bixby nodded her head.

"Your mom is not the best cook, and I am trying to save everyone's taste buds. I think she may have bitten off a little more than she could chew," Miss Marmalade said in a tactful voice.

Bixby broke out into laughter, and Marmalade followed suit. "Finally, someone who agrees with me!" Bixby said.

Mrs. Timmons walked in with a twin in each arm. She went over to the table and plopped them each in a highchair.

"Thanks for watching my meal, Miss Marmalade. How do things look?" Mrs. Timmons asked.

With a quick glance and a returned smile to Bixby, she replied, "Things are looking excellent. I can't wait to cook with you in the future."

"I know, Miss Marmalade. I will let you in tomorrow. I just wanted to make something special for Bixby and Cooper's first day as a way of saying how delighted I am for them," she said with a sense of pride.

"I look forward to it," Marmalade said, wiping her hands. "Well, it looks like I'm done here. I'll go and fetch Mr. Timmons."

Miss Marmalade removed her cooking apron and placed it on the hook beside the door as she shimmied out of the kitchen towards the Launch Rooms.

The kitchen did smell delightful, and her mother seemed to have a newfound joy working with all the new gadgets and mechanical oddities that made up her posh cooking area. Mrs. Timmons was full of life as she turned her attention from dinner to her daughter.

"Bixby! How was your first day? I want all the details: books, boys, teachers—all of it," Bixby's mom chirped.

"Ugh, Mom. Really?" Bixby again had to remind herself that moms could be almost as awkward as dads.

As Bixby began to set the table, she told her mom all about the exciting things she'd experienced being in the Launch

Room. Bixby conveniently left out the parts where she'd been bullied, the Business Draft, and how everyone was mad at the Timmons for living in Pinnacle Manor.

After Mr. Timmons sat down at the head of the table and said grace, everyone filled their plates with fried chicken and mac-n-cheese. Bixby repeated her day to her dad, who then told everyone about his day.

"Mr. Dragonthorp himself gave me a tour of the new offices. Did you know that the Bucksberry System was named after the Dragonthorps's childhood dog?"

The rest of the story that Mr. Timmons told was mostly common knowledge, but it made her dad happy, so Bixby simply smiled, nodded, and inserted an occasional "amazing" to make her dad feel good.

As he finished his tales of what it was like to work inside the Vixaterian 4000 Executive Offices of Dragonthorp, Inc., Bixby couldn't fit in another bite. She had puzzles in her room that needed solving, anyway.

"May I be excused?" Bixby asked her mother.

"Is something wrong, honey?" her dad inquired.

"No, no, nothing like that. I just have a lot of homework from my first day that I didn't finish during study hall, and I don't want to fall behind," Bixby replied, turning to her father.

"Wow, you really are taking this new school seriously, huh? I think it would be okay if you cut out of dinner early to get caught up, but just this one time," Mr. Timmons said, rubbing his daughter's head in approval.

Bixby felt that he was trying to connect with her but also give her space. Oddly enough, the grudge that she'd planned on holding onto for a while was quickly slipping away. She appreciated him more for the gesture but decided to keep those thoughts to herself for now.

Bixby hopped up, thanked her mother for dinner with a kiss on the cheek, and scurried out of the kitchen.

Back in her room, Bixby immediately reached for the small box with no handles or hinges that she'd found in the dining room. She ran her hand along the simple carving she'd read earlier: OPEN ME WITHOUT BREAKING ME.

Her grandpa had a similar box on a shelf in his workshop. It was the first puzzle Grandpa Timmons had ever taught Bixby how to solve. So, picking this one to start working on came naturally.

Lying on her bed, Bixby turned the box over in her hand.

"How are you going to open a box that has no lock, yet *is* locked, but has no keyhole or key, Bixby?" said a familiar Scotsman's voice as she concentrated.

Without breaking focus, Bixby explained the box to Harvey. "This is a puzzle box, Harvey. The trick to opening a puzzle like this is that the lock is on the inside. By sliding levers, holding it a certain way, or rotating knobs or handles, the box unlocks from the inside."

"Let's see you open it then, Smarty Pants, if it's so simple."

"I'm working on it, *Crabby* Pants!" Bixby said, mocking Harvey's crass tone and Scottish accent.

As Bixby worked her fingers over the box, she grasped one of the four round feet at the bottom and began to twist. It sounded as if she were winding a clock. After about seven turns, the foot clicked, halting in place. Out of the top of the box, the seal that had the "Open Me..." phrase popped up about a half-inch above the crest of the box.

"You did it, Bixby!" Harvey cried.

"Not yet. It just means I found the next step," Bixby said, focused on what to do next. Her first instinct was to turn it like a key. Bixby knew how to get back to this step, so she did exactly what her instincts told her. As she cranked the plate clockwise, the plate locked in place so that the words were now upside down. After a second, the box made a loud click, and the plate returned to its original setting, clacked back into position, and the foot of the box quickly unwound.

"That was quick. What's the next step then, Bixby?" Harvey said with some excitement.

"Start again," Bixby said, frustrated.

"What do you mean? The box moved again."

"Yes, Harvey, it moved back to its original settings. Anytime you make a mistake, the box resets," Bixby explained.

"Oh, well, that stinks now, doesn't it?"

Bixby rewound the foot, and the plate reappeared. This time, Bixby looked at it more closely. In two spots around the edge, she could see some worn patterns just above and below the O in WITHOUT. Bixby put her fingers right where the plate was worn and thought a moment.

"If I turn it, the plate resets. What else could I do if I put my fingers right here?" She wondered aloud, placing her thumb and index finger over the worn metallic shield. Then, she thought about what might happen if she pulled the plate instead.

As she started to pull the plate, Bixby noticed that the only thing attached now was a small rod connected to the bottom of the plate that ran into the heart of the box. She kept pulling until the plate finally came to a stop about two inches above the box. She waited as the plate spun around several times and then slammed itself back into the puzzle. This time the words were upside down. With this, the bottom panel smacked open and flopped against Bixby's hand. As she slowly turned the box over, the panel that hung open revealed a four-digit number combination lock, and the flap had writing carved on the inside of it.

With bated breath, Bixby read the inscription out loud: I built this box when I was two and a half years old, and my older brother was still in fifth grade.

Confused, Bixby read the inscription over and over. "That doesn't make any sense to me, Harvey. Do you have any idea what it means?"

"Don't ask me, Bixby. I can only keep you company. My program doesn't allow me to do any helping with those contraptions, remember?" Harvey said, sounding resigned to that fact.

"Okay, Bixby, what would Grandpa say?" Bixby self-coached, standing on her bed. Then she lowered her voice and tried to sound as much like an elderly man as she could. "Well, there, kiddo, it's a riddle. That means that part or all of it has two meanings."

"Harvey, which of the Dragonthorp boys was the oldest?" Bixby asked.

"Ah, something I can answer. Daemon was the older of the two boys. Came out two minutes before the Grand Master," he proudly replied.

"Daemon had the business smarts, and Cody was the book smart one, and, of course, this is Cody's house, so this is his puzzle," Bixby said. "So, if Daemon, the eldest, was in fifth grade, that would actually make him a little younger than me. How could his younger twin brother Cody be only two and a half years old, then? Think, Bixby!"

"Why don't you just guess a number, and when you get it wrong, guess again?" Harvey asked.

"Because, Harvey, if I guess wrong, I will have to start all over again from the beginning. With my luck, I will have to go through all ten thousand numbers to get it opened. That would take forever," Bixby said, slightly frustrated. "Tell me the basics about Cody and Daemon, and maybe something will come to me. My grandpa always said to talk it through."

"Well, they were born to Andrew and Alicia Dragonthorp in 1972," Harvey started, and Bixby quickly rolled the dials to one-nine-seven-two. The trap door slammed shut, and the box returned to its original state.

"Sorry that didn't work," Harvey replied as Bixby re-twisted the knobs and plate. "They were poor starting out, as Mrs. Dragonthorp couldn't work, and Mr. Dragonthorp's business wasn't doing so well. On Cody's first birthday, he took his two dollars of birthday money to a pawn shop where he bought an old clock and turned it into a fishbowl for the family's pet goldfish. One night at dinner, a neighbor saw the fishbowl and asked if Cody would make one for his nephew. The neighbor gave Cody ten dollars for his work. That was Cody's first invention. My, he was a brilliant—"

"Wait a minute," Bixby interrupted as she sat up on her bed. "Cody was a one-year-old when he made his first invention?"

"Well, no," Harvey said awkwardly. "Cody and Daemon were four years old, according to normal timekeeping, but their birthday is February 29th, so they have a birthday every four years. They were born on a leap year."

"*That's it!*" Bixby shouted. "They were ten years old and in fifth grade when Cody made this box. But, because their actual birthday was only every four years, he made this box when he was two and a half years old." Spinning the dials as fast as her fingers could move them, Bixby entered zero-two-two-nine.

The flap on the bottom of the box pulled shut, almost pinching Bixby's fingers. The inside of the box began to shake a little, prompting Bixby to place it flat on her bed. As she scooted back to watch the box gyrate, the knobs at the bottom extended to a few inches long. The "Open Me" plate rose up and rotated to reveal what looked like two eyes at the bottom of the shiny gold surface. The crease where the lid would normally open crept up and exposed what looked to be a mouth. Then it barked, yapped, and hopped as a note started to roll out of the animal's mouth.

"Congratulations! You have solved my Bucksberry puzzle to honor my dog. Please take your reward, as you will need it to solve my slide puzzle." Then, the dog dropped something from out of the box onto the bed.

"Looks like the dog just made a mess of your bed. That dog, Bucksberry, was always pooping on the carpets. I will get Miss Marmalade to come clean up the mess," Harvey said, disgusted.

"No, Harvey, it's a gold coin," Bixby said, shocked. "The note says I need to use it to solve the puzzle on the wall."

Bixby's gaze immediately shifted to the jumbled painting that hung above the fireplace. She quickly popped off of her bed and went over to the wall to see what she had to do with the coin.

"Has this painting always been here?" Bixby asked, examining the fireplace.

"The room is exactly how the master left it, except the bed was smaller," Harvey replied.

"Do you remember where Cody put these coins to work on this jumbled painting?" Bixby asked.

After a brief pause, Harvey said, "To be honest, Bixby, I don't remember ever seeing that jumbled painting above the fireplace, but my systems show something was there. I cannot seem to pull up what it looked like while the Grand Master lived here. This room is a complete blank for me. Sorry."

"It's okay. This puzzle thing is what I like to do more than anything else in the world. I'll figure it out," she replied.

Bixby grabbed the small stool that was at the edge of her bed and placed it at the base of the fireplace. She ran her hand over the mantle and then underneath. She examined the underside of the mantle on the far-left side just below where the stone had nearly stopped.

"What's this?" she whispered as her finger traversed a small opening. It wasn't cracked—it was more like someone had purposely cut the hole to place it there. Bixby held the coin up to the hole. An exact fit.

"Here goes nothing," she said under her breath. Bixby felt like she was about to drop this coin into an old-school video game at an arcade. As she let the coin go into the gap, she held her breath, waiting to hear the coin clink to the ground. Then, she slowly took a step away from the hearth. A loud noise like a boulder smacking against another boulder behind the wall rang out through the room. Bixby jumped onto her bed across the room, and one of the squares in the puzzle went from being flat on the wall to sticking out four inches.

"One of the pieces of the puzzle is ready to move, Harvey!" In a flurry of joy, Bixby danced and shouted on her bed.

Just then, the door flung open, and Mr. and Mrs. Timmons burst in. "Is everyone all right?" they asked.

Bixby hadn't really thought about the fact that the noise she'd made would be heard by the entire house.

Bixby dropped to the floor, but before she could say anything, Harvey answered the Timmons's question. "Quite alright. Miss Timmons has solved a riddle and won the right to change her room around a bit. It is a game we are playing. Terribly sorry about the ruckus."

"Well, then, let's try to keep it below a small roar, you two," Mr. Timmons replied. "Glad to see that you're having fun, Bixby," he said with a smile, ushering Mrs. Timmons out of the door before closing it.

"Arthur said that with the way you are programmed, you are not allowed to lie," Bixby said as soon as her parents were out of the room.

"We are not able to lie, Bixby. Tell me what part of my statement was a fib? You solved a puzzle which gave you the right to change the painting on the wall a little bit. And," he said, drawing out the word, "if I am not mistaken, even though I cannot directly help you, I did provide the information that led to the riddle's defeat. Therefore, we are playing the game together."

"Clever," Bixby replied, silently appreciating Harvey a little more. She took note of his seamless sleight of tongue deception. He was brilliant at it.

Again, the door flung open. This time, it was the Bulldog. Without a greeting, he simply stated, "Miss Timmons, your schoolwork is not yet complete. Enough games, Harvey, until she completes her assignments. That will be all." The door closed behind him as he exited.

"I really don't like him," Bixby grumbled.

"Goodnight, Bixby. I will leave you to your homework and then off to bed with you. We can continue the game tomorrow. I will dim your lights when you're ready to hit the hay," Harvey said.

With that, Bixby spent the next hour quickly finishing her schoolwork on her Holo-Writer and wasted no time readying for bed. Her only problem, as she crawled under her covers, was that she could only think about her new adventure. Could these be the clues that would bring Cody back? Had she really outsmarted all the other caretakers in a few short days of being at Pinnacle Manor? Bixby's mind quickly shifted to how she was going to spend her one-hundred-million dollars. Her mental list was exhaustive, to say the least, with all of the technology, gadgets, puzzles, her very own launch room with a Holo-Suit, which would include the most advanced doodads, and whatnots that could be added.

The thought of being on the right path alone produced an outbreak of emotions, but as she finished tossing and turning in anticipation, her gaze finally settled on the well-worn leather journal that sat on her nightstand. Grandpa gave most of his life to puzzles and riddles. All that she knew about decoding secrets came from a few memories, and the pages of his journals passed down to her dad and now to her.

Into the empty air, Bixby whispered with pride, "Grandpa, I totally got that puzzle all on my own. How did you like that?"

With one last plop on her pillow, she grabbed the book of Grandpa's words and tucked it in close. She grinned widely and fell asleep dreaming of what lay ahead, but what lay ahead was outside of anything a dream could contain. Bixby knew this because scorched into the outside of the journal that she now had snuggled close read:

Dreams can only take you as far as the morning. Adventures can take you as far as you push yourself to go...

CHAPTER SEVEN

TIPTON AND HIS SECRET WEAPON

FOR THE NEXT few weeks, Bixby did the bare minimum at Holo-School Prime. Her days consisted of launching into school with Headmaster Gabhammer hovering over her every move, attending each class and taking notes, getting razed by Wesley and his sister Penny Dagger (along with their friends), eating a lunch that consisted of turkey, cheese, and hot sauce sandwiches, and finally, going to study hall with Tipton.

Once she unlaunched from school, she'd race out of her Holo-Suit and continue to search Pinnacle Manor for different puzzles, taking them back to her room and attempting to solve them with limited help from Harvey. At school, Bixby even invited Tipton to help when she was stumped. Though he wasn't really much help in figuring out the pieces, he was a whiz kid on everything Dragonthorp.

"How is it even possible that you know all these little things about the Dragonthorps, Tipton?" Bixby asked. "Even Harvey doesn't know this stuff."

Under his bashful smile, Tipton admitted, "Okay, so when I was a kid, my dad took me to one of those 'Take Your Kid to Work Day' outings. While we were there, the Foreman stops my dad and asks how soon he can start on the first Launch Room. My dad goes all nuts because he has never even been spoken to by an executive, let alone asked to be on a major project. So, as the Foreman is leaving, this guy rolls up to my dad all weird like. He's talking to himself and looks my dad right in the eye and says, 'When you are in there setting the light capacitor, do not touch the green wire while touching anything else.' Then he makes this weird zapping noise, says, 'Our little secret,' and walks off. A week later, Dad's rigging up the light capacitor. It was set up so that he had to hold onto the wall where the light is supposed to come into the room to brace himself."

"You know an awful lot about technical specs and how things work for visiting one day with your dad," Bixby interrupted.

"After that day, I spent all my time in enrichment studying blueprints that my dad would upload for me. Very exciting stuff," Tipton replied. "Anyway, then Dad had to reach down and grab the green wire to connect it to the circuit board. Last thing he must do before the Launch Room would work, right? My dad said the image of the crazy dude making the *zap* noise flashed in his mind, and then he realized that it was a design flaw. If he connected the wire to the circuit board with his hand anywhere near the light capacitor, he would have arched himself with, like, fifty thousand volts of electricity.

"Come to find out, Cody Dragonthorp was the dude who gave my dad all the info. Then, Cody told his brother that it was my dad who figured out the flaw. The next day, my dad had a full-time job with a contract and everything. I've been obsessed with how cool Cody was to people ever since. My favorite place to get info is the Cody Club online. There are currently fifteen members from all over the world..."

"Like Pippa," Bixby interjected.

"Maybe. Anyway, I totally want to invent things and solve problems like Cody Dragonthorp...at least one day. For now, I guess I can do it on the side, seeing as I'll be drafted doing some stupid computer work."

"Why don't you design something that would allow you to come over to the house and help me solve all these puzzles," Bixby said casually.

Bixby could see Tipton's eyes grow freakishly big at her suggestion. "I've been working on them for almost a month, and I'm only a third of the way done. Each puzzle has to do with part of Cody's past, and you and Harvey are the only ones who know enough to help me solve them," Bixby said, trying to add context to her invite.

"Right. Well, I could come over if you want. I promise I won't mess up the settings at your house...Nobody's ever asked me to come over before," Tipton replied bashfully.

Bixby sat straight up in her chair, knowing there were only a few minutes left in study hall before the room would go dark.

"You're wrong. All the settings of the Manor turn back to the crummy default every time someone rings the front gate doorbell. It makes me so mad, especially when I'm in the middle of a puzzle, and the Manor shifts back to its original form until the delivery person, news reporter, or obsessed Cody fan goes away. Each time, I have to redo every puzzle because completed puzzles are the one thing Harvey can't save," Bixby said, agitated.

"Seriously, Bixby, I picked up a ton from my dad before... well, you know. Anyway, it was one of my first inventions when I decided to be like Cody. It's a mini chip that I hid in a coin because of its metallic properties, as well as the ability to easily conceal. If you had the coin there at Pinnacle Manor, I could get into my Launch Room, and the chip in the coin would link to one of your Launch Rooms, letting me appear in Pinnacle Manor as a hologram. The system wouldn't do any changing because it only searches for people who are actually there. I've been waiting forever to give it a try!" Tipton said, almost shouting towards the end.

A loud roar of, "*Shhh!*" immediately followed, and Tipton blushed when he realized he had disturbed the entire study hall.

Bixby quickly grabbed Tipton's Holo-Writer and began writing the address of Pinnacle Manor in it. "Tipton, I need you to overnight one of those coins to me as soon as you get out of your Holo-Room. I'll cover the cost, but make sure that the package doesn't look suspicious. The Bulldog checks everything that comes in the house."

"Bixby. I'm in the Cody Club—you really don't think I already know your address?" Tipton asked.

Just as he finished giving Bixby a little sass, the Friday bell rang, and the room went dark.

Bixby ran to her room, stripped off her Holo-Suit, and immediately started her puzzles. By the time she fell asleep that night, she'd solved two more puzzle boxes and a Rubik's cube of sorts. Only twelve more puzzles to go, and she now had a secret weapon coming tomorrow to help.

Bixby ripped open the package that was delivered to her house at 10 a.m. sharp. Inside were five dollars and one cent and a note that read:

Thanks for lunch, Bixby!
Your friend,
Tipton

Bixby grabbed the coin and immediately sent Tipton a Holo-Message, telling him to log in as soon as he could. She stood in front of the bathroom mirror while brushing her teeth, her wild hair standing up and her PJs still on. Just behind her, Tipton suddenly appeared, neatly groomed and smiling. Bixby nearly jumped out of her skin.

"*Tipton!* You scared the snot out of me!" Bixby shouted.

Beet red and now facing away from the mirror, Tipton stammered, "I may have forgotten to tell you that when I initially appear, it's designed to do so within ten feet of the coin. Maybe you shouldn't bring that coin into the bathroom...ever."

"I think that is a great idea, Tipton! Anything else you should've told me?"

"How about I wait in your room while you get ready?" Tipton said, then dashed out of Bixby's bathroom.

After about ten minutes of getting ready, Bixby opened the bathroom door, feeling presentable.

"I'm really sorry about that, Bixby," Tipton said.

"It's okay. We really didn't have much time to talk about the coin," Bixby said, knowing it wasn't Tipton's fault for showing up so suddenly. "Okay. So, how about some puzzles to get rid of the heebie-jeebies?"

"That sounds awesome," Tipton replied, relieved to be changing the subject.

"Aye, who are you talking to, Miss Timmons?" said a familiar, cranky voice.

"Harvey, I would like you to meet the newest member of the team. Harvey, this is Tipton Ellerby. Tipton, this is Harvey...my house," Bixby said.

Tipton looked around the room and then nodded a greeting into the air.

"Wait a minute. I didn't sense any extra humans in this house, or I would have reset the settings to default," Harvey said, panicked.

"It's okay, Harvey; he's a hologram. Just as you used technicalities on keeping me out of trouble for making noise the other night with my parents, we can say that *technically* he is not really here, so you don't have to reset the house. That means, technically, he can help us find Cody and bring him back," Bixby said, grabbing one of the twelve remaining puzzles.

"Technically, you're right, Bixby," Harvey said after re-scanning the room. "Clever girl. Very clever indeed."

Upon hearing Harvey's response, Bixby tossed the cylinder in the air, smiled, and with a new twinkle in her eye said, "Let's get started."

For the next ten hours, the trio stopped only for bathroom breaks and food. They hunted the entire house, finding puzzle boxes tactfully hidden in plain sight throughout Pinnacle Manor. Tipton launched and unlaunched each time Bixby slipped into another room as to not get caught by Arthur, or worse, her parents.

"Found one," Tipton said, pointing to a bookshelf in the den.

Bixby's eyes went up at least twenty shelves to the gizmo all the way at the top. "No way am I climbing up that shelf." Bixby gulped. "Harvey, can you shrink the shelf so that I can reach it?" she inquired.

Harvey made the adjustment quickly.

"Where did it go?" Tipton asked when the shelf made its way down.

"It seems that if I change the room in any way outside of the original settings created by the Grand Master, it disappears," Harvey said with a curious tone.

"Looks like you'll have to climb, Tipton," Bixby encouraged as Harvey reset the room.

"Sorry, Bixby; I'm a hologram," said Tipton.

85

The thought that holograms were not tactile frustrated Bixby because it meant she had to face her biggest fear in order to reach this puzzle: heights.

"I...uh, don't do climbing things," she admitted, embarrassed. "Would you do it, Hucklebee?"

Before Bixby even finished the question, Hucklebee was halfway up the shelves ready to help. Bixby had dodged a bullet by having a fearless H-bot help.

For the rest of the day, they solved finger traps, cryptex, and even one that had to be cracked using Morse Code. Harvey, though unable to help solve the riddle directly, was able to educate them on what letters meant what sounds. They had even more fun doing all the work while listening to many of the old spy records on Cody's shelf. It made them feel more like detectives. Each riddle required Bixby to remember something she had learned from Grandpa Timmons, knowledge of Cody Dragonthorp, and—every once in a while—plain, dumb luck.

Right around 9 p.m., footsteps could be heard coming down the hall. They'd solved eleven riddles and only had one box left.

Knowing it was getting late and recognizing that the Bulldog wouldn't abide by the same technicality exceptions as Harvey, Bixby grabbed Tipton's arm.

"You've got to go—now! Thanks for the help, Tipton. I'll Holo-Message you tomorrow when we start to try to solve the last puzzle," she said as the footsteps came closer.

Seeing that she was in a rush, he quizzically scratched his head, "Um...Okay?"

"I'll explain later, but you've got to go. Now!"

Just as Arthur turned the big brass knob on the door to give his usual bedtime speech, Tipton vanished into thin air.

"Ten minutes until lights out, Bixby," Arthur said.

Bixby let out a sigh of relief.

"That was close," she mumbled.

With that, Bixby bid goodnight to Harvey, changed into her PJs, and tried to fall asleep pondering how to open the last puzzle—a glass cube filled completely with what looked to be plain water. What made it hard to sleep was the possibility that the answer to Cody Dragonthorp's ten-year, one-hundred-million-dollar puzzle was attached to solving that cube.

She had no idea where to start.

CHAPTER EIGHT
ONLY TIME CAN TELL

EARLY THE NEXT morning, Bixby wandered down the hall to the kitchen, cube in hand. Since she was alone, it reset to her modern-castle settings. She went to the fridge, pulled out some leftovers, and made a bacon, egg, and cheese sandwich covered in her favorite ingredient: hot sauce. She placed the water cube puzzle in front of her and sat, chomping and staring.

"What have you got there, Bixby?" Hucklebee asked, startling her.

"Sneaking up on people again, I see?" Bixby replied.

"I will have to buy some louder shoes, even though these are so comfortable," he said with a chuckle.

"Hucklebee, what do you know about Cody Dragonthorp and water?" Bixby asked.

"Well, nothing, really. Other than Worthy Lake, which the Grand Master never swam in, and the water that comes out of the faucet," he replied.

"So, there was no fear of water or drowning? No passion to swim? Anything like that ring a bell?" Bixby asked through a mouthful of food.

"Nope, can't say I recall anything of the sort. The Grand Master had a dedicated schedule he liked to follow, being that he was autistic and all. Any changes to the schedule and he would get...well...utterly annoyed. Swimming wasn't on the schedule, but bathing was done every night at 7 p.m. sharp. Does that help?" Hucklebee said, openly wishful.

"No, I don't think so," Bixby said as her shoulders fell. "Thanks for trying, though."

"Anytime. That's one of the Grand Master's old puzzle boxes, eh?" Hucklebee said, eyeing the cube.

"Yeah, I found them in my room, and they all seem to have to do something with Cody's...I mean, the Grand Master's, life. I can't figure this one out, though. It's just a square glass with water inside, but nothing about Cody has anything to do with water."

"You've got me, Bixby. I'd put it in a pot and boil it. Maybe it will open up?" Hucklebee said.

"Maybe," Bixby said, wondering if the solution was that simple.

Though it was the most promising idea she had received, Bixby was hopeful her teammates would have some input as well. She finished breakfast and headed back to her room through the Great Hall. The house was quiet this Sunday, like normal, since her mom had made plans to take everyone antiquing—something Bixby always turned down, including today.

Instead, she summoned Harvey and Holo-Messaged Tipton that she was ready to tackle the final box. Within a few moments, everyone was assembled and staring at the three-inch by three-inch cube filled with the clean, clear water.

Over the next three hours, the team not only proceeded to put the box in the fireplace to boil it, as Hucklebee had suggested, they also smashed it on the ground, put it in the freezer, spun it on its corner like a top, sang to it, and stood on it. Still, the glass never broke, and the liquid inside never changed.

"I'm totally out of ideas," Tipton said, dejected.

"And I can only help you with your experiments," Harvey said.

Bixby stood on her bed, frustrated and needing to think. "Think, Bixby. Think," she said, tapping her head. "What would Grandpa say?" Again, in her best old man's voice, she started speaking out loud: "Every riddle has a key phrase, key word, or simply a key to solving the puzzle. The problem is finding which one you are looking for and how to apply it."

"How often would you say you talk to yourself, Bixby?" Tipton asked with just enough sarcasm to not offend her.

Realizing how crazy she probably looked, she bent to her knees on the bed and shared, "My grandpa always taught me to look at all problems from different angles when I couldn't figure it out. For me, the best way to solve a puzzle is to recite one of his famous Grandpa-isms while standing on something or doing something I usually wouldn't. I know it seems goofy, but it's what works for me. It's like he invented a whole rulebook for puzzle solv—" Bixby stopped.

She dropped down to the ground, flat on her belly, and stared right at the cube.

"What is it?" Tipton asked.

"This isn't the puzzle. It's the key," Bixby said, her mind reeling.

"Wait, you're saying that cube unlocks something?" Tipton said.

"Harvey? I need you to find something in the house. Can you do that for me?" Bixby asked, confident she was on the right track.

"Finally, something I can do. What is it that you are looking for?" Harvey replied.

"You told me that Cody's first invention was a clock that he turned into a fish tank, correct?" Bixby said.

"Aye, first thing he ever built."

"Somewhere in this house, there is a clock that hasn't been working for years...if it's worked at all since you've been here. Where in the house is it?" Bixby asked.

"I don't even have to do a digital search of the items in this house. I had Hucklebee put that old thing in storage when the Grand Master went missing. He had it above the fireplace in the Great Hall. I never understood why he loved that broken piece of junk so much," Harvey said.

"Have Hucklebee bring it here immediately," Bixby stated in return. "I'm going to get a snack from the kitchen, and then we are going to solve this thing."

After another turkey, cheese, and hot sauce sandwich, Bixby returned to her room where Hucklebee stood, beaming with pride, next to his find: a clock that was three feet tall and two feet wide. Bixby, Tipton, and Harvey all agreed it was definitely the biggest eyesore they had ever seen. Random lines and circles had been carved into the metal, which rusted almost completely through. The hands on the clock both dangled at the six. There were what looked to be mouse holes in the material that once was the backdrop for the timepiece. Where a complete array of stained glass had been, only two small squares remained intact.

"It looks like it hasn't been out of a basement in a hundred years. Gross," Tipton said as he walked around it. "So, where does the cube go?"

Bixby had already started searching for the answer to that very question. On her hands and knees, she circled the clock, examining every detail and carving, all the while holding her breath to avoid the stench.

"There has to be a way to open the back of this clock," she said.

"So, the clock is the puzzle box?" Tipton inquired.

"Ding, ding, ding," Bixby said. "We have a key, and now the puzzle box. We need to figure out how they work together."

Her first attempt was to move the hands to 2:29, the day of the Dragonthorp twins' birth. The hands fell limply back to rest on the six at the bottom of the clock. Then, she tried looking for a latch or a lever that would open the back panel, but there was none to be found. For the next hour, they each tried something different, but nothing seemed to work.

"Maybe we should get a hammer and pry the door open," Tipton said.

"If I thought that it would help, I would totally agree with that plan. The clock is in bad shape, and yet the back door won't budge. Everything is broken. The carvings are just a bunch of lines and circles, and it smells like rotten garbage. Maybe this isn't a puzzle box," Bixby said, feeling defeated.

Hucklebee, who was standing in the corner watching as the team tried to decipher the clock, suddenly piped up. "Begging your pardon, Bixby, but are those *just* lines and circles?"

Bixby and Tipton shot Hucklebee a questioning look.

"Well, what I mean is...Harvey and I run on a computer system, and all of our data comes to us via ones and zeros. It's called binary. Each series of ones and zeros means something, and for your sake, it can be translated into words, pictures, sounds, and so on. But for us, it's just a string of ones and zeros."

Tipton took his turn to smack himself on the forehead. "How did I not see that? Cody was so smart, he could probably read and write in binary. You and I couldn't possibly be able to read it, but Harvey and Hucklebee could."

Tipton and Bixby both looked at Hucklebee.

"I reckon it'd be best if Harvey does the scanning and then uploads it to the Holo-Writer?" Hucklebee quickly said.

"Trying awful hard to join the team there, aren't ya?" Harvey quipped. "At least you recognize my talents."

"It's okay, Harvey. You've helped solve several of the puzzles in one way or another. With four heads focusing on a puzzle instead of three, we have a better chance of solving Cody's riddles and possibly getting him back to Pinnacle Manor," Bixby reasoned.

Without agreeing or disagreeing with Bixby, her Holo-Writer lit up and started to spit out ones and zeros.

"Oh, you're going to like this, Bixby," Harvey said as the Holo-Writer's screen went blank.

"*Well?*" the rest of the room said in unison.

The screen lit back up to show a 3D picture of the clock, which started to move. Slowly, the clock rotated, and at each point, it stopped, and a certain part of the clock moved in a specific direction. Immediately, Hucklebee lifted up the clock, and, as each scene played, Bixby did exactly as instructed. The final move was to set the clock to one exact time; Bixby used 2:29. Hucklebee set the clock back down, and the new team of four waited with great anticipation. Within moments, they were rewarded. With a loud click, the back of the clock sprang open. A perfect three-by-three-inch slot appeared inside.

"Get the cube, Tipton," Bixby said in awe.

"Hologram," Tipton said, reminding Bixby that he couldn't really grab anything.

"Right," Bixby replied as she retrieved the cube. "Moment of truth?" she said, placing the cube back in its old home.

Bixby latched the door closed, and they all took a seat in front of the clock. As if someone had turned on a switch, an electric pulse could be seen through the holes in the front of the clock. Little bolts of lightning went all around the glass of the cube. The bolts seemed to follow a pattern etched into the glass. One bolt looked like a fish, another took the shape of a computer, and another the face of a clock.

The gears started to spin, and the clock began to repair itself. The tarnished and rusted metal turned into magnificent, brushed silver. The backdrop of ripped fabric grew seamlessly back together. Little crystals sprouted in the empty holes where stained glass used to be. Vibrant blue and green glass soon filled each empty space. The dingy, old smell was now replaced with the pleasant scent of oil running through the system. The gears were clicking and clacking faster and faster, and the hands on the clock perked to life, immediately turning themselves to 12:18.

Tipton and Bixby checked their phones: 12:18. It had kept perfect time.

As the clock settled into the normal rhythms of what a clock should be, two doors slid open, and the cube inched forward and locked into place. The water was glowing neon blue, and a small flicker had begun. Two fish—holograms, most likely—swam around in the little blue cube. They were fish like no other, with their beautiful, flowing fins, elaborate color array, and luminescent trail they left as they swam. Cody must have created them especially for this clock.

In stunned silence, the team stared at its brilliance. However, just like all their other successes, this one, too, would be short-lived, and a coin soon rolled out of a small slot in the lower right-hand corner of the clock. It wobbled to a stop next to Bixby's shoe. It was the final coin needed to solve the slide puzzle above the fireplace mantle. Bixby looked at the coin and then looked a few seconds more at the clock. She took the coin as she stood up.

"You guys ready to see where the slide puzzle leads us?" Bixby asked.

"*Yes!*" everyone said with excitement.

"Okay. Hucklebee, can you please place that clock on the nightstand next to my bed and then come over here?"

Hucklebee shot her a quizzical look.

"You came up with the solution to the puzzle, so it's only right for you to put the coin in the slot on the mantle," Bixby said, handing him the coin.

Hucklebee reached out reluctantly as if Bixby were going to pull the coin back as part of a trick, but she didn't. She simply said, "Welcome to the team."

As he dropped the coin in the slot, a familiar *thump* occurred when the coin reached the bottom. The wall made its usual rumblings, and the final piece to the stone slide puzzle became visible. This time, though, part of the wall next to the fireplace slid away, and a small touchpad appeared with the exact mixed-up image of the slide puzzle above. Bixby approached, and as she ran her fingers across the screen, the puzzle moved above her head.

Most puzzles took mental focus and being able to think outside the box, but slide puzzles were easy for her. When first learning how to solve puzzles, Bixby had taken to the Internet to complete more and more of them, eventually becoming bored by the common patterns used. This one, however, interested her immensely because of its enormous size and lack of a picture. The puzzle seemed to be a series of random colored lines.

As Bixby started to slide the first piece of the puzzle into a more "unmixed" position, she heard the van door slam with two boys crying at the top of their lungs. This puzzle would have to wait. Mr. and Mrs. Timmons were home from antiquing, and Bixby was not ready to let them join in on her fun.

"Sorry, guys, we'll have to put a pause on this puzzle until I can get my parents out of the house long enough to finish it."

"Leave that to me," Harvey said. "That is something I can help with."

CHAPTER NINE
AN INVITATION LIKE NO OTHER

IT HAD TAKEN Harvey three days to develop his plan, but he was eerily good at strategies of disguise, and he executed this new plan perfectly. Bixby was to get out of enrichment at exactly 2:45 p.m., and Mr. Timmons had to work until 5 p.m. and thus wouldn't hear the stone puzzle pieces move in Bixby's bedroom from his concealed Vexaterian 4000. Harvey had planted the idea in Miss Marmalade's program to talk to Mrs. Timmons about bringing the twins down to the beachfront next to the dock for some sandcastles and swimming, reminding her that they lived in Pinnacle Manor. It could be summer practically all year long if they requested it. Mrs. Timmons jumped at the idea of being able to go and work on her tan, but she worried about having dinner ready for the family. Hucklebee immediately stood up and took one for the team, offering to take care of dinner while everyone was having fun. Finally, after much anticipation from the team, Harvey was able to clear a two-hour and fifteen-minute window where Bixby could work on the massive slide puzzle.

Sprinting from her Holo-Room to her bedroom at 2:45 sharp, Bixby quickly changed out of her Holo-Suit and texted Tipton to come over. Harvey closely monitored everyone at the other end of the property as Hucklebee knocked on her bedroom door.

"I thought you had to make dinner?" Bixby exclaimed. "Mom is going to be super mad if there's nothing to eat when they come home."

"Don't worry. In one crockpot, I have a roast that's been cooking most of the day, and I just dropped some homemade mac-n-cheese in another crock. They should both be done right at five," Hucklebee said proudly.

Bixby smiled at Hucklebee's ingenious plan to get around having to spend all afternoon slaving over a hot stove, then she quickly returned her attention to the touchscreen. She realized the puzzle was even harder than she'd imagined as she feverishly slid the pieces around. Each piece could fit with at least two others, which made keeping track of what had already been done almost impossible. Tipton, Harvey, and Hucklebee sat for well over an hour, waiting and guessing between themselves as to what the picture might be.

"Wait, Bixby, stop!" yelled Tipton. "I see it!"

"See what?" Bixby said, stepping away from the touchpad.

Tipton ran up next to Bixby. "Look, each puzzle piece has extra lines written on it in different colors, but if you match only the middle green lines and ignore the other colored lines, the pieces match up," he said, tracing his fingers over the green grooves.

"Green was the Grand Master's favorite color," Harvey chimed in.

Knowing how to solve the puzzle, Bixby worked at a heated pace. It was a five-by-ten puzzle with forty-nine tiles to move around, and Bixby was in the zone. She could now start to see what she was drawing but had only thirty minutes left until her parents would return home per Harvey's recent update to the status of things.

It took longer than she wanted, but eventually Bixby slammed the last piece into place and jumped back to stand with the rest of the team and admire the photo. As if someone had started to erase the other colored lines, they disappeared one by one, until just the green lines were left. Blotches of color began to appear on the stone canvas, and the picture was clear. It was Cody sitting at a desk, putting together a clock fish tank.

"Cool...but that's it?" Tipton said, slightly bummed.

"That can't be it!" Bixby shouted, running over to the touchpad. She'd spent days dreaming about how the one hundred million dollars would free her and her family from the bonds of being a caretaker. Bixby desperately wanted to go back to her old life; this time without the financial limitations. However, the touchpad simply read:

An Invitation Like No Other

ALL GOOD THINGS COME IN TIME. THANK YOU FOR PLAYING.

"No!" Bixby cried. She slumped down on the wall. "I thought we were going to find Cody."

"We're home!" shouted her father from the Great Hall.

"Your dad's out of his Holo-Room and heading this way, Bixby...I'm sorry, I was hoping to find The Grand Master, too," Harvey said in a quick but somber voice.

"I better get going," Tipton said sadly as he flashed and disappeared.

"And I had better get to finishing dinner," Hucklebee said, then slipped out the door and loudly greeted Mr. Timmons. "How was your day, Sir?"

In the background, Bixby could hear Mr. Timmons talk about his wonderful Discovery Department and how productive they were today, but it was broken up by her sniffles.

"I know you don't think so right now, Bixby, but I believe in my heart that if anyone can find the Grand Master, it will be you. I haven't had this much hope in anyone since he went missing. Please don't give up. We are all counting on you," Harvey said softly.

Then Bixby was alone with her thoughts and tears.

Bixby washed up and made herself presentable for dinner, which was good for what little Bixby ate. Mostly, she pushed her food around her plate and tried to figure out where she'd gone wrong.

Cody wouldn't have gone through all that trouble to build an elaborate puzzle system just to end it with that message on a touchscreen, would he? The rest of dinner was a haze, a mixture of polite conversation infused with thoughts of disappointment. As Miss Marmalade cleaned the dishes and Mr. and Mrs. Timmons took the twins for a bath, Bixby said her goodnights to everyone and slowly walked back to her room.

Arthur didn't even have to give his nightly bedtime countdown because Bixby had already finished her homework and crept under the covers. She was too upset and exhausted from the past few weeks of puzzle solving to put up a fight to stay awake and think. Moments after the lights were out, Bixby found herself mesmerized by the two fish in the clock next to her nightstand.

She didn't realize how quickly she fell asleep. She did, however, realize that something had woken her up.

Clack.

Bixby was surrounded by near-darkness as she shot up from her slumber. The fire was low, giving off a warm glow as she took a mental inventory of the room around her. Moonlight beamed through the gigantic windows, and Bixby glanced at her new fish clock that read exactly midnight.

"Harvey, is that you?" she asked with a groggy whisper.

"Bixby...it is the middle of the night, and even computers like a little shutdown time to cool our hard drives. My systems show no disturbances, and everyone else is asleep," Harvey grumbled in a low voice.

"No, seriously, I heard a noise. Like someone opened a door," Bixby insisted. "Turn the lights on!"

The room lit up. She rubbed her eyes and started searching. The door was still latched shut, and everything was on the shelf just as she had left it. She turned to the windows. Each was shut tight.

The slide puzzle, she thought to herself and took a few steps back. Nothing had changed. Cody was still at a desk putting together another clock fish tank. Then, out of the corner of her eye, she saw something had changed. The words on the touch-pad were now different:

ALL GOOD THINGS COME IN TIME. NOW IT'S TIME TO WORK.

Bixby and her team had missed the obvious yet again. Cody was autistic and did things on a strict schedule. He ate at the same time, he got up at the same time, he wore specific clothes on specific days, and he did his work at specific times during the day. The only way to access the next part of the puzzle was to wait until it was time—Cody's time.

Bixby hunted for whatever had opened. She pushed on wall panels, tugged on bookshelves, and even tried to lift her bed up. Nothing budged. She jumped up on her bed, stood on one leg, and started reciting Grandpa-isms in her best Grandpa voice: "If you catch a fish this big, always say it was a few inches bigger; it makes the story a lot more fun. Hard work is like going to the dentist, nobody wants to do it, but those who do feel a whole lot better than those who don't."

Bixby paused for a minute.

"Ah, none of those help," she said, eying a spot on the floor to jump. Then something out of the ordinary presented itself. While she was lying in bed, all she could see was the fire in the fireplace. Now that she was standing on the bed, above the flames, she could see the wall behind them, where there was an opening about six inches wide in one of the corners.

"Harvey, turn off the fireplace," she whispered.

Without making a sound, Harvey obliged. Bixby rushed over to explore the new opening. As her face approached the crack, she could feel a cool breeze that smelled like an old library—slightly stale and with notes of old books.

"Harvey, what is in this part of the house?" asked Bixby.

"I do not have access to anything past the fireplace except the hallway," Harvey said with a little more curiosity.

"Interesting...a secret tunnel inside of a computer system. Cody gets cooler and cooler," Bixby said to herself.

She rushed to her Holo-Writer and immediately Messaged Tipton: *911. COME OVER IMMEDIATELY!*

A minute later, she received a Holo-Message back: *This had better be good. It's midnight.*

"Oh, Tipton, my robust friend, you are going to be the talk of your Cody Club," Bixby said, speaking to herself again. "Better wake Hucklebee. We have work to do."

Five minutes later, the whole team was assembled back in Bixby's room and staring into the fireplace where a newly formed void had appeared in the corner.

"Okay, so you have a hole in your fireplace," Tipton said through a sleepy fog.

"It opened at midnight, and the words on the touchpad changed, now saying we have work to do. It means we have to go into whatever is in this tunnel," Bixby said.

"I totally get the point here, but who works at midnight? I am starting to not like Cody," Tipton grumpily replied.

"Oy, mind your mouth, that's the Grand Master you're talking about!" Harvey barked.

"*Shh!*" Hucklebee and Bixby said in unison.

"Put on your big boy pants and get ready to go into the deep, dark tunnel," Bixby said sternly.

"I'm afraid you are on your own with this one, Team. I am a program with parameters of just this house, and that tunnel is not on my list," Harvey said, disappointed.

"Actually..." Tipton piped up. "You could project yourself through the coin I gave Bixby into any form you want."

"How long have you known about this, you round, little booger?" Harvey snarked, still cross at Tipton for speaking negatively about Cody.

"*Shh!*" Hucklebee and Bixby demanded again.

He repeated himself in an angry whisper: "How long have you know about this, you round, little booger?"

"Listen, Harvey. I'm sorry I never thought about making you a living being. Just read the program, and you'll be able to see how to manifest yourself into real life. As I said before, you can use one of the house's Launch Rooms to project yourself through the coin," Tipton said.

After a few minutes of prep work, Harvey said, "Okay, here we go."

The rest of the team looked around the room, and, right in front of the fireplace, a boy roughly fourteen years old appeared. "What do you think?" he said in Harvey's grumpy voice.

Instantly, everyone broke out into quiet laughter.

"You can't be serious, Harvey?" Bixby made out through her giggles and snorts. "You look like a kid and sound like my grandpa."

"Aye, if you want me to go down in that hole, I'm not going to be an old man," Harvey snapped.

"But you sound like one."

"And?"

"And Cody made you the way you are because you either reminded him of someone, or he liked your personality. Right now, you look just plain ridiculous," Tipton said.

"All right, all right."

The boy disappeared and, a few moments later, an older man appeared. He wore a pair of dress pants, a sweater vest, a tweed jacket that had patches on the elbows, and a matching flat cap. He reached into his pocket, pulled out a pipe, lit it, and said, "Well, what are you namby-pamby kids waiting on?" He pushed open the back of the fireplace to expose the dark, spiral stairwell leading downward. His appearance matched his voice perfectly this time.

"After you, Bixby," Tipton said in his usual timid voice.

As she stepped out onto the stairwell's platform, a motion sensor must have been triggered. A series of lights turned on one by one, leading down into the abyss. The four adventurers leaned over the edge to watch and see how far down they had to go.

"That's helpful. Anyone want to guess how many stairs there are to the bottom?" Bixby asked, joking.

"Tell you what, Bixby, you climb down and text me when you get to the bottom," Tipton replied. "That way, I can catch a nap."

"You go, too, or you get cut from the team," Harvey said. "Don't be such a baby."

The team made their way to the bottom. They arrived at a large door with another fishbowl clock carved into the massive wooden structure. There was a touchpad on the sidewall with a four-digit code. Without hesitation, Bixby typed in zero-two-two-nine.

"*I'm sorry. That is incorrect. You have three more attempts,*" the panel read.

"Try one-nine-seven-two, Bixby; the Dragonthorps's birth year," Tipton suggested.

I'm sorry. That is incorrect. You have two more attempts.

"What do you think, Harvey?" Bixby asked.

"Well, the door opened at midnight. Two-four-zero-zero?" Harvey guessed.

Reluctantly, Bixby typed the numbers into the keypad.

I'm sorry. That is incorrect. You have one more attempt.

With a sense of desperation, Bixby started to ask questions and state facts out loud: "Okay, so we know Cody has autism, and he uses numbers that are easy to remember or close to him. Not his birthday or birth year like we used before. Not the hour in which he likes to work, and there are no numbers on the door or time on the clock. *Ahh!*" Bixby growled up the stairwell.

"What about the number of stairs?" Hucklebee said.

"What about the number of stairs, Hucklebee?" Bixby asked.

"Well, I thought there was really a bet about how many stairs there were, so I kept count," Hucklebee admitted.

"Well, how many were there?" Harvey grumbled.

"One thousand and ten. It is kind of like his binary code, don't you think? One-zero-one-zero," he said, sounding hopeful.

"Are we all in agreement that this should be our last try? I mean, spikes could shoot through the ground and kill us," Bixby said, half-joking yet slightly worried.

"Actually, it would just kill *you*, Bixby...We are all holograms and machines," Tipton corrected.

"*Not* making me feel better, Tipton."

Bixby cringed as she approached the touchpad. Holding her breath, she started typing: one-zero-one-zero.

The moments went past like hours as the team waited for the room to do something awful to Bixby and Hucklebee. Then a loud series of metal smacking against itself allowed the massive wooden doors to swing open by themselves. Each team member exhaled, knowing Bixby and Hucklebee were not going to get impaled.

An Invitation Like No Other

From behind the colossal doors, lights turned on one after another again, revealing a long hall of bookshelves on either side of the room. Except this time, they were not lights but torches jetting out of the sides of the bookcases. It looked like something out of a medieval castle, with the red carpet stretching from one end of the room to the next. The walls were made of gigantic castle stone just like in the Great Hall.

"Wait, this must be right under the Great Hall," Tipton said as he realized the similarities of the space.

Walking through the doorway, they could see that the bookcases stopped two hundred feet from where they stood, but there was a second-floor balcony with another staggering number of bookcases that went the entire way around the room.

"Bixby, your kitchen would fit in great right off this room, eh?" Hucklebee said with excitement.

"Yeah, it would," Bixby replied. "Cody seems more and more awesome as this goes on, doesn't he?"

"His puzzles also seem to be getting harder as we go along, too," Tipton added.

"Way to ruin the mood, sport," Harvey said, poking at Tipton.

"Listen here, you grumpy, old computer. Keep it up, and I'll reprogram you to be wearing a baby's diaper every time you appear," Tipton fired back.

"You two need to start getting along, or I'm kicking you both off the team," Bixby replied over her shoulder at the bickering boys.

Both understood that not having time to shutdown was starting to wear thin on their attitudes.

Harvey straightened. "Aye, I'm sorry, Master Tipton."

As the group made their way down the long red carpet, they were amazed by the collection of books. There were tens of thousands of books in cases that needed rolling ladders to reach the top shelf. They didn't have libraries like this in Snagelyville. Or anywhere Bixby had ever been, for that matter.

Tipton inhaled deeply through his nose. "I love the smell of books."

"Do you think he read all of these?" Bixby asked, hoping one of the three Cody experts could answer.

"Probably," Hucklebee replied. "He had...has one of those eidetic minds."

Bixby gave a look as if she had no idea what Hucklebee was talking about.

"So, let's say he reads a book. His mind takes a snapshot of each page, each word, and each letter and never forgets any of it. It's probably why he could read binary code. He could read a large book in the amount of time it took him to flip the pages," Hucklebee said, starting to sound excited. "He was a walking computer."

Bixby nodded as Tipton wrote down that fun fact in his mini Holo-Writer, probably to take back to his Cody Club.

As they approached the far end of the hall, there was a large writing desk scattered with all kinds of rolled up pieces of paper and books flopped open. A small ball of light started to flicker and hover in the middle of the brown executive leather chair in front of the desk. The group stopped in their tracks. The light began to grow, and in a flash, there was a figure sitting at the desk, writing on a piece of parchment.

"Grand Master!" Hucklebee cried out and ran to hug the figure. As he reached the desk to wrap his robot arms around Cody Dragonthorp, he tumbled over the chair and landed face first with a thud on the hard desk. His arms were wrapped only around himself. The excitement faded quickly as they all realized that it was only a hologram. Hucklebee brushed himself off and made his way sadly back to the trio. The chair rolled to its original position, and the ball of lightning grew back into the shape of Cody Dragonthorp. Everyone leaned over to see what he was writing, but they realized that he was speaking the words as he went.

To whomever solved my first riddle,

Thank you for taking an interest in my puzzles. They make me happy, and I hope they made you happy as well. Now that you know me a little better, I have an offer to make you. Of the five houses I created, like the one you are currently in, I require a player from each to compete in a series of riddles. At the end of each riddle, the last person to finish will be eliminated until only one remains. Become the Riddle's Champion and I will give you alone the secrets of Holo, both present and future.

If you aren't already aware, this is a prize that will change your life and the world.

I must also warn you that although the riddles you solved to get here came with no risk, the puzzles in the contest will contain no small amount of peril, and the dangers will increase as the game goes on.

Knowing this, if you wish to be the contestant in my riddle to represent Pinnacle Manor, please sign below.

Cordially,

Cody Dragonthorp
*X*_____

With that, Cody disappeared, but the letter and quill pen remained on the desk where he had left them. Bixby froze as she tried to process the offer. She loved puzzles and riddles, but could she really be good enough to solve Cody's riddle? He was the smartest, richest man alive, and she was an average teen from the slums of Snagelyville. Winning the secrets would also mean a hundred million dollars, which would quickly change life for her and her family. And what did he mean about Holo secrets? It all intrigued her very much as she continued to drift away in thought.

"Bixby?" Tipton interrupted.

Snapping to, she saw that all eyes were on her.

"Aye. We are all looking at you, Bixby," Harvey said. "I'm a program, he's a robot, and that kid doesn't even live here. That just leaves you, missy." His words eliminated any question as to who could sign that paper.

"I do like to solve riddles," Bixby said.

Her mind reeled in disbelief that she had the chance to unlock the greatest mystery ever.

"I don't know, Bixby. He did mention 'peril' in his letter; that doesn't seem too inviting to me," Tipton retorted.

"But the Grand Master has to be brought back," Hucklebee pleaded.

"You can just walk away from all of this and just enjoy Pinnacle Manor for as long as you've got it," Tipton encouraged.

"It will be easy for Bixby. She has already solved this one with little trouble; what are a few more puzzles going to hurt?" Hucklebee volleyed back.

"He is right. I know the Grand Master, and even though he could make things challenging, being as clever as he is and all, he wouldn't really harm anyone," Harvey added.

"So, you think I should sign it, Harvey? You think it's worth the risk?" Bixby said.

"Aye."

"And Hucklebee, you think there is a reason why he decided to use riddles, and that I'm the right person to solve it?" Bixby questioned.

"I think that for whatever reason, the Grand Master needs to be rescued, and hiding in a riddle was the only way he could think to do that," Hucklebee said confidently, looking her directly in the eyes. "You're the best chance we've ever had."

Bixby smirked a little, not knowing how to take Hucklebee's assessment.

"What about you, Tipton?" Bixby asked.

"No idea. I only know silly facts about Cody to take back to my Cody Club. I thought it was going to be like an online search or something like that, but these guys are right: Cody was awesome to my dad. He was always looking out for the people of his company and the little people. But...in the last two weeks, I've made the closest thing to a family I've had in a long time. Even the old bag of bones over there is all right," he said, pointing over to Harvey. "I hate the word 'peril,' but knowing the secrets of Holo and one hundred million dollars is pretty tempting. It's a risk *you* have to take, not us."

"Would your dad sign this piece of paper if it meant rescuing Cody?" she asked.

After an agonizing few moments of staring at the ground, thinking about the question, and missing his dad, Tipton stopped kicking the carpet, raised his head with watery eyes, and nodded a simple yes.

Bixby realized she was only asking the questions to confirm the decision she had already made the moment she solved the first puzzle box. She breathed in deeply, and just as heavily, she let it out. "I'm not sure I like the 'peril' part either, but for a hundred million dollars and the secrets to Holo, I think I'll take that risk. Plus, I am a sucker for a good riddle."

She marched over to the desk and, using the X that Cody wrote, she signed:

Bixby Timmons

With that, the paper flew up into the air as if it were attached by a string. It then folded itself up and exploded into a little ball of lightning.

"That settles it. We have a riddle to solve," Bixby said proudly.

"We also have school in the morning, Bixby, and it's already three a.m.," Tipton reminded her.

"Well, guess we'll see what tomorrow brings," Bixby said to the group.

With that, Tipton and Harvey disappeared. Hucklebee and Bixby marched up the one thousand and ten stairs back to Bixby's bedroom. Not a word was said the whole walk up.

In her bedroom, Hucklebee slowly closed the fireplace. Bixby wasn't quite asleep as he started to slip out the door; he stopped and looked over his shoulder and whispered, "I knew you would save my best friend the moment I met you."

Bixby just hoped peril meant that she wouldn't have to lose her life to save his, but she'd already signed on the line.

In another manor, far away, the lights flipped on in a bedroom covered in black silk and red trim. The fireplace was adorned with a lion's head mounted above its mantel, and black mahogany bookcases encompassed the room. The man sat up and demanded, "How *dare* you come into my room at this hour of the night. If you don't have a good reason for doing so, I will send you straight to the scrap yard this instant, Robot!"

"Sir. We have a problem. Pinnacle Manor has been activated. The Riddle is about to start," the H-bot replied.

Anger turned to amusement in an instant. "Time to learn your secrets, Cody."

CHAPTER TEN

A NEW COOL KID

THE NEXT MORNING morning, the alarm clock on Bixby's cell phone seemed to go off every two seconds. With the intent of just turning off her phone, she pulled it close to her face and saw the following: *You have 62 New Holo-Messages and 602 Text Messages*

Bixby struggled with the covers as she brushed her hair out of her face and sat up. She gasped at all the messages from news reporters, morning talk shows, afternoon talk shows, and even famous rock stars and athletes. All of them wanted to do an interview or just hang out. She was still watching the Holo-Message from her all-time favorite Holo-Tuber Tess Jaxson, who was inviting her to be a guest on her next episode when Bixby's door flew open. Her mother, followed by her dad, raced into her room.

Bixby's mom was rambling on about, "How could you go and do something like this without telling us? I have a mob of people at the front gate buzzing like crazy trying to get you to come out."

At the very same time, Mr. Timmons was like a little schoolboy, drooling over the idea that his daughter was the one who'd cracked Cody's code. "How'd you do it? Did Grandpa's puzzles help you solve it? Tell me everything!"

Mrs. Timmons continued to rattle on over her dad's questions. "The school called, and there's a two-hour delay so they can update their firewalls to prevent reporters from hacking their way into Holo-School Prime. Who told you that you could play a game when you have important schoolwork? You aren't even old enough to enter into a legal contract. I am calling a lawyer this afternoon and getting you out of this fiasco right now!"

Bixby's eyes shifted back to her dad. "What was Cody like? I need a step by step walkthrough of how you solved the first riddle."

Mrs. Timmons jumped in and grabbed Bixby's arms, looking for bruises. Taking the conversation back, she said, "Are you hurt? Of all the irresponsible things you could have done; what if you would have been hurt!"

"I have been searching this house in all my free time trying to find a starting spot like Grandpa taught us. Man, I am so proud of you!" Mr. Timmons finished in the heated back and forth that was starting to make Bixby's brain hurt.

"*Silence!*" scolded an old man with Harvey's voice who stood in front of the fireplace. "I'm merely a *computer program*, and even I have a headache from all of this racket. I can only imagine what Bixby is feeling...Tell 'em, Bixby."

Mrs. Timmons tightened the neck of her robe, appearing uncomfortable after she noticed that Harvey now had a form. "I don't think you have a say in this, Harvey."

"I was there when she solved the riddle, so I think I am in this as much as everyone else," he replied firmly.

"When did you get a body?" Mr. Timmons interjected.

"Tipton helped create it for him. It allows us to not just talk to the air when we need him," Bixby explained while Mr. Timmons continued to stare in amazement.

"Who is Tipton?" Mrs. Timmons asked.

"He's a boy from my class who's an expert on technology and everything Cody Dragonthorp," Bixby said.

"He was here?" Mr. Timmons asked, scanning the room for places that this boy could be hiding.

Bixby briskly moved on. "Long story short, I was bushed when we first moved in, so the only change I made to the room was a bigger bed. I looked around, and there were all these puzzle boxes on the shelves, just like the ones Grandpa used to make. As I solved each one, a gold coin came out, and I had to place them here in the fireplace," Bixby said, gesturing to the touchpad, "which unlocked a piece of a puzzle that is now solved and—"

"And that's brilliant," her dad interrupted.

"Go on," Mrs. Timmons said with her arms crossed.

"Last night at midnight, the touchpad opened a secret passage behind the fireplace, and we followed a staircase down to a huge library, where a hologram of Cody wrote a letter asking for someone to solve his riddle. It's no big deal. He's hiding some sort of secret in a riddle." Bixby was careful not to mention the part about "peril" to her parents.

"The Riddle will be hard, but Grandpa taught Dad and me how to solve riddles, which means I can totally do this. We are Timmons—riddle solving is what we do. It'll be cake."

"Plus, if she wins, we get the Grand Master back, and she gets a hundred million dollars," Hucklebee politely added.

"A hundred million..." Mrs. Timmons whispered. Her voice trailed, but she soon reverted to the role of a concerned mother. "I don't know, Bixby. I'm still a little nervous about all the attention you're going to be getting."

"Ah, what could a little game hurt?" Mr. Timmons said, thrilled by the fact that riddles were *indeed* right up their alley. "Bixby, as a family, you must let us help you. No more going behind our backs. We want to trust you, but you have to also trust us."

Then, to Mrs. Timmons, he added calmly, "You know, we've been needing to do stuff as a family again. This is perfect for all of us to work on together."

Bixby jumped on the lifeline her dad had just given her. "I can keep you informed, and all of us, including Harvey and the H-bots, can win this."

"Maybe," Mrs. Timmons said. "We'll talk more about this over breakfast."

"And no more hiding in your room with holographic boys," Mr. Timmons scolded.

Bixby blushed. "Ew...Tipton?"

"Get ready for school. It is probably going to be a very long day," Mr. Timmons said, ushering Mrs. Timmons out the door.

"Doing this as a family. I like the sound of that, kid," Harvey said, heading for the door. "That was more than kind of you to call us family."

Bixby smiled. "You know, as a hologram, you don't have to walk everywhere."

"It does well for these old bones," Harvey quipped.

Bixby started to dread all the unwanted attention she was about to get. Still, she showered, slipped on her Holo-Suit, and made her way down to the kitchen for breakfast. Miss Marmalade was making pancakes; she gushed as Bixby walked in the room.

"The brave girl who is gonna' save the Grand Master must be starving," Miss Marmalade bubbled.

"Thanks. They smell great. What kind are they?" Bixby asked.

"Oh, I didn't know what you wanted, so I made eight different types. I also packed you two turkey, cheese, and hot sauce sandwiches for lunch," Miss Marmalade said.

Bixby was already a bit uncomfortable with the overly nice things people were doing for her, and she hadn't even left the house yet.

Hucklebee raced into the kitchen. "Harvey, make a TV anywhere, and turn it on channel seven!"

A TV appeared just above the table and turned itself to the correct channel. On the screen was a model of perfection with peppered black hair, stylish black glasses, and a puffy chest set in a well-tailored, color-changing Pedrodean business suit. There was no doubt from his appearance that the figure was Daemon Dragonthorp. He was a spitting image of Cody, only way more athletic without a hint of bashfulness. He was in midsentence of a greeting as the TV came on.

"...and to all those who have been hoping and praying for the safe return of my brother Cody. After ten years of aimless searches by both the authorities and people like you, my sleepless nights will hopefully come to an end. Earlier this morning, I received confirmation that the only way to bring back my brother was to enter a dangerous game of riddles."

Bixby cringed at the word 'dangerous,' looking at her mother, who was briefly distracted by Darby, who was pulling on her coffee cup.

"We do not know specifics about who is controlling this riddle, but it is the first tangible lead we have had in over a decade. What we do know is that each of the five houses that Cody created—Black Rock, Plumberry Isles, Pinnacle Manor, Verruckt Overlook, and Dragonthorp Estates—are to choose one person to compete in this riddle. At the end of each level, the last house to complete the tasks shall be eliminated from the competition. The final house standing at the end of the Riddle will not only save my brother's life but also safely bring back the man who created the Holo-System; a system that has made all of our lives easier."

Bixby was a little surprised that Daemon hadn't mentioned anything about the secret that Cody had offered the winner.

"The reason I bring this up publicly is because this riddle will affect each and every one of us that use Holo on a daily basis. The rules read as follows, 'Once the Riddle is afoot, and a Riddle contract is signed, the remaining houses must also follow suit and select a contestant to play the game. If a house does not select a contestant to play in the Riddle, that house and all who live in it will be terminated permanently from Holo. In addition, a selection of one-fifth of the world's population will be deleted permanently from Holo the next time they log onto their system.' This is, undoubtedly, a threat to our way of life. We, as keepers of the houses, must act for the safety of our families and the livelihood of the people we now represent—whomever they may be."

"That is not good," Mr. Timmons said. "If someone can't log into Holo, not only will they not be able to go to school, but they won't be able to get a job anywhere, either."

Daemon's speech went on.

"All names shall be submitted no later than this Sunday, April eighteenth: three days' time. The Riddle will commence on the thirtieth. Two names have already been agreed upon as contestants. In my old age, I am unable to compete in this contest; although, I truly wish I could do this for Cody's sake. The initial one-hundred-million-dollar reward offered for the safe return of my brother will now go to the contestant who completes these games and successfully negotiates the return of my brother. If you wish to have the honor to compete for the Dragonthorp family, defend the wellbeing of one-fifth of the world's population, and a chance at one hundred million dollars, please contact Dragonthorp, Inc. by noon tomorrow. That is all."

With that, a quirky reporter jumped in front of the camera and began to commentate about Daemon's speech. Bixby, no longer hungry, pushed her plate away. Her mind reeled at the idea of her family losing access to Holo, not to mention one-fifth of the world's population without access to school, work, or even enrichment.

"That seemed a bit dramatic from the letter Bixby signed," Hucklebee mumbled as Bixby turned and realized her whole family was now standing behind her, dumbfounded. "I mean, it was paraphrased," he corrected.

"I thought you said this was going to be, 'just a riddle,' Bixby! There's way more at stake than solving a riddle here!" Mrs. Timmons said.

"I'll petition Mr. Dragonthorp to let me go into the riddle in Bixby's place," Mr. Timmons offered.

"Not happening, Cooper Timmons!"

Bixby only heard her mom call her dad by his whole name when she was very upset.

"It's not a big deal, Mary," her father replied to her agitated mother. "It's a riddle; all I have to do is go in, try to win us a hundred million dollars. If I don't win, people can still log onto

Holo, and we get our lives back. Easy-peasy," he finished casually.

Bixby could see her mom contemplating it.

"I'm not quitting on this riddle," Bixby said.

"You have to, Bixby. This is something that should be handled by grownups," her mom said, clasping Bixby's shoulders.

"This is completely not fair. I solved the puzzle boxes. I found the library, and I got this far in the riddle. You never trust me to do anything."

"Bixby, that is not true. We allow you to..." her mother cut in, but before she could finish, Bixby continued.

"It was totally okay if Dad was going in and solving riddles, but because I'm a teenager, you don't think I can do anything. That's why I solved all the riddles around this dump without your help—you always jump in and take over," Bixby said with a raised voice.

"Watch your tone, young lady," Mrs. Timmons said with a pointed finger.

Bixby turned her attention to her dad. "You know I can do this. You and Grandpa made me a great puzzle solver. I can do this if you'll just trust me," she pleaded.

"I don't know if you should be handling so much..." Mr. Timmons started before he was cut off.

Arthur stepped into the doorway and announced, "My system received an update this morning. I'm afraid that, according to the rules, Bixby has no alternative but to compete. The document is binding. She now competes for Pinnacle Manor as our champion, and her one-fifth includes the entirety of Snagelyville."

"Wait. *What?*" Bixby shouted.

"I'm sorry to inform you, but you are now Holo-Basic's only hope to maintain access to Holo and the cash prize," he informed as if one were as valuable as the other. "Now, I have two Launch Rooms ready and waiting for those of you in Holo-Suits. Please hurry, or you will both be late." There was no hint of sympathy in his monotone voice.

Bixby's old friends, classmates, and neighbors raced to the forefront of her mind like a tsunami. She couldn't move.

Mr. Timmons furrowed his brow. "I want to take a closer look at these so-called rules when I get home. Until then, let's keep a cool head about all of this."

"I don't like any of this at all, Cooper," Mrs. Timmons said, standing by her disapproval as Mr. Timmons dispersed to change into his Holo-Suit.

Seeing that her dad was leaving alone, Bixby saw her chance to plead her case. She raced after him, catching him in the Great Hall as they made their way to their rooms, out of earshot of the kitchen.

"You know I can do this, right, Dad?" she inquired.

"Bixby, it isn't that I don't think you can do this. That's not what's bothering me. In fact, I know you can win this whole thing," he said. He stopped and looked Bixby square in the eye. "I'm your dad, and I have always wanted what is best for you. That also means I want to protect you. This is all happening so fast that your mother and I need to take time and talk about how we can trust you while we also do our best to protect you."

He finished as he pushed his bedroom door open. "Does that make sense?"

Bixby understood him, but it didn't mean she liked it. With a shrug, she left him at his door.

Bixby waited for the puff of air to breeze across her face as the Launch Room turned on. As she opened her eyes, she was alone in the hallway with a familiar face hovering above her.

"Good Morning, Ms. Timmons. I see that you have already created more work for me than I prefer, which is very much unappreciated. All students will be launched directly into the seats of their first-period classroom from now on to avoid the commotion of having you around. Though you have now put yourself in the spotlight, I expect your schooling not to falter. I don't like you or your low-breeding kind. You bring attention to where it is not wanted. I have also taken the liberty of separating you and your new adversary to avoid complications as you two play your games. Now, please go to your classroom and avoid disturbing anyone to the best of your abilities."

With that, Gabhammer did his usual about-face, folded his hands behind his back, and began to walk away.

"My newest adversary?" Bixby shouted after him.

Without stopping or turning around, he announced, "Mr. Dagger will be representing Black Rock, and to my knowledge, he despises you. He has no intentions of letting you out of the first round."

"Idiot. Wesley is the one who is in trouble," she said under her breath.

She closed the door behind her. The classroom was already to capacity and went dead silent upon hearing the door latch. Everyone's heads swiveled toward the back of the room to stare at Pinnacle Manor's champion. Bixby hurried to her seat and slumped down next to Tipton.

"You're not going to believe the morning I've had," Tipton said jovially as Bixby pulled out her Holo-Writer. "My Cody Club wants to make me president of the club. Two hundred new applicants also want to join. I've had four girls ask me out on a date, and I have like a thousand friend requests on my Social Page."

"That's great, Tipton. I've had my family, along with like a billion other people's wellbeing, threatened if I don't compete. Gabhammer was all in my business this morning, more so than normal. Oh, and by the way, Wesley Dagger has already started his trash-talking," Bixby said, tilting her Holo-Writer to the side so that Tipton could read what was on it: *I hope you watch where you step.*

"Oh, man. Sorry, Bixby. I wasn't even thinking about that. At least you'll get to be famous on Holo-TV; that's pretty cool, right?"

"I haven't even convinced my parents to let me compete in the Riddle, let alone go on any famous Holo-TV shows," Bixby replied.

"Really, Bixby?" Tipton questioned. "You have no clue, do you?"

Bixby stopped typing. "About what?"

"Cody's personal website went live last night with a countdown on it. The Riddle is going to be Holo-Streamed... everyone is going to be watching it live," he finished, filling in the blanks.

Even though Mrs. Gable had already begun the lesson for the day, Bixby's mind churned as a plan began to hatch on how she would convince her parents to let her compete.

"Hey, Bixby," Tipton said, snapping his fingers in front of her Holo-Writer screen. "Class is over. You okay?"

"I'm fine, but we only have a few days to make a game plan, and I need your help. There will be a meeting over dinner at my house tonight. You're going to be there," Bixby commanded.

"What about your parents? I guess I could try to see if I could only turn on the chip's audio but leave the hologram out," he whispered to himself.

"Actually, you're welcome to dinner tonight. Mom invited you, and I think she's making chicken. Five o'clock, and don't be late," Bixby said, knowing that most everything she had just said was a bit of a white lie. "No more talking about the riddle until we're out of school. Who knows who's on whose team."

Tipton nodded with excitement and terror.

For the rest of the day, Bixby's Holo-Writer was constantly interrupted by well-wishers, autograph seekers, and even more threats from Wesley's camp of goons. School was hard enough for her without distractions, but now it was nearly impossible.

Her last class was still study hall, and the bench she and Tipton usually sat alone was suddenly full of people supposedly *studying*. Wesley Dagger and his moron parade were sitting at their usual table, making choking motions and playing dead. She wasn't sure if Wesley had grasped the concept that the riddle was for real, and he was going to face the same tribulations as the rest of the house champions. Bixby turned to find another place to sit.

Mrs. Gable had pulled study hall duty today, and Bixby was sure she would have a solution to all the extra attention.

"Mrs. Gable? I was wondering if Tipton and I could work on something here at the head table that didn't involve the rest of the ninth grade?" Bixby asked.

Mrs. Gable replied with her usual jolly charm: "I think I have these papers to grade, which involves you two doing your homework and figuring out how to beat that bully at those puzzles. Go ahead and sit right there. You won't be bothered."

For the rest of study hall, Bixby and Tipton did their schoolwork and communicated the old-fashioned, un-hackable way. Pen and paper.

Bixby: When I get into the Riddle, I need a way to talk with you and everyone else, but I don't think you can be in there with me.

Tipton: OK. So, do you need me to find a way to make the coin either hologram and voice, or add a "just voice" setting?

Bixby: Yeah, but the problem is that it's going to be televised, which means if I can hear you, so can everyone else.

Tipton: I think I can fix you up with something, but it might not be pretty. Inventing something in three days and shipping it to you is kind of hard.

Bixby: Doesn't matter, as long as it's something we can hide in plain sight.

Tipton: How are we going to cover up the fact that you're talking into thin air? I can cover up us talking to you, but I can't cover up the fact that you'd look crazy talking to us.

Bixby: We'll have to think about that because, right now, I don't have an answer.

Tipton: What else do you think you're going to need?

Bixby's Holo-Writer lit up even though it was on the "Ignore" setting. A message was in her inbox:

RULES FOR CONTESTANT – Pinnacle Manor.

Bixby looked up and met eyes with Wesley, who must have received the same Holo-Mail. He gave her an evil smile and a wink just as the final bell rang. The room went as dark as Bixby's mood.

CHAPTER ELEVEN
THE PLAN

BIXBY SPENT ENRICHMENT solving every type of riddle she could think of. She even asked the computer to skip a few levels so that she could work on harder riddles and puzzles.

As the final light in the Launch Room stopped refracting, Bixby walked over to the wall and sat down.

"Grandpa?" she said as she looked towards heaven. "I'm going to need your help here in a few days. You always taught me to do what's right, in my mind, and in my heart. There's going to be at least one kid in there that will bully and cheat every chance he gets. The sad thing is, I'm sure he isn't going to be the only one. Help my group get the right answers, and if you could put in a good word with the Big Guy about keeping me safe, that would be much appreciated. Thanks...I miss you..."

With that, Bixby stood up, took a deep breath, and opened the Launch Room door.

"Verruckt Overlook announced their selected represent-ative for the riddle. You have a new friend," Hucklebee said with a smile as he stood next to Harvey.

"Hucklebee, when I'm inside the riddle, you're in charge of positive thoughts," Bixby said with a hint of sarcasm. "You'll be great at it."

"Really?" Hucklebee replied. "You want me to be in charge of something? Man, that's great news. I've yet to oversee any-thing outside of house chores!"

Bixby couldn't help but smile at Hucklebee's joy, and she knew she couldn't take it back now, even if her comment had been made in jest.

"Congrats, Hucklebee...Big responsibility you have there," Harvey said, patting him on the back and shaking his hand. Hucklebee just stood there, beaming, as Harvey chased after Bixby.

"Oy, can I be in charge of sarcasm, curse words, and comic relief?" Harvey said once out of earshot range of the newly appointed Happy Patrol.

"He needs something to do, and I'm sure I'm going to need a smile from time to time," Bixby replied. "Plus, in case you've forgotten, it was his counting that got us into the library last night."

"Aye, true," he conceded.

"I'm going to take a nap and then meet everyone for dinner and our planning meeting."

"Planning meeting? When was this scheduled?" Harvey asked.

"Just now," Bixby said as she began to walk away.

"Why do I think that it was a bad idea to teach you to stretch the truth?" Harvey inquired.

Bixby looked over her shoulder, scrunched her nose, and stuck out her tongue.

At 4:45 sharp, Bixby awoke to Hucklebee taking his new post very seriously. "Knock. Knock."

"You realize that you're supposed to save these for when I really need them, right?" Bixby said with a yawn.

"Come on. Knock. Knock," Hucklebee insisted.

"I'm thinking this is the only way to get to dinner," Bixby said, pushing back her blanket. "Who's there?"

"Hatch."

"Hatch who?"

"Oh, God Bless you, Bixby. Let me get you a tissue."

Bixby snickered and crawled out of bed before smoothing her hair and leading Hucklebee down the hall to the kitchen.

Everyone was already in the kitchen when she got there, and she had no doubt that there was an elephant in the room about to be addressed.

"Have a seat, Bixby," Mr. Timmons said as he directed her towards her chair. "Your mother and I have had a talk at length about this riddle. As I said this morning, I want to trust you, but this seems a lot bigger than someone your age should be involved with..."

"But Dad, I—" Bixby started.

"Let me finish, Bixby," he continued. "We want to trust you with this chance, just like every parent who lets their kid try out for a Holo-Sing-Off or Holo-Race. You're a great puzzle solver who deserves to compete, but we've never seen anything like this. So, we, as parents, don't know how to protect you from any potential dangers, which scares us."

Bixby was shocked at his bluntness.

"Without being sure that you won't get hurt, we don't know if it's wise to let you compete." Bixby's mom sounded like she was going to say no.

"I know how you can keep me safe and protect me," Bixby chimed in, knowing this was where she could win them over.

"Besides cutting the power to your Launch Room if I see anything I don't like?" Mrs. Timmons volleyed back.

"Hear me out," Bixby said as she sent a message on her Holo-Writer. Moments later, Tipton appeared in the kitchen. Based on the quizzical look on Bixby's mom and dad's face, Tipton could tell that Bixby had not actually told them he was coming.

"Um, hi?" he squeaked.

"So, you're the boy who's been sneaking into my daughter's room?" Mr. Timmons barked.

Terrified, Tipton said, "*Ahh*, she invited me. And they were there, too!" he added, pointing to Harvey and Hucklebee.

135

"Dad, Tipton is a Hologram, and he's my friend; that's it," Bixby said boldly as she slid in front of Tipton.

"I too can attest to the fact that Tipton has only been at Pinnacle Manor in the context of helping Bixby," Harvey interjected.

"I don't care, Harvey. I would like to be in control of who comes in and out of my home," Mr. Timmons grumbled.

Bixby could tell that her father's ire of the boy in front of him hadn't faded, even when Tipton pretty much melted into a cowardly puddle.

Fearing Tipton would unlaunch, she went on. "Dad, I promise I won't let it happen again. We need his help. Please, let him stay."

Bixby hoped that with her word and Harvey's affirmation that Tipton wasn't a threat, her dad would at least hear them out.

"It had better not happen again," he said in a strict voice while staring at Tipton.

"Yes, sir," Tipton squeamishly replied.

Knowing her dad wasn't going to kick Tipton out, Bixby quickly changed the topic towards the Riddle.

"Tipton is developing a way to allow all of you to communicate with me in the game using similar technology to what he's using to launch himself here right now," Bixby started. "If the Riddle is broadcast live on Cody's personal webpage, you'll be able to see and communicate with me inside the Riddle. You'll practically be right next to me."

Bixby's mom, who had been quiet during most of the conversation, spoke up again with her objection. "How do I pull you out if I don't like what's happening?"

"I don't think you can, Mom. That's where you must trust me, just like on Holo-Race when they have challenges," Bixby said as she put the unknown into her parents' hands.

"Everyone knows Holo-Race is staged," Mrs. Timmons huffed. "This is completely different."

"If I could promise you that nothing would go wrong, I would. However, it's new territory for all of us, and I promise I won't do anything foolish," Bixby said.

"If anything goes wrong, I will take a sledgehammer to that Launch Room's electrical panel and yank you out myself," she replied in her momma bear voice.

Bixby shot out an open hand. "Deal."

"Tipton? How is it that you plan to help us keep in contact with Bixby?" Mr. Timmons asked, still trying to figure out Tipton's motives.

"I can simply turn off the Hologram feature on the coin that Bixby currently has," Tipton started as Bixby removed his invention from her pocket and laid it on the table. "The voice transfer should work fine," he continued as everyone gawked at the simplicity of the transponder. "The only question is, how do we get it into the Launch Room without everyone seeing it?"

"Holo-Suits don't have pockets," Mr. Timmons said.

"Aye, then you hide it in plain sight," Harvey put in as he came out from the corner of the room.

Mrs. Timmons frowned. "How so? It can't be that easy."

"You hide it behind your family crest," he said.

"We don't have a family crest, Harvey," replied Bixby.

"What's a family crest, anyway?" Hucklebee asked.

"In olden days, you didn't know a family by its name, necessarily, but by its crest or its coat of arms. I was thinking maybe you could hide it behind something like this," he explained as he pulled up the screen on her Holo-Writer. Bixby glanced at what Harvey had created, and it did not fail her expectations. On the screen was a silver shield with a brown, rugged cross dividing the emblem into four sections. In each section was a symbol: a key, a crown, a lion's head, and a heart.

"When did you make this?" she inquired.

"Doesn't take long to sketch when you have a computer for a brain," he said, winking.

"What does this crest mean, Harvey?" Bixby asked with awe as she handed the paper to her parents.

"The cross in the middle is for faith. The key is what will help us unlock this riddle. The crown is for your leadership. The lion head is for your courage, and the heart is just that...your humungous heart, Bixby," he finished.

"This is perfect. Please have a patch made for me, and I'll wear it on my Holo-Riddle Suit to protect the coin," she said, knowing everyone would love the idea.

"Speaking of which," Miss Marmalade said, "it came today. I'll go fetch it."

Even Tipton had quietly found his way into the group and stated his amazement of the new crest.

Miss Marmalade quickly returned with a box. "Well? Go ahead. Open it already."

Bixby cut the tape and pulled out a Holo-Riddle Suit that looked almost identical to the one she already owned. However, this one had silver stitching throughout and looked to be already retrofitted. At the bottom of the box, there were instructions:

Contestant – Pinnacle Manor

This suit is custom designed for you. If anyone other than you puts it on, they will face both legal and physical consequences. Be advised: this suit will not activate until April 18th.

Good luck, Bixby Timmons – Pinnacle Manor.

Design Team

"They never send packages with nice letters without impending doom in them anymore, do they?" Bixby huffed as she stuffed the suit back in the box while her family looked on.

"Okay, let's eat up, shall we?" Mrs. Timmons suggested, breaking up the silence.

Everyone helped themselves to a plateful of food, and once around the table, the plan started to unfold.

"What do we know right now?" Bixby asked.

"Five houses, five contestants," Hucklebee said first.

"Only four puzzles to get to one person left," said Harvey.

"Holo-Riddle Suit will take you alone into the game zone," Mrs. Timmons said.

"You know the prize is a secret, while the money Daemon is offering is not. But you also know that if you don't play, people we know would lose everything," said Mr. Timmons.

"I feel like there are a lot of things we still don't know yet," Bixby interjected as she tried to process the data as fast as she could. "What do we know about my challengers?"

Harvey put up a digital board on the wall and pulled up a profile on each of the people who had already committed.

BIXBY TIMMONS – Pinnacle Manor
Height: 5'2." Weight: 128 lbs. Hair: Red. Eyes: Green.
Age: 14.
ENRICHMENT SKILLS: Science – Physics, Horticulture.
Riddles, Puzzles, Reading.
ENRICHMENT WEAKNESS: Technology, Time Management, Organization, People Skills, Physical Activities.
RANKING BY AGE GROUP: 12,180
Holo-School Prime: Class Z
Headmaster: Gabhammer III, Quincy Jeffrey
Achievements: None

"Really? They had to put weight on there?" Bixby grumbled.

"Is Headmaster Gabhammer's first name really Quincy?" Tipton snorted.

"Oh my. Twelve thousand, one hundred and eighty is a pretty high number, Bixby," Mrs. Timmons gulped.

"They don't count that third-place trophy from that spelling bee as an achievement?" Mr. Timmons interjected.

"Yes, well, very impressive, Bixby. You are definitely an overachiever, but for this task, we can help cover some of your shortcomings," Harvey heckled. "Now, let's take a look at your two known adversaries."

WESLEY DAGGER – Black Rock

Height: 5'8." Weight: 165 lbs. Hair: Black. Eyes: Hazel. Age: 15.

ENRICHMENT SKILLS: Martial Arts – Jujitsu. Science – Marine Biology, Physics. Diving, Math, Social Skills, Organization, Leadership, Business Management, Verbal Presentation, Multitasking, Communication, First Aid, Basket Weaving.

ENRICHMENT WEAKNESS: Hand-Eye Coordination, Anger Management.

RANKING BY AGE GROUP: 1

Holo-School Prime: Class Z

Headmaster: Gabhammer III, Quincy James

Achievements: Level 3 Black Belt, Science Fair Awards – 3x All-Around Champion. Dive Certified – All Depths. Eagle Scout – Youngest to achieve Eagle Scout status at the age of 7. Overall National Champion Basket Weaver.

President of three Organizations: Student Body, Young Leaders of the World, & Young Speakers Convention.

"Bah ha ha ha! Does that say he was a National Champion Basket Weaver?" Bixby howled. "Definitely have to save that one for the perfect time."

"I am glad you are taking this seriously," Harvey said with a scowl.

"Sorry. *Ahem*," she said, clearing her throat.

"Wow, Bixby, this guy is a rocket scientist with three black belts and temper issues," Tipton said.

"Yes, but any good woman knows how to use a man's temper to her advantage," Mrs. Timmons said. "When the time comes, dear, do exactly as I say, and I guarantee you that he will make a mistake. It gets your father every time."

Mr. Timmons replied, "Well, umm, you just be careful around this boy. He's a lot bigger than you are." Mr. Timmons was almost to his limit for the Riddle already with new boys in Bixby's life.

Harvey turned everyone's attention back to the board to look at the next opponent.

MAGGIE MURDOCK – Verruckt Overlook

Height: 5'1." Weight: 121lbs. Hair: Brown. Eyes: Brown. Age: 14.

ENRICHMENT SKILLS: Engineering, Metal Work, Survival Skills, Culinary Arts, Swimming, Matrix, Chess, Coding, Computer Development, Problem Solving.

ENRICHMENT WEAKNESS: Unstable Focus, Lacks Motivation, Short Tempered.

RANKING BY AGE GROUP: 4

The Plan

Holo-School Prime: Class ASD
Headmaster: Martinez, Gabriella T.
Achievements: Metal Works Student Artist of the Year, Survival Skill ranking of top 1 percentile, National 100-meter swim Champion 2nd place, Up-N-Coming Student Chef of the Year, Chess National Champion x4, Runner up x1.
Nationally Recognized Patents: 2.

"She could be your friend, Bixby," Mrs. Timmons started.

"Mrs. Timmons, I did some research before I came over. This girl's nickname is Mad Maggie Murdock. Rumor has it a kid once made fun of one of her metal sculptures, so she put a snake in his gym locker," Tipton said. "However, I was also told that she survived thirty days in the desert with nothing but a butter knife, a can of green beans, and the clothes on her back. She could be useful...if you stay on her good side."

"How much did you have to pay Marshall for that info?" Bixby asked.

"Two math homeworks," he replied casually.

"How much crazier could my group of new friends get, right?" Bixby murmured.

"Yes, but remember: while the boy is not really that good at puzzles, he can do the physical stuff. Mad Maggie is small and maybe even a bit weak, but she makes up for it with what seems to be a brilliant mind. She's a chess champion, so she's always thinking several steps ahead," Mr. Timmons noted.

"Good point, Dad," Bixby agreed. "Who do you think I should trust, Hucklebee?"

"Us," he said plainly.

"Care to go deeper on that thought?" Bixby urged.

"Well...we will be in your ear for most, if not all, of the time," he said. "We will be able to see all the contestants even when you cannot because it will be televised. My guess is that we aren't the only people who will be talking to a contestant. So, I'd be very wary of anyone trying to be your friend, especially since they're all out to win—and there can be only one winner."

"Agreed, Hucklebee," said Bixby.

"Tipton, did you figure out how we'll communicate without me sounding crazy talking into the air?" Bixby asked.

"I think so. We can sew the coin under the patch that Harvey is going to make of the family shield. It will transmit a signal to an old hearing aid I found. It'll be impossible to see because it gets jammed way back in your ear. The only problem is that if you have to do any swimming, even if we can make the patch waterproof, it may damage the hearing aid," Tipton pointed out.

Next, Tipton grabbed his Holo-Writer and had Harvey put the 3D image up on the info board.

"As for the part where you talk to us, I found one of the military-grade neck mics at an online surplus store," Tipton said. "Navy Seals use them on missions because they're durable and waterproof. It's like putting a black Band-Aid over your vocal cords. When you adjust the suit to something that you would like to wear in the riddle, it will have to be something that will cover up the bottom of your neck. It will pick up even the smallest whisper. So, to not look crazy, you'll have to talk through your teeth without moving your lips much. I know it's pieced together, but we can upgrade as I have time to invent."

"I think it will work for now," Bixby said in approval of Tipton's plan.

Bing! The board lit up again, and a new face appeared—a picture of another girl.

"Oh no...not her. Anybody but her," Tipton said with the sound of defeat.

"She looks harmless, Tipton," Bixby replied as the girl's profile flashed up on the screen.

MARIN ST. JAMES – Plumberry Isle
Height: 5'4." Weight: 142 lbs. Hair: Black. Eyes: Brown.
Age: 16.
ENRICHMENT SKILLS: Science – Chemistry. Puzzles, Riddles, Time Management, Physical Fitness, Computer Coding, Music, Organization.
ENRICHMENT WEAKNESS:
RANKING BY AGE GROUP: 1
Holo-School Prime: Class M
Headmaster: Von Schmitt, Max Dr. Gen.
Achievements: Classified

"Classified?" Mr. Timmons exclaimed when he reached the bottom of the profile.

"Does that mean she has no weaknesses?" Bixby asked.

"This girl is two years older than you; how is that fair?" her mother questioned.

"Marin is the first kid who volunteered for the military school version of Holo-School Prime. I heard from Pippa that they're training super soldiers at that school. Her list of skills is probably pretty watered down as well. All I know is, that girl has been training for a game just like this," Tipton offered.

"What I don't get is, why is this competition only for kids?" Mr. Timmons said with a questioning look. "I mean, where's the rulebook to all of this? Arthur, didn't you say there were some kind of rules?"

That reminded Bixby of the Holo-Mail she'd received when she was in school. She grabbed the Holo-Writer, logged on, and clicked on the email. The screen went fuzzy, and then a digital voice came through the speakers: "The Riddle, in which five contestants must play, is simple. These are the only rules." At that, the voice stopped abruptly. Then the screen spat out a list of rules:

- Only one contestant shall be selected to represent each of the five (5) houses.

- Each contestant must launch from their corresponding house.

- No contact is to be made between contestants until inside the Puzzle.

- Once the first contestant is chosen via Pinnacle Manor, the rest of the houses must choose a contestant within three years of age, to the day, as the contestant from Pinnacle Manor.

- The receiver in the Holo-Riddle Suit is fully functional.

- Weapons may not be brought into the gaming platform from outside the Launch Room.

- Once in the Riddle, there will be no return until that level is complete.

- All contestants must cross the finish line to be able to leave their Launch Room.

- The last contestant to complete each level will be eliminated.

The screen went blank, and the Holo-Mail disappeared from her inbox.

"That answers my question," Mr. Timmons said.

"Is everything okay, Bixby?" Hucklebee asked quietly.

Bixby could feel her face go pale as the cold sense of uneasiness crept up her spine.

"They turned the receiver fully on in the suits," Tipton whispered back to Hucklebee, low enough not to be heard by her parents.

"I don't know what that means," Hucklebee said, clueless.

"Fully functional means that if Bixby gets hurt in the riddle, she will also get hurt in the Launch Room," Tipton whispered back, knowing exactly what had caught Bixby's attention.

"Now all we need is the name of Daemon Dragonthorp's contestant, and we can finish strategizing," Bixby's mom said. She started enjoying the competitiveness of the game a little, oblivious to Bixby's recent realization.

"Sorry, dear, we won't know Mr. Dragonthorp's contestant's name until shortly before the launch. I work for Dragonthorp, and he never shows his cards too early. It gives him the advantage he's usually looking for," Mr. Timmons said.

"I still don't get why people from each house have to compete," Mrs. Timmons said.

"Probably because they're the only five houses that Cody created," Tipton said nonchalantly.

"I guess that makes sense but not completely. What do the houses have to do with anything?" Mr. Timmons asked.

"Well, each house was a gift from Cody to the board members when the company started to take off," Tipton replied. "The first one was Plumberry Isle, developed and gifted to a retired General for his work in getting the systems sold in the military community. He was also the guy who put up the money for the first Bucksberry system. Daemon thought it was a good gesture; Cody just liked to build things and give them away, so everyone was happy. Plumberry was the first house that could be digitally shifted by a central system. Other than that, there were no special features.

"Verruckt Overlook was the second house to be created by Cody. Supposedly, Maggie Murdock's dad did a lot of the engineering work on the original design of the Bucksberry systems. That house was the first to have H-bots in it. It made life a lot easier for the people living there." Tipton continuously flipped through his Cody Club notes.

"Then he created Black Rock, which was given to Dagger for his work as the company's right-hand man. It was similar to Verruckt. The only difference was that it had the ability to support digital shifts throughout the property. Nothing major, but instead of the house being the only aspect to change, the landscape was now in play. He then built Dragonthorp Estates for his brother to thank him for helping kids get a free education. It was built to have identical systems to that of Black Rock in every way, except the landscapes were larger, and the systems were upgraded for more memory.

"Finally, he built Pinnacle Manor. Nobody really knows if he built Pinnacle Manor for a specific reason, or if he just wanted another private oasis, but he only spent a few weeks here before he disappeared," Tipton finished, closing his Cody Club notes on the rundown of the properties.

"So, one member from each of his creations has to play in this game for no apparent reason, except to learn about Holo's secrets? What secrets? It all sounds a bit fishy to me," Mr. Timmons said, scratching his chin.

"I think that's enough planning for me tonight. I'm going to go lie back down," Bixby said, then pushed her dinner away, got up from her chair, and left the room.

"What got into her?" Mrs. Timmons asked.

Bixby's mind raced as she curled under her covers. How was she going to beat kids who were better than her? What if she let her family down? What if she let Grandpa down? How far would she be able to make it? Why would they turn the pain receptors on if it was just a simple riddle game? What if she never came out of the launch alive?

The puzzles that had brought her joy just a few days earlier had now become her nightmare.

CHAPTER TWELVE
LEVEL ONE: LAUNCH DAY

OVER THE NEXT two days, Bixby focused on solving puzzles and doing a little physical conditioning. Harvey also had her doing self-defense training to make sure that if she needed to protect herself, she would be able to. Tipton had the hardware he developed delivered early on the twenty-ninth. Miss Marmalade was able to sew the coin under the patch that Harvey had created. Mrs. Timmons was eagerly trying all the recipes she could to make food that would be easy to store and good for her.

Bixby had made up her mind that once inside the riddle, she was going to find only one ally. Two was too much work, and it left her susceptible to be the odd man out if the other two decided to move against her. One, therefore, was an easy number to manage.

Mr. Timmons did as much nosing around that he could at Dragonthorp, Inc., but everyone knew he was the father of Pinnacle Manor's contestant. Nobody wanted to lose their job for helping the Timmons family instead of their boss, so there seemed to be a hard line that nobody was willing to cross. He did, however, notice that some of the gadgets that he had been working on in the Discovery Lab, as well as the overseers to those devices, were no longer under his authority. To the best of his knowledge, he had not been demoted, but he had no doubt that someone wanted to keep his access to resources limited. With little access to new discoveries and tons of busywork, he might as well have been demoted, though.

Tipton's snooping proved to be more valuable.

"It was pretty easy to get the info on the final contestant," he bragged.

"Well, spill the beans already!" Bixby replied as she punched and kneed a dummy into submission.

"His name is Greg Tracy. His records are not released because Dragonthorp has not officially acknowledged him as their candidate, but he is definitely who they will pick. I had to do ten coding assignments for Marshall Groves for him to tell me, so I know it's solid. From what I've seen just by running his name online, he's a letterman athlete in six sports, does tons of work for homeless shelters and food kitchens, his father is a preacher, he goes camping like every other weekend, and he's generally liked by everyone in his school based on comments on his Social Page," Tipton finished.

"He sounds like the complete opposite of Wesley. Maybe he could be persuaded to be an ally?" Bixby wondered.

"Right now, he is still your adversary, and you will know more about him soon enough because you have four hours till launch, Bixby," Harvey interjected. "Why don't you go get a shower, rest, change into your Holo-Riddle Suit, and meet in the kitchen for dinner?" Harvey said, starting to clean up the defense props Bixby had been trying to beat up. "We will work on the intelligence gathering and update you as we know."

"I can live with that," Bixby said. She took her fighting gloves off for the last time. Her nerves were still a little high, but the more information she was able to be fed about the others, the more she felt like she could fit in.

Bixby sat on the end of her bed and read a few Grandpa-isms to calm her nerves.

"Many people want to be brave, but when given a chance to practice their bravery, most people pass on that opportunity."

"There will come a time when you are presented with the chance to do something the easy way and the right way. The easy way will always lead to momentary satisfaction...It is the right way that will shape who you are."

"Faith and family above all else. Having faith in something you can't see is very difficult, so He gave you a family to practice with."

"I read that book a million times myself," Mr. Timmons said from the half-opened door.

"When I read it, I feel like I can do anything. Grandpa always knew the right things to say," Bixby said, already decked out in her Holo-Riddle Suit.

Mr. Timmons sat down on the bed next to Bixby as she handed the family heirloom over to her father.

"I remember when Grandpa gave you this book just before he passed," he started, his fingertips glancing over the faded brown leather cover.

"He was so proud of you, Bixby, and grateful for the time you spent together. I am sorry that I haven't been spending much time with you lately. Between you and me, Bixby, I wish I could go into that puzzle with you, but for whatever reason, it is you alone who gets this opportunity. I'm proud of what you're doing, but promise you'll be careful," he finished softly.

Bixby mustered a smile and a hug in return. As her head lay on his shoulder, she said, "I'll be okay. Besides, we're in this together. I know you guys will watch my back."

They embraced for a few more seconds, enjoying each other's company, but Mr. Timmons knew the Launch time was quickly approaching.

He stood, and with a deep breath, said, "Before I forget. Here are the snacks that your mom made for you. Just open and eat. When I say your mother, I mean Miss Marmalade made some and switched them with your mom's packets for fear of food poisoning."

"Thanks, Dad," Bixby said with a smile.

"Well, it's time. Ready?" Mr. Timmons said, followed by a nervous sigh.

"As I'll ever be," Bixby replied.

Just outside the door was the entire team. Mrs. Timmons was welling up with tears as usual and handed Bixby a turkey, cheese, and hot sauce sandwich. Tipton was doing checks on the signals between the suit and the earpiece. Hucklebee gave Bixby a brief look at the forty-six pages of antics he had to work with when Bixby needed a smile. Miss Marmalade was trying to stuff more food into her Holo-Riddle Suit, and Harvey simply looked on.

"Bixby, you will be launching from your normal Launch Room. I have it prepped for you now," Arthur said in his usual monotone voice. "Once inside, the door will be sealed shut. The only way to access you will be when you complete the level or if you…" Arthur stopped his sentence; even he knew that what he was about to say would not help Bixby while in the riddle. "When you finish the level, Miss Timmons."

Bixby went down the line and hugged each member of the team, one by one. Mrs. Timmons took her plate, and Tipton handed her the earbud that was connected to her coin. Harvey's Holo-Writer went off, and just as they expected, the name of Dragonthorp Estates contestant came across the screen: Greg Tracy. Blonde hair, blue eyes, and built like a sprinter. The five contestants were set, and in a few moments, they would all meet face to face.

"Miss Timmons, please enter the Launch Room or you will be late, as usual," Arthur said. "Good luck," he said simply as he closed the door.

As the door latched shut, the remaining group sprinted down the hall to the Great Room where Harvey had a gigantic Holo-TV hanging over the mantle already tuned in to Cody's live stream.

Bixby closed her eyes before the first light ricocheted into the room and off her Holo-Riddle Suit. The puff of air was quick this time. She kept her eyes closed and let the rest of her senses enter the hologram first. She could smell the inside of a new car. She could feel the road rumbling under her feet. She could hear the tires roll along on the asphalt and knew they were going extremely fast. Bixby opened her eyes and saw that she was in the back seat of a stretch limo. Alone. Through the window, she could see a busy highway around her. Just to make sure it was all real, she pushed the down button, and immediately wind streamed through the car window.

"Okay, Team, this is the real deal. Can you see what I see?" Bixby said through her teeth.

"We read you loud and clear, Bixby," Mr. Timmons replied.

"Is there a driver?" Tipton asked, trying to get started.

"Um, I don't know. The tinted window between us is closed, and the button to open the window is missing," Bixby said as she began looking for another way to open it.

"Bixby, turn out all the lights in the interior. To see through that glass, you have to make your side of the window darker than the other side. Next, cup your hands over the window, blocking as much light as you can, and see if you can see anything," Tipton said.

Bixby turned off all the running lights, the disco ball, and the ceiling lights and did as Tipton suggested.

"Okay, guys, there's no driver, but I see a GPS in the dash. It says a hundred and ninety-two miles to my destination. That's all I see," Bixby relayed.

"That doesn't make any sense. Why would they launch you in a car to start the riddle and make you wait over three hours to begin?" Mrs. Timmons interjected.

"I agree. That makes no sense," Bixby said, suspicious. "Let's think about this. They obviously don't want me to talk to anyone. I can't get out of the car or stop it because we're on a freeway, and I have a time limit, it seems."

"Are you saying the riddle is the back seat of a limo?" Miss Marmalade asked, patting Darby on the back.

"Well, I don't think we should wait three hours to find out," Bixby said as she started to touch things in the limo to see if anything happened when she did. The seats didn't budge. There were no carpet snags or seams. The dials on the overhead did exactly what they said they did. Each cup holder was filled with a dirty glass. The fridge was filled with water only, and the ice bucket had ice.

"What am I missing?" Bixby mumbled to herself.

"How about starting with the knobs? How many are there?" Mr. Timmons asked.

"Five," Bixby said before starting to examine each one at a time.

"First button is a stereo that seems to get only one station: Classic Rock. The climate control makes hot air when turned to the red side, and cold air on blue side. The disco ball button turns the lights on and makes the disco ball spin faster or slower. Next, there's the running floor light switch that turns the lights on and off. Lastly, the ceiling lights that adjust to on, off, and color change," Bixby listed.

"Grab an ice cube and see if it's ice or something else," Harvey suggested.

"It's just ice," Bixby said after barely touching it to her tongue.

"This station is not really that good," Hucklebee said.

"I don't think it's time for a joke yet," Bixby said, stifling a smile as to not be seen by the world laughing at nothing. Bixby then double-checked each ledge for a latch.

"I'm serious. They have been playing that same terrible song for the last ten minutes, and it is not really that great of a song," he said with a bit of a pout.

"Genius!" Bixby whispered through her teeth.

"I am?" Hucklebee said, surprised.

"What did you find, Bixby?" Mr. Timmons asked.

"I thought the glasses were a little dirty when I first looked at each of them, but they're the key," Bixby said. She reached for the bottles of water in the fridge and filled up each glass to their smudged lines.

"What's she doing?" Mr. Timmons inquired through the finger he had pressed to his lips.

Then she grabbed an ice cube and wet her fingers.

"Brilliant, Bixby!" Mr. Timmons shouted the moment he made the connection. "It's a music lock. She has to line the glasses up in the order of the tune playing on the radio. The hard water lines are where she has to fill up the glass to make a certain note."

Bixby quickly ran her finger around the rim of each glass to ring out a note. One by one, she shuffled the glasses in the order that they needed to go to match the tune on the radio. Bixby soon had them in the right order, and she played the chorus right along with the radio. When she finished ringing the last note on the final glass, the road noise, wind, and rumble all disappeared. It was as if the car had gone from ninety to zero instantly, but Bixby didn't feel the limo slow down at all. She slid back to the last seat and tried to roll down the window, but nothing happened. She reluctantly reached for the door handle and pulled.

Click.

The door popped open, and outside she could see four limo doors just like hers. Two of the doors were already opened. As she stepped out, she immediately recognized the bigger girl from her picture. Marin was standing at a table filled with food. Next to her, in a lounge chair, popping grapes up in the air and catching them in his mouth, was Wesley.

"Look who decided to show up: the girl who doesn't belong here," Wesley said with a snarl.

Marin spun, seeming almost irked that Bixby had opened the door. "I had you pegged for fourth. Doesn't matter. I beat him, too."

"By like three seconds. Don't get all high and mighty," Wesley said as he chomped another grape.

"How long have you been here?" Bixby asked.

"Scoreboard's up there. Looks like we beat you by a good five minutes," Marin said as she grabbed a chicken leg and sat down in the chair adjacent to Wesley.

Bixby made her way to the table but realized she wasn't hungry. As she began to turn away, her mother whispered into the microphone, "Bixby, eat something or at least put something on the plate. You don't know when the next chance to eat will be, and if you have to run, at least you can stuff it in a pocket." Bixby complied with her mother's wishes because she knew her mom was probably right.

As she finished completing her sandwich, another door clicked open, and a tall, handsome boy stepped out. Greg had perfect hair, jawbone, muscular arms, tattoos, beautiful teeth creating a perfect smile...but then he spoke.

"Oh, man! Fourth? Bummer! I was just jamming to the tune on the radio, thinking I had three hours to chill, and then that beat kept playing, and I was like, oh, *duh!*" Greg said in a Southern Cal, surfer dude voice. His grammar was like nails on a chalkboard.

Wesley jumped up from his chair and grabbed him in a bro-hug as if they were old friends. As they did, Wesley whispered something into his ear.

"You two meatheads want to share with the rest of the class?" Marin asked.

"Not really," Wesley replied.

"Well, at least it's three girls against two guys," Bixby said as she and Marin sat watching the boys slam food in their mouths and talk about school and girls.

"Not interested, Timmons. I can do this whole puzzle thing on my own. I don't need any help from you or any of the other hacks. I especially wouldn't listen to advice from someone ranked almost thirteen thousandth," she finished.

Bixby slumped back in her chair, knowing Marin was a dead end as an ally and that the boys already had a bond. Mad Maggie was going to be her only chance.

It took almost thirty minutes for Maggie to finally open her door. Irate, she kicked the door open and then slammed it shut with five more kicks to the outside of the door to emphasize how mad she was. She had absolutely no features that stood out to Bixby. Small in stature, dirty brown hair, no makeup or jewelry, and her clothes consisted of jeans, tennis shoes, and an oversized t-shirt.

"*Ahh!*" she screamed with a piercing voice. "If I hear that song ever again, I am going to punch someone!"

"That 'tude will get you friends quick," Wesley said while he and Greg laughed at her outburst.

"Shut it!" she shot back. She marched over to the food table, and within two seconds, she started screaming again, "Hey! Who ate all the fruit? I am a vegetarian! I can't eat all this processed garbage!"

Bixby furrowed her brow as she recalled all the turkey, cheese, and hot sauce sandwiches she'd scarfed over the last several days.

Wesley shoved the grape stems behind his back as he continued to smile at her outbursts. Bixby realized Maggie had missed half the table in her rage and stood up to see if she could help her find something she could eat.

"So, why do you guys think we were timed on how fast we solved the puzzle?" Marin asked once the tension settled down.

"Really? You're a super trooper, and you can't figure out that it's a time lapse?" Wesley said.

"What's a time lapse?" Greg asked.

"Seriously? You have a hundred and sixty-eight I.Q. On paper, you're the smartest one here, and you sound like you're as dumb as a bag of potato chips," Maggie said, probably as irritated at the sound of Greg's voice as Bixby was.

Knowing that Greg was a potential ally, Wesley cut the sour tone and sat back in his chair. "We're stuck in this bunker tonight, giving us a chance to make friends for the upcoming tests. Tomorrow we'll be released in the order in which we solved the limo puzzle," Wesley said. His gaze turned to Maggie. "That means Super Trooper and I have a fifty-minute head start on Mad Mags here."

Maggie glared back with rage in her eyes.

"Maggie, I found some hummus here if you want some. Gluten-free, GMO-free, and a hundred percent organic," Bixby said, hoping to stop a fight.

"Aw, everyone's favorite redhead to the rescue," Wesley jabbed.

Bixby began to nibble on her hair like she'd done the first day she'd met Wesley. "You bet, Wes. Gingers love to hang out and get to know people...almost as much as they love to wash their hair." Only Wesley got the jest.

For the next thirty minutes, Greg and Wesley chatted in a corner. That left Maggie, Marin, and Bixby to sit and stare at each other.

At nine p.m., five previously unnoticed doors slid open. Each of the contestant's names lit up above one of the doors.

"You each have fifteen minutes to wash up and get to bed before lights out," a voice on a loudspeaker rang out.

"Great, Arthur and Gabhammer have a triplet," Bixby said under her breath.

"See you losers in the morning," Wesley said to the girls.

Before walking into her room, Bixby quickly made another one of her signature turkey sandwiches. As she passed Maggie's door, she waved to get her attention, "Catch up as fast as you can. I'll leave clues." Bixby whispered from her doorway.

"Why would you help me?" Maggie whispered back.

"Maybe I'll need a favor later in the riddle."

Maggie nodded as Bixby ducked into her room and shut the door behind her.

"The news feed is dead, Bixby. I believe it's safe to speak freely. Good job today," a familiar voice rang out in her ear.

"Thanks, Dad, and thank you, Hucklebee. It was you that led us to that answer," Bixby said, delighted that she didn't have to talk through her teeth now that she was in her bunk.

"I think Maggie is a good person to have on your side," Hucklebee added.

"I think she's my only choice," Bixby replied.

LEVEL ONE: LAUNCH DAY

"As long as we are all doing a lot of thinking, I believe you need to get to sleep, young lady," Arthur summoned from the corner of the Great Hall. It was now a complete team effort.

"Thanks, guys, for watching over me," Bixby said, climbing into bed.

CHAPTER THIRTEEN
BREAD CRUMBS

Y OU GUYS UP?" Bixby asked the next morning, checking her earpiece while sitting in the dark.

"Yes, dear!" Mrs. Timmons answered, sounding concerned. "We're here. Are you okay?" she asked.

Bixby could hear the shuffling and clanking of coffee cups in her earpiece. She was imagining everyone bursting into the Great Room from the kitchen with breakfast in hand.

"I'm fine. The lights came on in my room, and a countdown clock has started above the doorway. I'm guessing I have ten minutes until things get started. I'm going to get cleaned up really quick, and I'll see you in a few," Bixby said before starting to wash her face.

"Okay, I'll have Harvey get everyone together. Your father and Tipton will be at work and school, so it is Harvey, Hucklebee, Miss Marmalade, the boys, and me for the first part of the day."

"Work? School?" Bixby was confused as to why her dad wasn't taking time off work to help her.

"I'm sorry, Bixby. Your father got an email from the foreman last night telling him that even though you're in the Riddle, he is to come to work or he would be...*let go*."

Those cheating Daggers, Bixby's mind fumed even though she knew she was also fudging the rules a little herself.

"Your dad will be home as soon as he can, and I'm sure Tipton will be as well. Until then, let's do this!" Mrs. Timmons cheered.

"That sounds good to me. See you in a few minutes," Bixby said, enjoying that her mother was all in on the riddle now.

Bixby double-checked that she wasn't leaving anything behind, then she stood at the door and watched the clock wind down: *Five...four...three...two...one...*

The bedroom door slid open.

The other four contestants stepped out in a hurry just like Bixby, but they were in the same gathering room as before. This time, there was no food or chairs—just an empty white room with a single door. Above the doorframe, Marin's name was lit up and another clock counting down.

"Told you it was to see who goes in first," Wesley said, proud of himself.

"Congratulations, genius," Maggie said sarcastically.

"See you slowpokes at the end," Marin said as her clock ticked down to zero.

When the door slid open, all they could see was a concrete wall as Marin disappeared inside the hallway. Wesley was quick to stand next to the door as he was only a few seconds behind Marin. The door again skimmed open, and just as fast as Marin was gone, so too was Wesley.

After a few minutes of nervous pacing, Greg broke through the silence, "You girls want to be a team or something like that?"

"What? Why would we break up your bromance with Wesley?" Bixby replied.

"Well, I figure if we work hard enough as a team, we can catch that Marin girl and knock her out the first round. Then it would be guys against girls in the next level," Greg said.

"Or...we could team up with Marin and knock the boys out over the next two rounds and then have a good old fashion girl fight to the end," Maggie said.

"I'm just saying that I'm game if one of you two, or both of you, want to be partners," Greg said, making it clear this was his final attempt at making a partnership.

Her mom spoke into her ear: "Bixby, your clock is down to ten."

Bixby spun around, and while Greg was admiring his biceps, she was able to catch Maggie's eye once again and gave her a nod. She then opened one of the pockets of her cargo pants and half-raised a plastic bag with a turkey, cheese, and hot sauce sandwich in it. Maggie immediately knew that would be how Bixby would help—she would leave literal breadcrumbs.

Three...two...one...

The door slid open, and Bixby dashed into the hallway just as the door closed behind her. To her left looked exactly the same as to her right. The hallway curved as if it were in a circle. Bixby immediately ran left and saw a spiral staircase leading down. Either way she chose would have led her to this point, so she ran down the stairs as fast as she could.

At the bottom, she only saw an open door to the outside. The room was circular, and beside the door, there was a shield like the one Harvey made for her and her family. This one had a dragon standing against a red background on it. Bixby stopped just to make sure this wasn't the first clue, but she quickly realized that there was movement outside the door.

She ran through the doorway to get a better look. The sky was dark and overcast with mean-looking clouds coming her way. Off in the distance, about eight-hundred yards, she could see a bridge like the one at Pinnacle Manor. One person stood at the base of the bridge, talking to a man in a black robe. The other was well on his way to the other side by now. Bixby swiftly tore off a small bread crumb and left it just outside the door.

"Bixby, remember it's probably going to be a long day, so just jog to the bridge," Harvey chirped in her ear.

"Gotcha," Bixby said, knowing how much she hated to run.

It took Bixby longer than she thought to get to the bridge, and as she approached, Marin was sitting next to it, holding her arm in pain.

"You okay?" Bixby asked.

"I'm fine. Just make sure you get this guy's riddle right," Marin said, showing Bixby her arm. It had a red rash where it looked like she was burned.

"The Grand Master would never create a puzzle where someone got hurt," Hucklebee said into her ear.

Bixby approached the man in the dark robe. A hood covered his face as if to hide his appearance. His voice immediately boomed as Bixby approached: "Answer my riddle, and you may pass. Get it wrong and the consequence will last."

The robed man then pulled a riddle from his oversized sleeve:

8, 5, 4, 9, 1, 7, 6, 10, 3, 2, 0
What is special about this sequence of numbers?

Bixby stepped away from the bridge for fear of thinking out loud and getting her arm burned. As she thought about the riddle, she could see Greg leaving the tower.

"Okay, what do you think?" Bixby questioned through her teeth.

"Oh, Bixby, I don't really know," Mrs. Timmons admitted.

"What if it is one of those substitution cyphers where each number represents a letter of the alphabet?'" Harvey asked.

"Maybe," Bixby said as she quickly started to draw in the sand the combinations. Each time it became clear that a word would not form, Bixby erased it and started again. Her heart raced faster with each time she had to start again.

Bixby thought she saw Marin eavesdropping out of the corner of her eye. Her penalty time was up, and Greg was quickly approaching; Marin must not yet have an answer.

"C'mon, Grandpa. Little help here," Bixby said, panicked as she erased another failed attempt.

Just then, Marin's head popped up out of her lap, and she dashed over to the man in black and whispered into his ear.

"What did she tell him?" Hucklebee shouted.

"I don't know, but Greg is here, and something I wrote triggered a thought," Bixby answered franticly.

"Well then, what did you write in the sand?" Harvey insisted.

"What's up, Bixby? This dude looks creepy," Greg said as he approached, which forced Bixby to erase her progress yet again.

Bixby gave a nod and thought it would be best if she didn't tell him about the burn and the time delay, hoping that he would make a hasty guess, not knowing it would hurt if he got it wrong.

Moving away from Greg and the bridge—determined not to help anyone else out—she started rewriting her last cypher in the sand.

"I'm not sure this is it," Bixby said, looking at the gibberish that she'd scribbled on the ground when Marin had come up with the answer.

She then looked at Greg, who was still standing by the man, and saw him whisper in his ear. A second later, he was off and running, having been allowed to go on.

"Great," Bixby mumbled.

"Finish writing each of the letters out," Harvey insisted, as he too was not confident they were on the right line of thought.

"Guys, every time I look at what I wrote, I only see that I've spelled out a bunch of nonsen...Oh, stupid Bixby," she said as she erased the work she had already written and started scribbling.

"What is it?" Mrs. Timmons shouted.

Without giving a reply, Bixby franticly wrote the best hint she could think of, at the moment, to help Maggie get the right answer.

Eight, Five, Four, Nine, One, Seven, Six, Ten, Three, Two, Zero

Bixby quickly tore off a huge chunk of her sandwich and left it next to the words in the sand. It was a risky move being in fourth place, and it wouldn't take much to fall into last, but she knew she might need Maggie's help sooner or later. Leaving the hint would hopefully earn Bixby's trust but also make Maggie solve the puzzle on her own.

Quickly, she turned and ran to the man in robes.

"They are in alphabetical order," she said confidently.

"You may pass," the dark voice boomed.

In her ear, Bixby could hear everyone cheering at her success. However, there was no time to waste celebrating, and out of fear that the robed figure would change his mind, she sprinted across the bridge.

"Thanks, Harvey, for telling me to spell it out. One point for you and one point for Hucklebee," Bixby said through panting breaths.

"You're welcome?" Harvey replied, unsure that he had done anything helpful.

As she reached the other side of the bridge, there was a trail leading into a forest. She had watched all three of the prior contestants run into the woods, so she proceeded to follow. Slowing to a walk shortly after entering the woods, Bixby took a quick look around. All she could see was the forest. There was no light coming through the canopy, and the path curved and disappeared up ahead of her.

She closed her eyes and let her other senses take control. The first thing she noted was the smell of dank, musty air, which complemented the moisture clinging to her skin. Then as she turned to start walking, she heard a sound off in the distance. She kept her eyes forward as she tried to listen to the direction of the noise. She also didn't want to alert it that she knew it was there. Off to her right, there was something moving along the path, and it was no more than twenty feet from her. She took a step, and then she heard a step mimic hers. She took three steps and three steps followed next to her.

"Something's in here with me, guys. I need you to keep an eye on the forest to my right," Bixby said, slightly panicked. "Something is walking along side of me. It stops when I stop and walks when I walk."

"I don't see anything, Bixby," Hucklebee said.

"I promise you that it's there. Please keep looking," Bixby said. Her pace was quick and steady now.

Greg had to be only a little way in front of Bixby, which meant that Marin was a few steps ahead of Greg, and who knows how far ahead the person she loathed the most was: Wesley. Even though the other two were more than capable of keeping up a jogging pace, Bixby knew Marin was hurt and would probably take her time on the next puzzle. Greg, however, seemed to be breezing through so far. He hadn't broken a sweat solving the limo riddle once he'd realized that it was the riddle. When he made it to the bridge, he didn't even flinch with his answer. That was a bit worrisome for Bixby. If Maggie couldn't catch up, Bixby might survive this level but would never make it out of the next. She started to jog again.

After what seemed like hours of hiking on the path, Bixby stopped cold in her tracks.

"*Ahhh!*" A masculine scream rang out up ahead of Bixby. One of the boys.

"Careful, Bixby, it could be a trap," Hucklebee cried out, sounding like he was watching a suspenseful movie.

"She can hear you, Tinman! Don't scare her like that!" Harvey shouted.

Bixby could hear a metallic clunk followed by Hucklebee screeching, "Ow!"

"It's okay, Harvey. I can see Greg and Marin up ahead," Bixby whispered. "But I don't see Wesley." She slowly strolled through a small clearing that allowed sunshine to peak through the trees. As she approached Marin and Greg, Bixby was on guard, because not seeing Wesley made her uneasy.

"You guys okay?" Bixby asked.

"For sure, but we now have matching burn marks," Greg said as he rubbed his arm and looked at Marin.

"Care to share how you got it?" Bixby asked, hoping he would tell her what mistake he'd made so that she wouldn't repeat it.

"Ah ha ha, I see what you tried to do there, Ginger. Na. If you make the same mistake, we'll all have matching rashes on our arms," Greg said.

Bixby made her way up to a stone wall with a boulder for a door. To the left were extremely dense thorn bushes and a matching pair to the right. The stone door was sealed shut with just a dark smudge where the handle should have been. The wall was at least fifty feet high and smooth like a river rock. Bixby turned away from the wall and found a log to sit on. It was just down the path, so Bixby could study her surroundings as she thought.

Greg threw softball-sized rocks at the door. Marin had flanked Bixby and appeared to be keeping an eye on both her and Greg, in case someone did something to open the door.

"I'm getting sick of Marin trying to swipe all the answers from us instead of figuring it out on her own," Bixby said into her microphone.

"Easy, dear. The more emotional you get, the less clear your thoughts will be," Mrs. Timmons said. Bixby could hear her mother's frustration.

"Grandpa...page sixteen?" Bixby said, knowing her mom was reciting from Grandpa's journal.

"Yep," Mrs. Timmons responded in a soothing voice.

Bixby sat staring at the wall for a few more moments. She couldn't help noticing that every time Greg hit the wall with a rock, it made an echo. At least she thought it was an echo at first. Bixby turned her head and spoke softly so that none of the other contestants could hear.

"The echo noise from the rock. Did anyone catch that?" Bixby asked.

"Yes, Bixby. Hard objects make an echo sound when they bounce off other hard objects," Harvey said sarcastically.

"No, listen again. It's like the noise I heard from earlier in the woods. It's mimicking the sound of the rock throw," Bixby said.

"Bixby, I'm lost at what you are getting at," Harvey grumbled, probably frustrated that he was not on the same page.

"Wait," Hucklebee said. "Rocks don't echo unless there's something for the sound to rebound off of?"

"Right," Bixby mumbled.

"That means the puzzle has to do with a mimicking sound...I think?" Hucklebee said inquiringly.

Bixby reached in her pocket and grabbed her sandwich and took a bite, making sure a decent-sized piece of bread fell from the corner of her mouth. As she lay on the log, looking up for a few moments, her hand slipped to the sides of the log to write one word in the dirt. She then stood up and looked at the door from right behind Greg so that he wouldn't suspect she was onto something. Marin slowly rose up from her position to get a better look at what Bixby was doing. The smudge on the rock was in the shape of a circle, but as Bixby glared harder, she finally made out what it was. Knowing that Marin was watching her every move, Bixby decided she had to distract her.

"I don't think rocks are going to work, Greg," Bixby started.

"Well, duh. It helps me think when I throw things," Greg said, sounding more and more like a tool and less like a child prodigy.

"Then, maybe a bigger rock will work?" Bixby added, hoping he would take the bait.

"Listen, *Bix*, let me do it my way, and you do it your way," Greg said, strolling over to a new patch of rocks that were slightly bigger. Picking one up, he tossed it in his hand to prove the extra weight had no effect on him. He arched back and hurled the rock through the air. As it smashed into the wall, the rock door slowly creaked open.

"Well, I hope you two ladies can hurl a rock that big," Greg said as he strolled towards the door.

As he pushed the door all the way open, he let out another cry of pain.

"AGGHH! What is going on man? I totally smashed this door open," Greg yelled as he rubbed his second burn mark.

"Actually, I did," Bixby said as she pushed her way through the doorway and the stone crashed closed behind her.

"Brilliant, Bixby!" Hucklebee shouted. "But how did you pull it off?"

"The riddle was about shadows. I wrote it in the dirt for Maggie to find. Your shadow does everything you do when you do it. So, in the woods, when I took a step, it took a step as well. I couldn't see my shadow because we were in the dark woods, but in this riddle, it let me know my shadow was there by copying my moves and making noises where it doesn't normally. When Greg was throwing the rocks, I heard the echo and realized there wouldn't be an echo without any walls for the noise to reverberate off. I also knew Marin was watching me, so I had to find a way to distract her. I confirmed it was a shadow riddle when I was standing behind Greg, and the smudge on the wall looked exactly like the shadow of a door handle. So, I couldn't turn the knob, but my shadow could. I had to make Greg move because his shadow was blocking mine from opening it. I figured if I could get him to move to the larger rock pile and throw a boulder, Marin would surely watch the first large rock as he threw it at the door to see if he was right. That gave me a split second to line the shadow of my hand with the shadow of the doorknob and make the turning motion."

"Simply brilliant, Bixby!" Miss Marmalade chimed in.

"Clever girl indeed," Harvey agreed.

"What did we miss?" hollered Mr. Timmons as Tipton and he ran into the Great Hall.

"Did you two just get there at the same time?" Bixby asked as she started down into a cavern.

"Well, yeah. I shot Tipton a text when I logged out of the office," Mr. Timmons said.

Bixby stopped in her tracks, "Did you say you texted Tipton?"

"Yes, Bixby. Tipton has agreed to message me each time he would like to come over, and I would text him confirmation. If he doesn't, I reserve the right to ban him access to Pinnacle Manor." Mr. Timmons said in a firm tone.

"And I agree to that completely," Tipton added awkwardly.

"Really?" Bixby said, dumbfounded at what she'd heard.

"Yes, really," her dad said. "Why?"

"That's just...I don't know. Weird."

Tipton broke in. "Okay, seriously, what did we miss? I saw you get across the bridge on my Holo-Writer, and then you were in the woods forever."

"Hucklebee, can you bring them up to speed?" Bixby asked as her short cavern hike came to an abrupt end.

Bixby's hands fumbled along the rock wall, pushing and pulling on every crevasse she could find.

"What are you doing, Bixby?" Tipton inquired, cutting Hucklebee off from speaking.

"I'm desperately hoping one of these grips has a secret latch that will open a door?"

"Why?" he asked in return.

"Because the alternative is terrifying."

It was no secret to Bixby's family that her next challenge also happened to be her greatest fear. Bixby was quite sure everyone watching her could see the dismay on her face as she stood at the base of a gigantic rock wall with no climbing gear. She was completely surrounded by rock walls, and up was the only direction to go.

"I hate heights," Bixby said as she slowly started up the wall.

It was comforting that every ten feet or so was a rock ledge she could stand on. Unfortunately, all those ten feet intervals quickly added up to a hundred in total. As she sat resting, Bixby could see that she only had a little farther to go. She tried not to look over the edge often. Each time she did, an anxious rush made her head spin a little. With a quick glance, she could make out Greg's blonde hair as he began to scale the wall. He was fast at work, and it took him no time to make it halfway to where Bixby was. Once the spinning stopped, she rushed back to work.

"I see you, Freckles!" Greg shouted as he started up the next ledge. "I have to hand it to you. The sleight of hand while getting me to throw that rock and distract Marin was pretty smart. She's still back there, confused. All I had to do was turn the handle while throwing a rock. It took a few tries, but it worked."

"I don't need your flattery, Greg," Bixby said as she started up the next ledge at a much slower pace than Greg. Her biggest concern was that Greg would catch up to her before she got to the top and give her a nudge back to the bottom. The idea quickened her climb exponentially. The last thirty feet, Bixby climbed without a break. Her arms and legs were close to the point of giving out on her. A quick glance down revealed that Greg was ten feet behind her and closing in fast.

"Almost got you, Bixby," he shouted.

Bixby scampered up the last few feet. Then she raced away from the edge as fast as she could, fearing that he would grab her leg at the last second. Once far enough away, she turned to see Greg come over the ledge and dust himself off. Bixby, with her back to a tree, took a defensive stance, ready to fight.

"Whoa, there. Hold on, Short Stack," Greg said as he held up his hands. "I'm on your side. It's Marin you need to worry about. She's the one trying to cheat our answers. I know you saw her watching us as we were working on how to solve the door. I knew it was you that opened it, but I took the shock to make her think I was clueless. I already knew it was a doorknob. I just couldn't figure out how to open it because my stupid shadow was blocking everything. All I want to do is stay in the top four."

"Why should I believe you?" Bixby said, not backing down.

"I guess you have no reason to, but if it's any consolation, I know you've been leaving clues for Maggie. I spotted you doing it the first time as I crossed the bridge and again when I was picking up rocks. If I wanted to guarantee somebody loses this level, all I'd have had to do is pick up your breadcrumbs and make sure Marin keeps up with us," Greg pointed out.

"Bixby, he has a point," Harvey said.

"Listen, Greg, I appreciate what you're doing, but I don't trust Wesley; therefore, I don't trust you," Bixby replied.

"Totally understand. I'm going to jog ahead now, and maybe I'll see you again before the end," Greg said as he walked past Bixby with a wide enough path to put her slightly at ease.

Once he was gone, she took a quick look over the edge, and to her surprise, there was Marin making her way up the wall.

"Careful on the top ledge. There are some loose rocks up here," Bixby hollered down primarily for Marin's benefit, but this tip was going to keep them both safe.

"Bixby, they're gaining on you. No more breadcrumbs," Mr. Timmons insisted.

"Probably a good idea," Bixby agreed.

"And it's getting close to dark, which means you'd better get out of that forest and find some shelter," Harvey added.

Bixby chose to run for the first time that day. As the sweat started to drip down her face after about a mile of running, Bixby wobbled to a stop and put her hands on her knees.

"I...am...so...out of...shape," she gasped.

"Bixby, I see light up ahead. You have to keep going," Tipton urged.

"No matter how fast you go, you're lapping everyone on the couch," Hucklebee cheered.

Though exhausted, Bixby let out a sizable laugh.

"Perfect timing, Hucklebee," Bixby commended.

"Uh...Bixby...sorry to cut the good times short, but I think it's time to start running again," Mrs. Timmons said. Bixby looked around at what she meant.

About two hundred yards behind her, Marin was almost at a full sprint. Immediately, Bixby's adrenaline peaked, and she turned and began to hustle. Just outside of the woods, Bixby could see an archway and a campfire blazing. She knew that was the final checkpoint for the day, and she wasn't about to let Marin beat her to it. More sweat dripped down her face; it burned as it rolled into her eyes. It was a useless endeavor to try to wipe the moisture from her face; it was now pouring down her brow in wave after wave. Marin had spent the last two years of her life conditioning, whereas Bixby had only spent the last two days. Marin was quickly catching up, and they were only twenty-five yards away from the wooden finish line. Bixby could hear the heavy breathing right behind her. The two boys who'd been lounging by the fire stood up, clearly interested in this finish. Fifteen yards. Ten yards. Five yards...Bixby started to stumble, so she dove towards the finish line.

With a face full of dust, Bixby rolled over to look at the timer hanging on the side of a covered wagon. Wesley's time was now only seven minutes faster than that of Greg, but it was the anticipation of her own time that she was now interested in.

St. James, Marin – 3rd place - 10:21:14
Timmons, Bixby – 4th Place – 10:21:15

Bixby's face slumped back down in the dirt as she realized defeat.

"Oh, man, that was wicked, dude!" Greg said, high-fiving Wesley.

"Nice job, G.I. Jane," Wesley congratulated Marin while strolling over to Bixby. "So close, Bixby," he said, crouching over her. "At least you'll get to sleep in while I'm busy whooping you all again tomorrow."

"Bixby, don't let that bully think he owns you. Stand up, and don't let him see any discouragement," Mr. Timmons said.

Bixby looked up, met Wesley's eyes, and laughed mockingly. "Did you see that? That was fun."

As she started to sit up, she glanced at Wesley's arms as his sleeves had slid up. Noticing that Bixby could see part of his forearms, he quickly adjusted his shirt back down to his wrists. Wesley had at least four burn marks up each of his arms.

Getting to her knees, she said, "What a rush, huh?"

Before anyone could answer, Marin was there, reaching her hand down and helping Bixby to her feet. "Nice race, Bixby. At least you made it exciting," she said.

Bixby wasn't sure if it was a compliment or a jab, but she nodded in agreement, nonetheless.

After five minutes had passed, Bixby could make out a shadow coming from the woods. It was Maggie, who started to jog as she saw that the end was near. It took her a few minutes to reach the finish line, but when her time came up everyone realized that Wesley had maintained his lead by seven minutes, and Maggie had decreased her deficit by nearly thirty minutes.

The five battered contestants sat around the fire, and for the first hour, nobody said a word.

"Hey, Maggie," Greg said, breaking the silence, "do you have any wilderness treatment for burns? I got two today."

"Only if you have some aloe," she replied in a less grumpy mood than yesterday.

"Man, I felt so dumb getting burned twice at the same riddle," he followed. "And, Bixby, I tried to pry the door open with a stick. That's how I got my first burn."

Wesley suddenly became curious enough to join the question and answer session. "What was your answer on the bridge that got you burned, Marin?"

Knowing that everyone already knew the solution to the riddle, Marin felt safe enough to answer.

"I was trying to be sarcastic and asked the guy if he was able to give any hints," she said. "I guess he took that as an answer and told me that I had to wait five minutes to guess again."

Maggie chuckled.

"Does pain make you happy, twerp? Because I can give you something worse than a burn," Marin growled.

"Are there marshmallows anywhere? I would love to have a s'more," Bixby said, desperate to diffuse the tension.

"Nobody likes it when you do that, Bixby. Let Maggie stand up for herself," Wesley said angrily.

"Okay, okay...I just wanted a s'more. Sheesh," Bixby said, sliding down to the far end of the log. Bixby thought about asking Wesley about his burns to put him in his place. She decided, however, that it was not in her best interest to add fuel to the fire.

Regardless of how Wesley saw it, Bixby's question had calmed the moment, and everyone started to look for food in the wagons that had their names on them. Inside Bixby's, she found a lunch box with a three-digit combination lock on it.

"I just want to eat!" shouted Maggie. "Not another puzzle!" she huffed, smashing the box on the side of her wagon in frustration.

Bixby quickly rotated her box in her hand. When she found her riddle, she started to laugh.

"What's so funny?" Greg asked, trying to pry his box open with his hands.

"I'm sure eventually you'll all be smart enough to realize there's a puzzle on the bottom. Well, actually, it's a joke my grandpa told me when I was a little kid," Bixby said.

Everyone flipped their lunch boxes over, and Greg read aloud, "Why didn't anyone want to sit at the lunch table with the number seven?"

They all turned and looked at Bixby for the punchline. "I'm going to tell you because I think this has less to do with the riddle than with someone having fun with us."

Bixby quickly rolled her dials to check and make sure that she was correct. Her box popped open right away. She looked up and said, "Because seven *eight* nine." She'd been hoping for a laugh, but none came.

Everyone hurried to get their box open as if it was part of the bigger puzzle they were completing. As they spun their dials, Bixby noticed a small square medallion in the bottom of her box. On it was engraved:

1st place mini-puzzle.

Bixby said nothing as she grabbed it and slipped it into her pocket. Quietly, she ate her turkey, cheese, and hot sauce sandwich with a bottle of water. Everyone else scarfed down their food just as quickly.

"Do you think we'll know when we're approaching the final leg of this level?" Marin asked while spinning a drumstick in her hand.

"Well, if you're in last place, you'll know when you're eliminated," Wesley inserted.

"No, really. Will we know that it's the finish line for this level or just another day complete?" Marin asked.

"I'm guessing we'll know," Greg said. "I mean, either there will be people celebrating that they made it to the next round with you, or—*boom*—you're back in your Launch Room, the loser."

"When I saw you guys sitting around the fire, I was sure it wasn't over. I mean, if I was eliminated, why wouldn't the program just stop after the first four crossed the line?" Maggie asked.

"Because the rules said that you have to finish the level in order to leave your Launch Room," Bixby said.

"I can't listen to this garbage anymore. Why would you even start if you weren't going to give all that you have?" Wesley said as he stood up and dusted himself off. "We are here to compete. May I remind all of you that there is a hundred million bucks at the end of these stupid riddles? Just because Greg is Dragon-thorp Estate's contestant doesn't mean it won't go to whoever helps get Cody back. I, for one, don't care where the finish line is, as long as it's me crossing it first." With that, he walked off into the darkness.

Nobody spoke; instead, they just stared at each other, letting the realization sink in that they were not friends. Bixby knew she had earned a favor from Maggie, which made her the closest thing to an ally. That was all she could hope for in the first day.

Twenty minutes later, the same monotone voice came from everywhere. The announcement was also just like the first time they'd heard it: "Twenty minutes until lights out. Please turn into your wagons at this time."

As the rest stumbled to their wagons, Bixby stomped out the fire.

"Psst. Bixby," Maggie hissed.

Bixby turned to see Maggie right behind her, trying to talk so that nobody would notice as she repacked her lunch pail. "You're a good person, Bixby. Thanks. I won't forget it."

Bixby kicked one more scoop of dirt on the pit, and as she turned again, "Don't mention..." but Maggie was already gone.

Bixby then headed into her bunk where she listened to the sounds of the wildlife outside and started talking to the family.

"Thanks again for everything you all did today," Bixby started. "Hucklebee, your joke was right on time. Tipton, you have my dad texting and on social media, which I think I'm thankful for. Miss Marmalade, thank you for taking care of the boys and the food while everyone else was watching me. Mom, excellent heads up on the race at the end, and, Harvey, you got the first puzzle for us. Dad, thank you for encouraging me to get up and dust myself off. As a team, I would say we totally rocked today."

"Sleep well, Bixby. Your mom and I love you," Mr. Timmons said as the Holo-Feed went dark.

CHAPTER FOURTEEN

WATER GAMES

BIXBY AWOKE TO the sounds of people talking. At first, she thought maybe she'd left her earpiece in her ear, and it was her family. It didn't take her long to figure out that it wasn't them, but rather Marin and Greg having a contest. Bixby pulled the bottom of the wagon cover up to see what was happening. Marin was busy stacking stones on top of each other while Greg heckled her.

"Dudette, you're going to need to stack fourteen if you think you're going to beat me," Greg said, lounged back against a log. Above the archway just behind him, the start timer to today's leg of the journey was counting down from thirty minutes.

Bixby rolled over, and her stomach growled. She searched her wagon for more food, but there was nothing to be had. Then she remembered the snack packs that Mrs. Timmons and Miss

Marmalade had put together. She reached into one of her pockets and grabbed out a few bags and laid them out on her bed. Two bags read 'Breakfast' two read 'Lunch,' but only one read 'Dinner.'

"Hmmm, maybe I dropped it," she thought. Bixby grabbed one of the breakfasts and read the small print on the label: *Freeze-dried. Open and eat.* Bixby quickly tore open the snack pouch and looked inside. Much to her surprise, it was filled with freeze-dried eggs, bacon, and biscuit crumbs. There were maybe two handfuls in the pouch, so she ate each morsel as if they were the last crumbs she would eat for days. When she was finished with the small packet, she felt surprisingly full.

The time clock made a ringing noise as it hit fifteen minutes. Wesley was already stretching and doing calisthenics to loosen up. Marin was working on her second try at stacking fourteen or more stones on top of each other, Greg had his eyes closed and was humming some tropical song, and Maggie could be heard snoring from a mile away.

Bixby quickly slipped her earpiece in and did a quick soundcheck.

"Everyone awake?" Bixby whispered.

"Your father was called in to the office early this morning, and Tipton is at school. Your mother is with the boys. One of them is running a fever, and Hucklebee stayed up all night watching to make sure the system didn't wake you up early. He is recharging now," Miss Marmalade explained.

"All right, you and Harvey it is," Bixby said as she approached the fire pit.

"Big Red! You want in on this little bet?" Greg said as he sat up on the log. "If I win, Commando over here has to give me her entire movie collection. She says it's up to five hundred and twenty-three movies."

"But when he loses, he gives me his Cody Dragonthorp clock. Handmade and one of a kind," Marin said in rebuttal while stacking rock number eight.

"I don't think so," Bixby replied, knowing she had only been in Pinnacle Manor for a few months. She had nothing of value to give to a silly bet like this.

A much louder horn went off at the five-minute mark, and Wesley was now sitting Indian style, doing breathing exercises. Everybody's heads turned as Maggie finally rolled out of her wagon with her hair a wreck, sleep in her eyes, and clothes completely wrinkled.

Greg howled at her appearance. "Welcome to the land of the living, Zombie Face."

"There's like a billion people watching you, Maggie. At least pull yourself together before coming out of your wagon," Marin snarled, reaching for stone number twelve.

Maggie seemed to pay no attention to their pokes at her appearance but simply looked around the campsite as if she was hoping for something.

"No coffee in this puzzle?" she said with a yawn.

"Seriously, you think there's going to be coffee? You're twelve years old and shouldn't be drinking coffee, anyway. It'll stunt your growth," Marin said.

Bixby held her hand over the pocket that had her food pouches hidden in them. Bixby knew that she'd most likely been the only one to eat this morning.

"Almost fifteen," Maggie said as she started to stroll back to her wagon. "Wake me up when it's my turn to start."

Just as she reached the wagon wheel, she bent over and picked up a large rock that was by her ladder. "Someone could break an ankle on this thing," she said as she threw it over her shoulder towards the fire pit. The rock hit the ground, bounced up and smacked up against the log that Marin was sitting on while trying to stack the fourteenth stone. It hit the log just hard enough to break Marin's concentration for a split second and the stones came crumbling down.

"I'm going to kill her," Marin said under her breath, her teeth clenched and her hands each balled around a stone.

Bixby couldn't help but smile as she watched the bully get what was rightfully coming.

Whomp! Whomp! Whomp! The timer started to ring out as it counted down from ten to zero.

"See you suckers later," Wesley shouted as he disappeared down the trail. The clock reset, and 7:21 appeared and began its march downward.

"That's me, ladies," Greg said as he stood up, dusted himself off and did a little running in place. "Oh, and I will expect my movies within a week of this whole thing being over," he smiled, rubbing his soon-to-be victory in Marin's face.

Marin smashed the rest of the stones back to the ground and mumbled, "Hundred million bucks will buy them back."

Greg's time quickly counted down, and he was heading out with an eight-minute, ten-second lead over Marin and Bixby.

In a few moments, Bixby's day would start, so she tried to stretch out her sore legs. Marin sat down next to Bixby and asked, "Why are you sticking up for Maggie and helping her, Bixby? She's nothing but trouble."

"Why are you bullying her and trying to be my friend?" Bixby replied.

"I'm not being a bully. She's rude and needs a little discipline in her life," Marin said in a tone that reminded Bixby of a drill sergeant. A flashback of Marin's secret military profile gave Bixby a little understanding as to why Marin seemed angry all the time.

"If anything needs discipline, it would be the grammar coming out of Greg's mouth," Bixby added, trying to ease the tension.

"See, there you go again with your sarcasm. They're going to take you out of this competition if you don't start taking this seriously," Marin urged.

"Bixby, you have twenty seconds," Harvey interrupted.

"Maggie, get up! You're next!" Bixby shouted towards the wagons. Then she turned back toward Marin: "I'll take that into consideration. Thank you," Bixby said in the sincerest voice possible and then made her way to the arch.

It didn't take Bixby long to fall even further behind Marin. It wasn't because the path was hidden. Bixby could see that it led across a mile-long stretch of desert and straight up the side of a sand dune. The problem was everyone was running, and each step made Bixby's legs burn even worse than they already were. She stammered to the platform as she reached the crest of the dune. The view was something off a postcard from a vacation. Bixby was now looking down along a coastline with crystal clear water.

"Oh, I'd vacation there," Miss Marmalade marveled.

"Me, too," said Bixby. "As long as it didn't involve anymore running," she gasped.

"I have your training regimen all set up for you when you get home," Harvey added.

"Thanks, Harvey. Let's just hope I survive that long," she said.

Bixby started down the dunes toward the water. Looking around the beach, she could see three people off in the distance. Bixby's mind immediately raced to the idea that she was about to catch up to all three of the people ahead of her. If she could get the riddle right, she could take the lead.

Reaching the lead group on the beach, she saw that Greg was frustrated and dragging a boat in from the shore.

"Did you see that? I almost went down to Davey Jones's locker, man!" he shouted.

"Too bad you didn't. I could have kept my DVDs," Marin replied.

Wesley was by himself a little farther up the bank, trying to keep his work secret. Bixby ran to the table on the beach in front of the water and read the note written out in crayon:

What you seek,

Is the flag I ask.
Six items will help
To complete your task.

Bixby looked up, and in the distance, out on the water, was a platform with five flags waving. Each one had a contestant's name on it. The waves were heavy and deafening as they repeatedly crashed down. There was no way she would be able to swim out to the platform. Wesley was a champion swimmer at his school, and he obviously hadn't made it; he sat soaking wet next to a kayak. In a hurry, Bixby spun around to find her six items. Just up the beach, she saw a small kayak with her name written on the hull. Sprinting now, she made her way over to where the kayak was and glided down to her knees into the sand. Her kayak was upside down, so she flipped it upright. Underneath the tiny boat were four more items: a life vest, a hand towel, a rope, and an oxygen tank.

"That is only five things, Bixby. The riddle said six," Miss Marmalade said over the speaker.

"You're right," Bixby said as she loaded everything into the boat and started pulling it down to the waterfront.

"What do you guys think?" she asked.

"I think it's suicide if you go out into those waters," Harvey said.

"Thanks for that thought, Harvey," Bixby replied nervously as she looked out at the ferocious waves crashing down just offshore. Unlike for Harvey, this was real for her.

"Oh, *gruahh*, I mean, we'll figure something out," Harvey said.

"It's clear that nobody understands this puzzle. So, it must be more than just swimming or kayaking out there. I'm sure I have to use every piece for this to work, and..." Bixby stopped.

"What is it?" Harvey demanded in her ear as she inspected the boat.

"There's a two-inch hole in the dead center of the bottom of the boat," she said. "Either my boat's been tampered with or that's why Greg said he almost drowned."

"All right, how are we going to make this thing float?" Harvey asked.

"How about you stuff the rag in the hole and use the air tank as a propeller. I saw it in an old spy movie," Miss Marmalade proposed.

"That leaves out the rope and the life vest. Plus, we still don't know what the sixth item is yet," Bixby said, cautious of her answer. "I think Greg was trying to use that same method when we saw him wash back up," she added.

"What about tying the life vest to the bottom of the boat and using that to block the hole?" Harvey asked.

"Okay, that might work to keep the boat afloat, but how do I paddle to get out there?" Bixby questioned.

"Maybe that is the last thing: a paddle. Has anyone figured out a paddle?" Mrs. Timmons asked. Bixby could hear her humming a lullaby she used to sing to Bixby when she was younger. *"She must be rocking the twins in the stroller,"* she thought to herself as she took a brief moment to think of how nice it would be to be there with them.

"Mom? How are the boys?" Bixby asked.

"They're fine. Wyatt was running a fever this morning, and Darby was a little fussy, but they're better now that they're down for their naps," Mrs. Timmons explained.

"Focus, Bixby," Harvey said, committed to the task.

"Sorry about that. We were watching you in the bedroom, and I just love that beach," Mrs. Timmons added. "I have no idea how to get that boat floating, dear. Can you ask for another one?"

"No, Mom," Bixby said, knowing her mother meant well. Then she noticed Maggie tumble down the sand dune.

"Great. Here comes Maggie. Everyone's even now," Bixby said. "I'm at a loss. I can't keep the rag in the hole because the waves will just push it out, and the boat will sink. I can't use just the oxygen tank and life vest because the vest isn't really that big, even if I tie it around me with the rope. The waves will rip it off when I go out there. Plus, it would be impossible to hold the tank and swim."

For the next fifteen minutes, Bixby stumbled through five more possibilities of how to keep the boat afloat and use as many of the elements as she could. Nothing seemed to fit well enough to risk going out into the powerful tide. Her frustrations began to well inside almost to the point of crying. "I don't know if I can do this, guys."

"Bixby, I've got it!" screamed a voice racing down the Launch Room hall. "Oh, man, I've been swamped at work, and the Foreman has taken almost all of my work crew away, so we are crazy busy! I've been waiting for my lunch break to log off and help you."

"Dad," Bixby said a little more loudly than she probably should have. She lowered her voice and continued, "Never mind that; what's the answer?"

"Right. The final element you need is the sand."

"Sand?" Bixby echoed.

"Here is what you have to do...It will be tricky, but it will take all six elements to pull it off. The ocean waves are crashing in on the surface, and it looks like the tide is coming in. With waves that big, it is going to be impossible to get to the platform on top of the water in this riddle. However, the water must go out. It does that under the surface of the surf, right where it meets the sand. That's the undertow," he started to explain.

Her dad was saying she would have to swim underwater to make it to the platform. "Are you crazy? It's like a hundred yards off the coast. I can't hold my breath that long."

"Right you are, Bixby, but that is where the tools they provided come into play. I need you to do exactly what I say, step by step, Bixby. First, make sure no one sees what you're doing."

Bixby shifted in the sand a little so that the boat blocked the view from Maggie and Wesley. Then she made sure she was seated so that Marin and Greg didn't have a clear shot at her work.

"Next, fill the middle of the hand towel up with sand. Then grab all four corners up together and give it a spin so that the sand makes a ball inside the towel. Do you have it so far, Bixby?" Mr. Timmons asked, making sure Bixby could keep up.

Bixby rushed to follow his instructions. "Okay, I have a ball of sand inside the towel," Bixby replied.

"Big enough to block the hole in the kayak?"

Bixby opened the towel back up and stuffed a little more sand inside just to make sure it was enough. "Plenty," she confirmed.

"Okay, now wrap the rope around the towel with a good, tight knot. We don't want that to let loose," Mr. Timmons instructed. "Next, Bixby—and this is the important part—put the other end of the rope through the hole inside of the kayak and out the bottom, and then tie it to the life vest in a way that you can release it quickly."

Bixby quickly pushed the rope through the bottom of the boat as instructed and then made a loop at the end of the rope to buckle the life vest to. All she had to do was unclip the life jacket's buckle, and it would free itself.

"Okay, done. Now what?" Bixby asked.

"Put the air tank into the kayak down where your feet normally go, and then you are ready," Mr. Timmons said, followed by a big breath.

"I don't get it, Dad," Bixby said, confused.

"Don't be scared, Bixby, but this is what you will have to do to get out to the flag," Mr. Timmons said. For the next two minutes, he explained current, buoyancy, undertow, and the order in which Bixby had to apply those scientific principles in order to achieve her goal.

"Bixby, it's the only way to use all the elements to get to that flag like the riddle says," Mr. Timmons said. Bixby could tell by the shakiness in his voice that even he thought what he was telling her to do was madness.

"Don't forget to take your earpiece out and hide it somewhere," Harvey interjected. "Tipton said it would not hold up in water."

Bixby had almost forgotten.

"I'll see you guys on the other side," she said as she reached in her ear, knowing her dad was right about how to get to the flag. He had spent his whole life as a scientist and computer specialist. When he wasn't at work inventing new ways to get computers and robots to do spectacular new things, he was buried in science magazines in the hopes of connecting old science with new.

She slipped her hearing aid under a seashell while the others were messing with their own plans to get their kayak to the platform.

"Okay, Grandpa. Now is when I need a little help from the big guy upstairs. I would like to come out of this alive and in one piece," Bixby said. Then a new thought came to her: she had the opportunity to take first place.

Maybe I belonged here after all.

Bixby grabbed the back of her kayak and started pushing it towards the water's edge. As she pushed out for her maiden voyage, her teammates either sat at the edge of their seats or paced as Bixby shoved off. She grasped the rope and pulled the sand tightly against the bottom of the boat to keep as much water out as she could as she waded waist deep.

The waves were violent and unforgiving. The first one she encountered punched the boat into Bixby's gut and toppled her end over end, back to the shoreline. Determined, she jumped up and pushed right back into the water. Bixby was able to wade out to about twenty feet before more waves crashed down over her head. She grabbed the side of her kayak and tightly gripped the rope.

This was as far out as she was going to make it on the surface, so she released her grip on the rope. She could tell that the boat was taking on a lot of water now, which was part of her plan. As she looked up, a monster of a wave was heading right for her. She started to mentally brace herself because this was the wave she needed to convince the others that she was in trouble. She jumped up on the side of the kayak, hoping she'd speed up the sinking process with her weight. The wave was still growing in strength as it barreled towards her. Fifty feet now. Bixby climbed into the boat, wriggling about in order to force more water into the hull.

On the coast, the other contestants could now see that Bixby was in trouble and started cautioning her about the wave that was racing towards her. Bixby knelt into the water-filled kayak that was now inches from being completely submerged. The wave was about fifty-five feet tall and a mere five seconds away from smashing her into oblivion. With a last gulp, the boat steamed towards the bottom of the ocean floor. Bixby, taking one last giant breath, disappeared under the water with her ship just as the wave crashed down on top of where she had just been floating.

The onlookers on the beach and at home watching on Holo-TV, all gasped. Everyone was certain that Bixby couldn't have possibly survived a wave like that. Even Greg rushed to the water's edge and began searching for Bixby's body to appear.

"*Bixby!*" he cried, his eyes shifting from left to right.

Even though everyone at Pinnacle Manor knew the plan, they couldn't help the rush of anxiety as they waited for what seemed to be hours.

Mrs. Timmons was crying now with her hand over her mouth, muttering, "Please God, say she isn't hurt," over and over again.

Mr. Timmons couldn't breathe as he paced, knowing that he was the one that had asked her to do this. Never in his wildest dreams had he expected her to confront such a ferocious wave. The little Timmons boys had sensed the tension; Hucklebee and Miss Marmalade were consoling their tears with bottles and toys. Harvey could do nothing but stand in place—cold, even for a computer program.

Ten feet under the water, Bixby had the boat turned upside down on top of her. She quickly seized both sides of the kayak as the life vest desperately tried to float to the surface. It was being held back by a ball of sand in a towel jammed in a hole at the bottom of the boat. With one hand and elbow, Bixby was able to keep the kayak steady as she quickly reached into the foothold where she had stored the tank and cranked open the valve.

As her lungs started to burn, the fear of drowning started to creep in on her. The air was trapped inside the capsized boat, unable to escape. The sand was like a cork, keeping her precious oxygen from fleeing through the hole, as the life vest was keeping the cork in place. Bixby quickly pulled herself up to the air pocket that was getting bigger as the air tank continued to flow.

"As soon as you feel the kayak pulling towards the surface, turn off the tank, or the boat will pull you to the surface," Bixby could hear her dad repeating in her head. There wasn't a huge amount of breathing room between the water and the upside-down hull after the tank was off, but she could live with a few inches of air. Realizing her dad's idea worked, Bixby let out a scream of joy and relief.

"Just like a mini-submarine," she said, repeating how he'd explained it. "Now find the platform."

Bixby took a breath in and went back under the water, holding on to the boat so that it would not get away from her. She located the huge chains that were holding the platform steady in the raging ocean. Bixby popped her head back up in the oxygen and started pushing the kayak into the direction of the chains. Just like her dad had predicted, the water at the bottom of the ocean was not pulling her into shore, but quickly pushing her out. She had to hurry. The oxygen wasn't going to last forever.

Maggie was sitting next to her boat, crying. "I don't want to do this anymore," she said.

Marin and Wesley were still hard at work on their boats to make them seaworthy enough to handle the waves. Greg continued to pace the coast, looking for signs of life.

"Will you stop it, Greg? She's gone, and there's nothing you can do about it," Wesley hissed.

"Dude, not cool," Greg snapped back.

It was the first time anyone had heard Greg sound upset, maybe even a little mad.

"She didn't belong with us, man. She obviously wasn't smart enough to compete. Now man up and move on," Wesley shouted over the crashing waves. "Or don't. Doesn't matter to me either way. That'll just make it easier for me to win with you giving up."

Greg's face burned red now as his fist balled up at his sides.

"Holy Moly! She's alive!" screamed Maggie.

Everyone quickly glanced up and down the coastline to see where she'd washed ashore.

"No, you dopes, she's on the platform!" Maggie yelled as she pointing out to sea.

"You have got to be kidding me," Wesley said, as Bixby stood pulling her flag down from the pole.

"How...We saw her go under...I don't...," Marin stuttered to herself.

Bixby waved to her competitors and jumped from the platform with the small life vest clutched in front of her. As she bobbed back up from the water, she simply body surfed on several waves until she was safely back onshore.

"I suppose you're not planning on telling us how you did that?" Greg asked, hoping Bixby was feeling generous.

"Ah, nope," Bixby said with a smile as she strolled over to the table with the riddle on it. Once she put the flag on the table, another archway rose from the sand, and a path revealed itself down the beach.

Bixby started walking towards the arches, but quickly, she realized she'd almost forgotten her earpiece. She made a small detour towards the shell that she'd hid it under on her way to the path. Kicking over the shell with her toe, she realized it was gone. She bent down, grabbed the shell, and rolled it around in her hand; it wasn't there. Next, she sifted her hand around in the sand—nothing.

"You looking for this?" a cold voice said from behind her. Wesley was now right above her with his hot breath beating down on her neck. From the corner of her eye, she could see that he was holding her earpiece. "I knew you were dumb, but deaf, too?" he poked. "I tell you what. Tell me how you made it to the platform, or you will be deaf in your one ear for the rest of this level," he threatened.

Bixby's mind reeled. He didn't know that it was a communication device to her team. He really thought she was deaf. Wesley must have seen her take it out before she went into the water.

"I can make it with one ear, Wesley," she replied quietly, hoping he didn't catch on to how desperate she really did need that earpiece. "But I'll make you an offer, take it or leave it. Or I'll go without my hearing aid, and you're on your own," she bargained.

"I'm listening," he said.

"I will tell you what the sixth element is and how to use it, in exchange for my hearing aid. You saw me go out, and I think you can put it all together when you know the final element and its use. Only offer," Bixby said.

It took Wesley a moment, but he knew that taking her offer was the best way to get past this riddle. He knew he could catch her in a foot race, so he dropped the hearing aid in the sand and grabbed her wrist. "Deal," he said, holding her there until she kept her end of the bargain.

"Sand. Sand is the final element. Use it to help plug the hole," she said as she grabbed the hearing aid from the ground with her other hand and bashfully put it in her pocket.

"Enjoy your head start. It won't last too long," Wesley sneered, releasing her. She could see in his dark green eyes that his mind was beginning to work on the puzzle with this new information.

Bixby turned and ran as fast as she could. She was still riding high on adrenaline from the ocean and her run in with Wesley. She would pay for it later, but for now, she sprinted as fast as she could through the arches and down the path.

CHAPTER FIFTEEN

CONFRONTATION

AFTER ABOUT A half-hour of running, Bixby stopped in order to catch her breath and connect with her team. As she pulled a few deep breaths into her lungs, she reached into her pocket and grabbed the hearing aid from within. It was covered in sand, so she worked quickly to clean it off before she put it back in her ear.

"Can you guys hear me?" she asked as soon as it was comfortably in its rightful place.

"Bixby, you did it!" Mrs. Timmons exploded.

"Good show, Bixby. You had us worried there for a moment when you took on the biggest wave in the ocean," Hucklebee said.

"I had to give them a show," Bixby replied proudly.

"For the record, I wasn't worried one bit," Harvey interjected.

"Thanks, guys. I couldn't have done it without Dad's instructions. Is he there?" Bixby asked.

"No, they called him back to work early. He had to leave while you were still underwater. I think they did it on purpose," Mrs. Timmons answered, knowing Bixby would be disappointed not to hear from her dad.

"But Tipton just got here," a cheerful Miss Marmalade added.

Without hesitation, Tipton exploded with information. "Hey, Bixby! You're not going to believe Holo-School Prime today. There are like three Holo-Writer hacks to watch the game at school. Everyone was following the live feed during class. It's driving Headmaster Quincy absolutely nuts. When you went under the water, the school totally stopped. Mrs. Gable couldn't contain herself, either, and put it on the Holo-Board. Nobody made a sound except for a few people who were crying and saying that you were dead. Then there were some rude comments by Wesley's sister, Penny, and her gang when you didn't come up after a while," he added. "When you climbed up on that platform, the roof of the building almost blew off. It was so awesome to watch. The whole Dagger Army slumped down in their seats."

"Wesley almost found out about our communication system," Bixby said. "He thinks I'm deaf in one ear, which means it won't take him long to figure out that it's not being used to help me hear. If he finds out that we're communicating with it, he's going to rip it out and smash it," Bixby said, concerned that she didn't have much more time with the system they had.

"Don't worry. I'm already working on something new. You're going to have to survive this level with what you have, though," Tipton said.

"I don't mean to interrupt, but are you going in circles, Bixby?" Miss Marmalade asked.

"I have been following the coastline on this path, so...I don't think so?" Bixby replied.

"Well, it's just the strangest thing. I feel like you keep going around that same clump of palm trees.

"I think you may be right," Bixby agreed. "I was so busy trying to keep running that I didn't really notice them."

"I think you should get off the path and head into those trees, then," Harvey voted.

"Does everyone else agree?" Bixby asked.

Looking around the room, everyone gave Harvey a nod, "Yes, Bixby. It seems like the most logical thing to do."

Bixby stepped off the path in high anticipation of getting her first burn on her arm; nothing happened. She started to jog a little bit, because if she had been going in circles, she may have given up a little of her lead, but quickly slowed back down to a walk.

"Man, I'm super thirsty," Bixby said, realizing she could barely moisten her mouth.

"It's a good thing those are coconut trees," Hucklebee said.

"Which trees?"

Bixby heard him tapping on what sounded like the monitor. "Those over there in a circle."

Bixby located the batch of trees he was describing. As she drew near, a smile engulfed her face. She could see volleyball-sized orbs hanging from the underside of the canopy of one. As she came to the base of the tree, though, her optimism quickly faded.

"They're like twenty feet off the ground. How am I supposed to get to them?" Bixby asked, looking around to see if there was anything nearby that could help.

"I think you're going to have to climb," Tipton said.

"Why is it always heights?" Bixby said with a sigh and a frown.

After a little bit of searching, she found a tree that leaned more than the rest and ran over to it. She bear-hugged the base of the tree with her arms, and, with a little leap, she shimmied up the bark with her legs wrapped tightly around the trunk. It took her almost five minutes to get to where she could reach the fruits—partly because she was now almost to the point of exhaustion, but also because she had never really tried to worm her way up a tree before. It was kind of like climbing the rope in gym class, except the rope was abrasive and a foot and a half wide. The tree was narrow at the top, so Bixby could wrap her legs all the way around the tree trunk. With all the might she had left, she started to bop the coconuts with her fist. After a few punches to the top of each coconut, they dropped to the ground. Bixby wanted to get a few down while she was at the top of the tree so she didn't have to climb back up again. Fatigue was setting in faster as Bixby looked at the four nuts that were now down on the ground. Content with her work, she made her way back to the sand.

Once again on the ground, Bixby grabbed a coconut...and just looked at it.

"Guys? I have no clue how to open a coconut," Bixby said, baffled. She turned one over in her hand.

"Oh, it's easy, Bixby," Mrs. Timmons said with excitement. "When your dad and I were on our honeymoon, there was this coconut shack. You would order your coconut, and these guys with really big knives would come over and chop the husks off the outside. Then, with the back of the knife, they would smack it along the middle of the nut, and it would pop right open for them. You can even eat the insides; they call it coconut jelly."

"Mom, I don't have a big knife," Bixby pointed out.

"You do have those jagged rocks over there," Tipton said.

Bixby took a quick look around. On the far side of the tree field was a pile of black lava rocks. Desperate to get the coconuts open to drink from, she stumbled over to the rock pile and found one with a sharpened point on one end of the stone. She lifted it with relative ease and brought it back to where her coconuts were lying. With the pointed end facing up, she buried the rock in the sand.

"Now, put the coconut above your head and drop it on the sharp rock point," Tipton said.

Bixby quickly followed his instructions. The first drop ripped right down the side of the husk and tore it in two. Bixby grabbed and pulled on the loose outer shell with all her might.

To her surprise, it pulled right off. Bixby stood up again and dropped it on its other side. This time, the rock pierced the husk as it bounced off, so Bixby tried a third time. After five drops on to the lava rock, she was able to tear off the rest of the husk, leaving her with just the brown nut left to crack.

"Okay, Bixby, I jumped on my Holo-Writer, and it says that a coconut has a weak equator. What you have to do is turn the nut sideways so that the oblong sides are parallel with the ground. Next, you will need to hit the equator of the nut against the rock and then keep rotating as you smack it. Eventually, the nut will crack, and you will need to put it up to your mouth and drink before it all drains out. Once you drink up all the water, you can open the nut completely and eat the white insides," Tipton read aloud.

Bixby was already starting to thump the brown nut against the rock as he spoke. After rotating the coconut around three times, she saw the juice splatter against the black rock, and she quickly held it up to her lips. Slowly, the water dripped in her mouth, and Bixby realized just how dehydrated she really was. She could feel that there was more water in the nut as she shook it, but it had suddenly stopped flowing out of the crack she had made. Looking closely, she could see there was something wedged into the opening of the coconut.

"Are there any bugs or animals that live in coconuts?" Bixby asked timidly.

"Let me look," Tipton said as he searched the web. "No. Unless the nut rots, usually the inside of the nut is free from any bugs or animals. Why?"

"Because something is wedged in there, blocking the water from coming out," Bixby said.

"Crack it all the way open and find out, Bixby. You have more nuts to open if that one has something living in it," Harvey said matter-of-factly.

Bixby stood up and held the fractured nut above her head, directly above the makeshift knife in the sand, then let it go. She stepped back in case something deadly sprung from the confines of the shell. Much to her surprise, though, the nut broke almost evenly in half and fell on either side of the rock. Within the one side of the shell was what looked to be an actual puzzle piece.

"Curious," she whispered to herself.

Bixby drew close to the newfound treasure, hesitated, and then reached in and picked it up. Without warning, the ground began to shake, and in the heart of all the trees, the sand parted, and a slab of concrete rose out of the ground. The new structure stood twenty feet wide, eight feet tall, and boasting five sides.

"That four seconds of rest was fantastic," Bixby said sarcastically as she dashed over to the new addition to the beach to see what was next.

She took a lap around the massive statue that was now in the middle of it all and started reading the names on each side: Wesley, Marin, Maggie, Greg, and, finally, Bixby. As she stepped up, she saw the chiseled shape of a large puzzle. Above the puzzle board was a giant square of equal size. Bixby took the piece and tried to match it up to a space on the board, but there were at least three possibilities. Bixby reached for the first spot that seemed to match.

The next thing Bixby remembered was being flat on her back and her forearm burning. Looking down, she recognized the red rash that was now searing.

"Bixby! Are you okay?" Harvey shouted.

"Yeah, I'm fine. I guess I thought you could put the piece in a spot, and if it didn't fit, you could try another one. Turns out, if you put it into the wrong spot, you get zapped," Bixby said as she poked at her wrist to assess the damage. "Essshh, these burns are no joke."

"That's it, I'm breaking the door open to your launch room," Mrs. Timmons barked.

"Stop it, Mom," Bixby said through her teeth. "I'm fine."

"No worries, Bixby, there's some first aid right there in those coconuts," Miss Marmalade started.

Bixby looked in the empty half quizzically.

"Put some of that coconut jelly on it to soothe the pain," Miss Marmalade instructed.

Bixby followed directions, and indeed the jelly felt amazing on the burn, but she had no time to waste enjoying the relief.

Bixby rolled to her knees and looked up at the board. The piece had moved up into the carved square where it stayed put.

"It must be where you store your pieces as you get them," Bixby thought to herself. She quickly grabbed another nut and began to work on opening it. Just as before, she drank out as much of the water as she could and then split the nut wide open. Bixby quickly grabbed the piece and headed to her rock face.

"It's the same piece," Bixby said, frustrated.

"Bixby? How many trees are there around you?" Miss Marmalade asked.

It was a strange question, but Miss Marmalade led her to this point, so she didn't hesitate to take a quick count.

"Twenty-four," Bixby answered.

"There are also twenty-four places to put puzzle pieces in that riddle," Miss Marmalade said.

"Oh, man, you totally had the same thought I did!" shouted a voice from up the sand. Bixby's lead had been short-lived, but she was now on track to solving this riddle.

"I was looking up here at the coconuts, hoping I had time to grab some electrolytes. Then I heard you scream from down on the beach and knew not to follow the path," Greg said.

Bixby fumed at the knowledge that her stupid mistake had cost her time.

"I'm not gonna lie, Ginger. I have seen some gnarly waves in my time, but when that wave came barreling down over you...totally thought you were a goner," Greg said as he plopped down on the beach, admiring the stone slab.

"Maggie was crying her eyes out, and Wesley was sure you were dead, too," he said as he started to take in the work Bixby had already been doing. "Anyway, it didn't take me long to figure out what you did after you disappeared under the water and came back up with the life vest. Problem is that now that you were able to get to the platform, everyone else figured out how to put together a gnarly submarine. The rest of them should be coming here post-haste. Tick tock, Red."

She knew that he was already aware that she was working on the next puzzle, and now she knew that everyone was probably close to catching up.

"I'm going to get me some of that water, and then I'll have to bust a move on this puzzle," he said, jumping up from his seated position and starting to scale his first tree.

Like a monkey, it took him no time at all to smack a few of the nuts to the ground. Bixby was already making her way up a third tree, and she only knocked one nut to the ground. Going down was much faster for Bixby because she could jump once she got close to the bottom. At her station, she made fast work of what she was doing. The piece came out quickly, and now she knew for sure Greg knew what to do. Bixby slapped her fourth piece onto the rock under her name and began to climb tree number five. At the top, she could see down the beachfront, and in almost a full sprint, came Wesley, followed closely by Marin. Off in the far distance, Bixby could make out Maggie dropping her flag down on the table. Greg must have tipped them off to not having to run the path when he strolled up the beach. Frustrated, Bixby was now enraged that she had wasted half an hour of time running the path instead of heading to the trees in the first place.

Wesley made sure to walk close enough to Bixby to give a nice kick of sand all over her. He snagged one of her coconut halves and buried his face inside, sucking on the jelly.

"Thanks, twerp," he said, then worked on drinking every last drop from her coconut. As he finished, he lowered the coconut and realized that the puzzle was right in front of him.

He made a lap around the monument and realized that Bixby had five pieces on her board, and Greg already had three.

"I appreciate all the hard work you did for me, Bixby," Wesley said. As he reached up to her board and went to grab a piece with each hand, Wesley was knocked down to his butt with a burst of energy.

Greg let out a laugh. "Dude, that would be cheating. Riddle seems to frown upon that, bro."

Wesley grumbled as he brushed himself off and admired his growing sleeve of burn marks up his arms. Bixby was on her way up tree seven as Marin came into camp. She did the customary lap around the puzzle and then a quick review of what the others were working on, and immediately dashed up a tree. Every once in a while, a contestant knocked down more than one nut on accident. It was an opportunity for others to make one less climb. Wesley was making a habit of stealing coconuts from just about everyone in the circle. Bixby would knock one down, and if Wes was close by, he would take it right out from underneath her.

Marin quickly fixed that problem. As Wesley walked away with one of her nuts, she reached up, grabbed another one from the tree and hurled it in his direction. The shot couldn't have been any more on target as it smacked him directly in the back of the head. His body fell limp to the ground, face-first in the sand.

"Captain Coconut, you knocked him out cold," Greg announced as he rolled Wesley over. "He's still breathing, but he's going to have a whopper of a headache when he snaps to."

Ten minutes later, Maggie stumbled her way into the trees and saw Wesley's seemingly lifeless body propped up against a tree, "Is he dead?"

"We're not that lucky," Marin said as she slid down the tree.

"He was stealing other people's coconuts," Bixby added, working on her sixteenth piece.

Maggie quickly figured out what she needed to do to solve the puzzle. She snatched a rock and placed it in front of her puzzle board. She then strolled over to where Wesley was working.

"I don't think he'll need these for a while," she announced as she gathered up Wesley's stolen nuts and brought them over to her camp to work. Nobody cared. Plus, Maggie had no clue which trees those nuts had come from, so she was bound to repeat herself several times.

An hour later, Greg started to put his puzzle pieces into place on the board. Bixby was on twenty-three and Marin was about to finish twenty-four. Bixby couldn't help but think how far ahead she would have been if she hadn't wasted thirty minutes of running. Maggie somehow was on her way, as well. A quick glimpse showed that she had at least fifteen pieces, and three of them were already in their correct location on the board.

"*Ah*, my head!" came a moan from the sand pile that was now Wesley's base. "What did you do to me?" he continued as he sat up.

"Coconut fell and hit you on the head. Lucky for you, Greg was nice enough to move you out of the way, or two more would have smashed your head open like a melon," Marin said as she pulled out her final piece and headed to the board.

"You better get going, big guy," Greg said as he put his tenth piece into its correct spot.

"You!" Wesley spat, getting to his feet and wobbly facing Bixby.

"What?"

"You hit me!"

"Me? You really think I had anything to do with it? I was nowhere close to the tree that you were stealing coconuts from," Bixby said, appalled.

"It's part of the game, you little runt. Learn to defend what's yours, and you won't need to bash me in the head with a coconut," Wesley said, his eyes cold with hate.

Bixby stood up with her last coconut in hand. She palmed it and assumed a defensive position that Harvey had taught her the day before she launched, "If it was me who bashed you in the head, then defending what was mine was exactly what I did."

"Really? You think you can go toe to toe with me, runt?" Wesley said, his jaw beginning to clench. "It's time to end you right here and now."

Another coconut zipped past his ear from behind. He spun around and saw Marin with a second coconut ready to throw.

"How big of an idiot are you? You know that coconut came from my tree. You were standing right below it. So, if you don't want another concussion, back off and start working on your own puzzle. By yourself," she said, appearing more than a little hopeful Wesley would charge her, instead.

With a dizzy head, Wesley turned to a tree. Outnumbered and far behind, he began to climb.

"Thanks," Bixby said with her nerves completely on edge.

"Don't thank me. You were the one willing to fight for my actions," Marin said, returning to her board.

Bixby drank the last of her water, stuffed one half of the nut in each of her pockets in case she needed them later, and planted the last piece on her board.

Bixby scanned the board and her pieces, and there was only one piece that was different than the rest. Without hesitation, she slapped it in the dead center of the board. From there, Bixby could hear Miss Marmalade shouting out pieces and locations faster than Bixby could grab them off the rock face and put them in place.

"This really seems to be your puzzle," Bixby whispered as she found the piece she was looking for.

"Oh, thank you kindly. I was once in this group of H-bot speed puzzlers online. I took second place in the one-thousand-piece puzzle category. It took me four minutes and twenty seconds," she boasted.

"Okay, then, what piece goes where next?" Bixby murmured.

One by one, Miss Marmalade continued to direct Bixby around the jumbled mess of pieces. Without missing a single piece, Bixby completed the puzzle in a few short minutes. The puzzle locked into place and became a clear picture:

Some use me alive.

Some wait till I've died.
My age is unknown,
Without looking inside.

"Hmm," Bixby hummed as she stood back to ponder the puzzle.

"How about a coconut?" Hucklebee said, trying to not miss the obvious again.

"That won't tell you how old it is when you open it up," Harvey said.

"What about an animal? You would use their skin and meat when they are dead, and they can be useful when they are alive. I bet there's a way to find an animal's age with some kind of fancy blood test," Mrs. Timmons suggested.

"That doesn't fit Grandpa's rules. 'The answer will answer the entire riddle precisely.'" Bixby said.

The sand began to shake, and another set of arches rose up from the ground. With a huff, Bixby could see her lead disappear. She quickly went around to his side of the puzzle to see if his answer was still there. The rock face was completely blank; there were no pieces, no empty square, and now no Greg. Marin was standing there next to her momentarily, then realizing that the answer was gone, she went back to her own puzzle board. Bixby followed suit.

"Any more ideas?" She slumped back into the sand.

"Bixby, I really do wish you had time to enjoy that beach," Mrs. Timmons said, concerned her daughter was getting frustrated. "That sunset with the trees, sand, and crashing ocean really was beautiful. When your grandpa was stuck on a puzzle, he would sit out on the rooftop and look over the city. Maybe you should take a second and look at that sunset?"

Bixby turned her head slightly towards the beach, but then it snapped back to the stone slab. With a start, Bixby leapt up from the sand. As she did, Marin started to run for the arches. She must have figured it out just before Bixby.

Bixby began whispering her answer to the rock face, but nothing happened, not even a burn.

"How do I give my answer," she pondered aloud.

"I think it wants you to write the answer above," Tipton said.

"Let me grab out my handy-dandy rock pen," Bixby said sarcastically.

Her head began to dart back and forth along the ground for some kind of rock, or stick, or...

Bixby loved it when answers finally popped into her mind. It was as if her heart had been shocked with pure adrenaline. It was the stone she had used to shred her coconuts. The water from cracking the nuts had leaked onto the stone turning it midnight black. She quickly scooped up half of a coconut, dug in with her fingernails, and scrapped out two fingers full of jelly. She went up to the rock wall and wrote on the empty square where her puzzle pieces used to be stored. The light grey stone turned charcoal grey with each wet letter she wrote in slime: TREE.

When she was finished, she stood back and hoped. As she thought, the puzzle board was sucked into the rock, and a blank rock face closed over top of it. Then, as quickly as the letters were written on the stone wall, they evaporated away one by one in the hot evening sun.

Bixby sprinted under the arches and for some reason looked back over her shoulder. There, standing in front of his board, was Wesley. His face filled with rage as he pounded his fist into his hand. A threat that everyone knew meant a beating was coming. Then Bixby saw Maggie and, for a moment, felt bad about leaving her there with him alone. There was nothing Bixby could do, though, so she just kept running.

Up ahead was a bonfire on the beach and a huge stone arch. Bixby knew that she had to put time between her and Wesley. With everything she had left, she ran until her lungs burned. She had given everyone thirty minutes back from the head start she had; she couldn't afford another second. Her legs were like Jell-O as she ran, but she kept going. Her final destination of the day was only a half-mile down the coastline. The waves were calm now, and she splashed through the water on her way to the finish line. It felt cool and soothing on her skin as the water was rolling down her legs. As Bixby crossed under the checkpoint, she didn't stop to see her time but instead ran right into the water, waist deep. She knelt down so that she could drench her sore arms from climbing the trees. It only took a second to realize the saltwater on her freshly burnt arm was not a great combination. She shot right back up, wincing in pain.

"Careful on that earpiece, Bixby Timmons," Tipton shouted. Bixby had almost forgotten they were there.

"This water feels good," Bixby said with a heavy sigh while watching the sun started to disappear over the horizon. "Well, when it doesn't hit the burn, at least."

Mr. Timmons returned home at about nine p.m., which had been, by far, his longest day ever at Dragonthorp, Inc. Visibly distressed, Mrs. Timmons ran over to give him a hug.

"Is everything okay?" she asked, inches from his ear.

"We'll talk when the feed goes down," he said quietly.

She nodded in understanding.

Tipton, Harvey, and Hucklebee were engulfed in talking to Bixby about how she'd come up with the answer to the riddle.

"It took me a second, but when Mom said something about how beautiful the sunset was, I had to shift to see it around the tree. Then it hit me. You can build houses and fires with the wood that trees provide when they're dead. They provide fruit, oxygen, and shade when they're alive, and the only really good way to tell how old a tree is, is to cut into it and count the rings," Bixby explained as she slowly waded back up on to the sand.

In the distance, Bixby could make out the last two contestants making their way up the beach. Maggie was in the lead, but she could see that Wesley wasn't going to let her beat him. Wesley passed Maggie with about twenty yards to go in their footrace to the finish line.

"I'm going to go check on Maggie," she said, cutting into her family's chatter.

Bixby ran up and caught Maggie as she tumbled to the sand. "You okay?" Bixby asked.

"Yes...just...need...to catch...my breath," she replied.

"Looks like you're all the way caught up to the group," Bixby said cheerfully.

"Still in last," she said after a few moments more of heavy breathing.

"Well, at least today wasn't elimination day, right?" Bixby said, still trying to make Maggie smile.

Her comfort wasn't working. As Maggie looked up at Bixby, her eyes were terrified, and Bixby could tell she was physically and emotionally torn apart.

"Bixby, I thought you died out there today, and when Wesley started making all of those threats...I thought when you left...he went nuts. He started smashing coconuts on the rocks, punched the trees. I wrote my answer on the rock and was getting ready to run to the arches, but then he started coming towards me, so I blurted out the answer so he wouldn't hurt me," Maggie said, tears running down her cheeks.

"Maybe it's better if I just lose this round and be done with this puzzle," Maggie said through sobs.

"Don't say that," Bixby said sternly. Her blood was now on fire. "You represent Verruckt Overlook. Those people are cheering for you, along with the people at your school. We won't let him bother you anymore—I won't let him."

Bixby took Maggie by the shoulder, and they walked, arm in arm, to the fire.

Greg and Marin were laughing as they talked of today's trials. They hushed as soon as they saw Bixby help Maggie down to the ground. She slumped against a log.

"Where's Wesley?" Bixby demanded.

"He already went to his hut. From the looks of it, he was pretty ticked off," Greg said.

"Wesley!" Bixby shouted towards his hut. She picked up a large rock and threw it at his door. The rock hit the window just above the door, which shattered it into a million pieces.

"Wesley, you don't scare us anymore! You're done picking on people, stealing from them, and being a bully! You hear me? *Done!*" Reaching down and picking up another rock, Bixby buried her feet in the sand and prepared for a fight. He never came to the door.

"Coward," she yelled as she walked back to the fire.

The friendly chatter was gone now. The waves and the crackle of the campfire were the only sounds in the night. Bixby had just declared war, and it was only level one.

Back at Pinnacle Manor, Mr. and Mrs. Timmons were finally alone in their room and were climbing into bed. Mr. Timmons spoke as calmly as he could to Mrs. Timmons.

"There was a note on my desk when I got back from lunch," he started. "They know we're helping Bixby."

"What did the note say?" Mrs. Timmons asked, concerned.

"It said, 'Stop helping her, or you're not going to be the first to have an accident on the job,'" Mr. Timmons said, voice wavering.

"Cooper! We have to say something," Mrs. Timmons said as she froze.

"Who are we going to tell? 'Dear Mr. Riddle Maker, the other houses know we're helping our daughter. Can you tell them to stop threatening us?'" Mr. Timmons replied.

"Seriously, though. What are we going to do?" Mrs. Timmons asked, grasping her husband's hand.

"Right now, nothing. Bixby can't find out. Nobody but us can know. If she finds out, she'll go to pieces, and that's the last thing anyone of us needs."

"We've got to do something."

"I know," he said. "Don't worry. I'll figure something out. But until then, I think I'll be forced to work sunup till sundown, which means that you'll have to lead the team."

"But—"

"No buts. Bixby needs us," Mr. Timmons said as he lay down, praying Bixby would understand.

She'd have to. There was no other choice.

CHAPTER SIXTEEN
BUMP IN THE NIGHT

BIXBY SHOT UP in bed. She looked around, heart pounding, and let her eyes adjust to the darkness. Moonlight shone through the now-broken picture window of her door. Despite what light managed to creep in, she couldn't see much else.

Carefully, Bixby eased across the room to where she thought she could see something on the floor, doing her best to avoid any broken glass. Below a small reading table, she found a rock with a note attached. It read:

YOU DON'T BELONG HERE.
STAY OUT OF EVERYONE'S WAY, OR YOU WILL END UP IN THIS LEVEL PERMANENTLY.

She grabbed the rock and held it tightly in her fist before creeping to her door, ready for a fight. Bixby turned the handle and stuck her head out an inch. She expected Wesley to be standing there waiting for her, but she saw nothing. Nobody's cabin lights were on, and nothing stirred nearby.

Wanting answers, Bixby stepped into the night, the cold sand pressing between her toes. She scoured the area for footprints but found only hers. She did, however, find a piece of driftwood and decided to take it as extra insurance against any future intruders before returning to her cabin.

Shutting the door behind her, Bixby reached for her earpiece, hoping someone was up at Pinnacle Manor who she could talk to. She'd barely moved when she heard the crunch of glass in the darkness, and then everything went black.

Bixby woke to the sounds of Marin yelling at Wesley to put out the fire.

Pain wracked her head as if somebody had put a knife in the back of her skull and kept twisting it slowly. As she went to reach her hand to her head, she realized her hand wouldn't move. Trying the other hand returned the same result. Her legs seemed paralyzed, as well. Bixby struggled to raise her head and soon realized she was tied to her bunk. As the blurriness from her eyes began to clear, she heard Marin's countdown start and a door slide open. She then heard the clock reset and knew she was now supposed to be heading towards the start line.

Maggie owed her a favor, and now it was time to cash it in.

Bixby tried to scream to grab the girl's attention, but she quickly realized she'd been gagged with a sandy towel and couldn't make a sound.

Terror gripped Bixby's heart. There were no cameras allowed in the sleeping quarters, so no one would know what had happened to her, and she could very well be trapped there forever.

Bixby strained against her restraints, but the knots held fast, and the ropes cut into her skin. She tried screaming again, but all she managed were muffled cries far too weak to get her any help. Worse, she could hear her countdown clock outside quickly running out of time.

Whomp! Whomp! Whomp! Before she knew it, Bixby's timer was down to zero.

"Hey, Bixby," she heard Maggie shout. "Where'd you go?"

Bixby thrashed and screamed in response, but nothing came of it.

"Take another step closer to that door, and I'll break your legs," Wesley's voice rang out. "If she doesn't want to wake up in time to race, then that's *her* fault."

Five minutes rolled by, and Bixby hadn't made any progress in getting free. As she fought for freedom, she had a new thought. Did her team know she was in trouble? If so, what could they possibly do about it?

The timer started to count down for Wesley. He must have been standing close to the cabin because she could hear him talking now to Maggie.

"I think you and me, Maggie, are going to go into the puzzle together. I don't want you cheating and waking our dear friend Bixby up."

"What if something's wrong?" Maggie pleaded.

"Not another step. Turn around and march."

"Bixby!" Maggie cried out. Bixby could hear from the struggle that Wesley had picked her up and was dragging her, possibly kicking and screaming, towards the start line.

Whomp. Whomp. Whomp. Maggie's time had come, and the door slid open. "*Bixb—*" and then they were gone.

The only thing left was the sound of the ocean. Her head was throbbing now, and all the screaming had started to make her dizzy. She was sweating profusely, and her vision blurred, and then the room went dark again.

"Bixby, wake up!" a familiar voice rang out. Bixby's eyes blinked open, and she assumed she was dreaming. "Bixby? Who did this to you?" Tipton asked.

Bixby could only muster a moan as Tipton was assessing Bixby's situation. She noticed that the gag was loose on her mouth while she had relaxed. Wiggling her head, she was able to push it free, but as she tried to reach up to rub her head that was still pounding, it was to no avail as her hands were still fastened to the cot.

"How did you get here?" Bixby asked, confused.

Bixby was still a bit fuzzy as last evening slowly came back to her.

"When I saw that you missed your start time, I knew there must be something wrong. So, I logged off Holo-School Prime—

which will get me a detention, by the way—and launched into your parents' house—which is going to get me killed for not getting approval by your dad," Tipton explained as fast as he could.

"Where is my dad?" she asked hazily.

"I checked his log because he wasn't answering his texts. He launched into work at 4 a.m. this morning," Tipton replied.

"What about my mom?"

"Your mom was with the boys, who were screaming their heads off. Anyway, Hucklebee was trying to find a quote to say for when you finally woke up, and Harvey was just staring at the screen, baffled by why you hadn't come out yet. I also knew that cameras couldn't be in your bunk room. Did I mention that I promised your dad never to launch into your room again? He's going to kill me."

"Tipton!"

"Right, so I launched in via the coin under your patch, knowing nobody would see me. Good thing, too. Looks like someone left you here for dead," he said. "The good news is that there is a way out, but you're not going to like it."

"Just untie me already!"

"Bixby, I'm a hologram, remember? I can only help walk you through how to get out of this," He started. "Oh man, someone smacked you on the side of the head really good."

"Tipton, how do I get out of this?" she demanded.

"The only way would be to really stretch yourself hard, and chew through the rope on your left hand." Bixby could see that it was tied closer to her face. With all of her might she tried to pull herself close, but the ropes tied to her feet didn't give enough slack. Slumping back on the cot, Bixby lay exhausted, trying to reach the rope.

"Any other ideas?" Bixby demanded in frustration.

"I'm looking," he said, his voice more worried now because he didn't see another solution.

"I'll do it myself," Bixby barked in frustration as she got her breath back. She had gone from hazy, to angry, and now to furious as she searched around the room. It took a minute, but she spied a piece of broken glass stuck in her driftwood off to the side on the otherwise recently cleaned floor. Apparently, whoever had covered their tracks after knocking her out, had missed it.

Energized at a potential solution, Bixby rocked the bed back and forth with all her might. For the first few pulls, the bed hardly moved. Once she got a rhythm going, she realized it was going to work, and she hit it harder and faster, like a drummer working herself into a frenzied beat. Then it happened: the bed went over its tipping point and took Bixby with it. The metal frame on her back didn't hurt because of the mattress, but the weight of the hunk of metal smashing Bixby's already sore head onto the rock floor sent stars through her eyes.

"Esh, Bixby!" Tipton shouted, wincing with sympathy pain.

She grimaced, but then her adrenaline kicked in as she started to shimmy towards the driftwood. Not wanting it to move from the wall, she lined the rope up with the shard of glass and pinned the club to the wall, and then started to saw.

"Wow, Bixby, you are brilliant. I didn't see that glass there."

Bixby kept sawing as she tried to drown out Tipton. Her first rope was free. No longer needing the glass, she moved furiously to the other arm with her newly unrestricted hand.

With a crash, the bed flipped to its side, and Bixby made fast work of her feet.

"How far behind am I right now?" Bixby asked.

"I'd say you're now twelve or thirteen minutes behind Wesley," Tipton said with a little hesitation.

Bixby wobbled to her feet. "I have to go," she mumbled

"Are you sure? Bixby, your head is cut up really bad."

Bixby located the coconut from the day before, on the floor of her cabin. Scraping out an almost dry chunk of jelly, she placed it on the gash along her head.

"Ouch!" She jumped as she applied it.

"That really looks painful. Are you sure you can stand?"

"I can't let everyone down like they're letting me down."

It took a second for Tipton to realize what she'd just said, and he looked like she'd hit *him* with a ton of bricks. "Nobody's let you down, Bixby."

"My parents are back to their normal life of ignoring me, you are useless as a hologram, the H-bots are hoping an idiot like me can bring back their programmer, when we don't even know if this is actually Cody's riddle, and now somebody is trying to kill me," Bixby said as she stumbled to the floor. Tipton stood there, stunned.

Bixby stood and grabbed her earpiece.

"Then you might as well eat before you run out. You'll need your strength since you want to be on your own," Tipton said with a long face as he disappeared.

Reaching up to her neck, she felt the voice patch that was there and knew that everyone had heard what she'd said and instantly regretted it all.

Her hand disappeared into her pocket and pulled out some food. As the flavors of meatloaf and mashed potatoes danced on her tongue, tears began to stream down her face. Maybe everyone was right...Maybe she didn't belong here...Why were people so mean? Why did she have such a big mouth...? She could just finish this level and go home and disappear. What if she just stayed here and never went back?

In her earpiece, a line of static started to buzz. She pulled it out to see if she had gotten it wet. To her, it looked like it was fully functional. The buzzing was still there and, as she walked closer to the door, she could hear someone's voice. The crackling over the voice made it impossible to make out what they were saying, so she stepped outside of the cabin to see if the sound would clear up. Bixby could tell that the farther away from her cabin she went, the clearer the voice became.

"Do you guys hear that?" Bixby asked, thinking someone was pranking her. Nobody responded.

At first, Bixby started to walk towards the ocean, but the signal almost went silent. She made her way over to the fire pit, and the signal began to grow. She knew now where the signal would be the strongest. As she stood at the threshold of the start of the day's puzzles, she could hear the voice loud and clear, repeating a message over and over: "If good, honest, and worthy people were to give up the fight, the world would be a bad place...Be strong, honest, and worthy because it gives us all a fighting chance," the deep voice repeated.

"Grandpa?" Bixby said out loud as the doors slid open. The voice went silent. She didn't know how or why she could hear her grandfather's voice, but her mind played the voice repeatedly in her head. Her heart started racing, and her blood boiled. Wesley was going to pay for what he'd done to her, Maggie, and anyone else he'd ever picked on. Her body rocked back slightly, and with the sounds of her grandfather willing her to continue the good fight, she began to sprint like she had never run before.

CHAPTER SEVENTEEN

CLAUSTROPHOBIA

IT DIDN'T TAKE Bixby long to reach the entrance to a cave filled almost completely with water. A quick look around left no doubt that this was the only way to go. There were cliffs on either side of the hole and steps that led right into the heart of the abyss. Bixby waded into the water, and it felt as if she had walked into a hot bath. Water rose up from below her; it must have been the start of a hot spring that was being fed from an underground stream.

The current gradually moved Bixby to the far end of the cave, the pace reminding her of the lazy river at Wallaby Water Works, an amusement park outside of Snagelyville. However, within minutes, Bixby started to speed down tunnels as if she had jumped into a tube slide. Within moments, she rocketed through the water and was forced to cross her arms over her chest and lock her ankles together, lest she lose a limb while shooting through the underground gully.

The rock slide tube widened, and Bixby caught sight of where she was headed: a gigantic lake some two hundred feet below.

"Oh, boogers!" Bixby shouted, plummeting down a sudden eighty-degree drop at what felt like sixty miles an hour. She could feel the freeze-dried food leave her stomach and rest just below her tongue.

The slide leveled out near the bottom, and Bixby skimmed across the water like a skipping stone. Coming to a rest in the middle of the lake, Bixby floated motionlessly, letting her stomach settle. Once she was situated, she took a quick look around and could see that there was a beach close by.

Bixby turned to the shore and started to swim her way over. While paddling, Bixby saw that the lake was completely encased by stone walls and a domed ceiling. The only light that came into the cave was coming from directly above, from a hole no bigger than her bedroom window back in Snagelyville. As the sunlight came in, it reflected off the water, refracting the light to the walls around it. In each wall there were millions of stones of all different colors, redirecting the light yet again. For a moment, she couldn't help but look around, but a crackle in her earpiece quickly reminded Bixby that she was in last place.

Once ashore, Bixby wanted to do a microphone check to see how much damage there was to her equipment. She also tried to apologize.

"Hey, guys...Um, I'm sorry for what I said back there."

All Bixby got back in return was a buzzing sound.

"Guys?"

More buzzing.

Bixby took the piece out of her ear and tried to shake it dry, but her efforts proved futile. It was completely soaked, which meant one thing: Bixby was on her own.

"Okay, Bixby, three tunnels to choose from," she said to herself as she eyed what she assumed was the next part of the riddle.

Without hesitation, she ran into the tunnel on the left. This puzzle seemed to not favor one direction or another when it came to choosing a path. The light from the opening rapidly disappeared, and now Bixby was alone in a cave in the dark. She felt her way around, and as she did, she realized the room seemed to be curved. Keeping her left hand against the wall, she kept walking. It didn't take long before Bixby was back out at the lakefront.

"That can't be right. It was a circular room," Bixby thought to herself. "What if I try another cave?"

Bixby rushed into the middle path, and it produced the same result—a circular cave. Her final option was to go right, and it, too, was totally round.

"I need to get some light in there," Bixby said to herself, looking around to see if there were any other options except for the caves. "But how? There's nothing in here to use."

Bixby did as she always did when she was in a conundrum; she tried to see the puzzle from a different angle. Without a wall to rest upon, Bixby decided this puzzle needed a handstand.

Once upside down, the caves looked almost identical upside down as they did right side up. Nothing seemed to be out of the ordinary, except sometimes when she adjusted her hand, she would land on a stone instead of sand. Bixby's arms finally gave out, and she tumbled to the ground with a thud. As she looked up, something was blinding her. She covered her eyes and sat up. The light was gone.

Bixby originally thought maybe she'd been hit on the head too hard the night before and was seeing things; however, when she looked down, there was light reflecting off something in the sand and onto her pants. Bixby got back down on her stomach to follow the light. It led to one of the rocks that was protruding from the beach.

"Bingo," Bixby said, jumping up. She quickly started unburying as many of the rocks as she could. They were each the size of softballs and weighed about five pounds, so Bixby could only carry about five or six of them before it was too awkward to move. She piled fifteen or so in the middle of the first cave she'd explored. Running back out to the beach, Bixby's next goal was to redirect light from outside of the cave to inside.

Back home, her family used to watch her grandpa's cat from time to time. She would take her cell phone case, hold it under the sunlight, and as she wiggled her phone around, the sunlight would refract off her phone and dance on the floor. The crazy cat would chase that uncatchable light for hours.

The sun was now coming in at an angle, so Bixby would have to turn the light about ninety degrees to get it to go into her cave. All the stones were round, but she hoped that the rocks were fragile enough to break in order to reflect the light. She grabbed one and threw it as hard as she could against the side of one of the cave's outside walls. The orb was so fragile that it shattered into a million tiny pieces on the ground. Bixby dropped to her knees and found another orb. This time, Bixby walked over to the wall with the crystal and tapped it on the wall like an egg. As she expected, it cracked fairly easily. Each piece splintered into six smaller pieces that were the size of a compact mirror. Standing under one of the beams of light, Bixby held a broken shard of glass, like her cell phone, and bounced the light towards the mouth of the cave.

After a few seconds of adjusting the angle, the light reflected from one mirror into the heart of the darkness and ricocheted off of fifteen globes. Bixby could see that the cave was now fully lit. Careful not to block the reflected sunlight, Bixby rushed into the well-lit room. It was just as she had predicted: a hollowed-out round cave. On the back wall, she could now clearly see her next task etched into the stone.

Find a door here,
Hidden from sight.
There is no handle,
Wish as you might.
To have it open,
Day must be night.

"Great, I have to wait until the sun goes down?" Bixby said to herself. "But, if that is the case, how did everyone else get through? We all left at the break of day, and it can't be any later than eleven a.m."

She knew she was missing something, but now she didn't have a team to talk to about it with because her earpiece wasn't working. She had to find a way to talk to her team...but how? She walked into one of the dark caves and asked if anyone could hear her. Her earpiece was a scrambled mess. It sounded like someone was trying to talk to her, but the voice was being drowned out by heavy static.

"Focus, Bixby Timmons. You can do this all on your own. We can't fall any further behind the group," she scolded herself. She walked back onto the beach and into the next cave. She reread the words on the wall, then plopped down in the sand next to the orbs and pondered for a little while.

"It's pretty clear that I have to wait until the sun goes down. I could turn the lights off in here, and then it would be like the sun went down, but that feels more like a step backward than anything else. I wonder if there's more to the riddle in the other caves?" Bixby said out loud.

A handful at a time, Bixby started to move the orbs into the middle cave to see if she could find something else. She picked up the last orb and walked out and then back into the middle cave. She then ran over to grab the shard that sat on the beach. As she bent over to pick it up, there was already a light being emitted from the caves, but it wasn't from the new cave. Bixby realized that her original cave was still giving off a slight glow.

"Stupid, Bixby!" she shouted as she sprinted towards the entrance.

She peered in, and there was a square that looked painted on the wall. The paint must have been glow-in-the-dark and needed some light to recharge its ability to illuminate.

As she rushed in closer, she saw that another riddle had been written inside the square:

0 1 2 3 4 5 6 7 8 9
How many times can you subtract the number 5 from 25?

Bixby knew that five went into twenty-five a total of five times, so she reached up and touched the number five. For the second time in the riddle, Bixby was jolted to her butt and another burn mark seared her arm. The jolt also reminded her of the large cut on her head that still throbbed. It was not the best day Bixby had ever had when it came to injuries.

"Okay...whew," Bixby said, then stood up and tried to ignore the pain. She shook her wrists and arms in the air, trying to wiggle the throbbing away, and then fixated on the riddle again. After the bolt of electricity pulsed through her, Bixby had recognized the answer was a play on words. She could subtract five from twenty-five *five* times to get zero, but really she could only subtract five from twenty-five *once* because after that, she'd be left with twenty.

"The answer is one," she said, convincing herself to touch the one. She closed her eyes and winced as she put her hand over the chosen number symbol. When she wasn't burned, she let out a huge sigh of relief, but she was a little annoyed that nothing big happened.

"Hey, I got the answer right. What's the next step?" she said out loud.

Bixby covered the one button again, but still nothing. She was petrified to touch another number. She knew one was the right answer, but now she needed to know how to press it. Her hand didn't work, so she thought maybe one of the globes would work. Turning to leave the cave, above the doorway was another saying that was lit up in glow-in-the-dark paint.

Try as you might,
Nothing can open it,
Except for the light.

Bixby knew exactly what she had to do. She sprinted out of the cave to grab the glass shards. Then she dropped one of them under the light that was coming through the opening above the lake, angling it towards the cave door opening. With a second shard, she ran over to where the light was being reflected. She caught the reflection on her chip and started to adjust it towards the number one on the back wall that was still glowing in the dark. She was careful not to touch any other number with the light, and as the sunlight illuminated just the number one, a rumble started in the cave. From under the sand, a cylinder rose up, and a hatch popped open. Inside the hatch, a flicker of light emitted. Bixby ran over to see where she was going next.

A ladder led deep below the surface. It was lit by a series of LED bulbs that went down as far as she could see. Bixby knew she was in last place and didn't stop to enjoy her victory over her most recent puzzle. Into the great unknown she quickly climbed.

The space between Bixby and the wall behind her was less than three inches. Occasionally, she would stop climbing down and rest her back against the wall as she took a moment to breathe. Her hope was that someone feared tight spaces and that this part of the puzzle had slowed them down.

Twenty minutes later, Bixby finally made it to the ground, where she saw a well-lit path with a small trickle of water flowing beside it. Exhausted from the descent, Bixby almost fell into the stream as she cupped her hand into the fresh water and took a few big gulps. Her ears perked up as she looked around. She wasn't the only one in this tunnel. As she listened closely, trying to block out the sound of the brook she was next to, she could now hear faint voices downstream. Leaping to her feet, she pushed on down the path. She knew she wasn't out of last place yet, but she was gaining.

Because the path was gradually steepening and then turning ever so slightly downward, Bixby could hardly tell if she was running farther into the cavern or if she was slowly treading up. All she knew was that it was a difficult run. There were places where the path's ceiling was short, and Bixby had to travel in a crouched position, and sometimes it was so narrow that she had to shimmy between rocks. Bixby never stopped pushing herself to keep going. The voice of her grandfather was now playing over and over in her head.

Be strong, honest, and worthy because it gives us all a fighting chance...

The voices were getting louder with every step. She could make out Maggie's voice, along with Marin and Wesley. Bixby was at full speed as she rounded the corner and saw the opening where the three of them were diligently working on another puzzle. She never slowed down as she located where Wesley was and barreled towards him.

Maggie looked up, confused. "Bixby?"

The sound of Maggie's voice in the cave made Wesley stand up and take notice, but it was too late. Bixby lowered her shoulder and, with all her speed and strength, drove her body right into the gut of Wesley. Both of them tumbled to the ground with a loud grunt. Wesley had no idea what had hit him as the wind was knocked out of him. He gasped for air, but nothing was going in. Bixby got to her feet and grabbed for a crystal orb that was nearby. She was about to smash Wesley in the head with it when Marin grabbed her and pulled her back.

"Bixby, what are you doing?" Marin yelled.

"He ambushed me last night in my room and tied me to my cot! He left me there to die!" she yelled, struggling to get free.

"Stop," Marin said calmly as Bixby tried to wiggle free. "You can't win this fight."

Wesley, now able to breathe, pushed himself up to his hands and knees.

"I didn't have anything to do with that," he said, assessing his pain. "I don't need to cheat to beat the likes of you."

"You broke my door window and cracked me over the head to knock me out," Bixby shouted, pulling free from Marin. "I never did anything to you, and you go and try to kill me?"

"Think what you want," he said, making his way back to his puzzle. "But if you come after me again, I'll put you down for good."

Maggie, now next to Bixby, looked at the cut on her forehead. "Hey, sit down and let me clean that up for you."

"No. I've got to start working on this puzzle to catch up," Bixby replied.

"I already have the answer, so if you let me clean you up, I'll give it to you," Maggie pleaded in a whisper. "It's the least I can do for all you've done for me."

Bixby nodded, and they went over to the small stream that trickled down the path.

"Man, he got you good," Maggie said, making quick work of the wound. She washed off the blood and old coconut jelly, and then from a pocket, she pulled out a pouch made of coconut tree leaves. As she opened it, there was a clump of fresh coconut jelly ready to apply. With two fingers, she scooped some out and carefully rubbed it over the wound. It hurt a little, but Bixby was still amped up on adrenaline.

"Good thing you got some coconut jelly on it when you did. This stuff really works wonders on scrapes and burns," Maggie said, seemingly trying to shift Bixby's focus away from Wesley.

"That pouch is pretty smart. I was just carrying around a half of a coconut," Bixby said, complimenting her.

"Thanks. The leaves keep the oils in the jelly from drying out as fast," Maggie said.

"We'd better get going," Bixby said. Her head was still sore, but the new coconut oil gave some relief.

"Okay, so while we're away from the group...the puzzle is pretty simple. Greg is kind of a hack at this whole puzzle-solving thing. He's smart but has no clue that he gives away the answer every time he's solving them because he isn't cautious about who sees," Maggie said. "It's very similar to the beach puzzle where you looked like you drowned."

"Keep going," Bixby said as she saw her pile of things.

"There's a bunch of bamboo sticks, twine, some flimsy paper, tape, a match, a piece of tinfoil, and a candle. The riddle on the wall says something about letting your light go free," Maggie told her. "It's called a Chinese torch. I used to make them with my cousins on the Fourth of July. What you need to do is make a big circle roughly ten inches wide with the bamboo sticks. Then make an X in the middle with your bamboo circle with two more bamboo sticks. Use the tape and twine for that. In the middle of the X is where your wick is going to sit." Maggie walked Bixby through several more steps as she finished instructing her on how to make a Chinese lantern.

"This last step is extremely important, Bixby. Light the lantern and let it start to float up. Once you have it rising, you must climb the wall with it. You can blow on the lantern, but *do not* touch it to make sure it goes up through that hole in the cave. If you get it to fly out of here, you get to disappear down that tunnel up there," Maggie pointed to the only exit in the room. "If you fail, you have to start again. The pieces show up after five minutes of waiting," she said. "This will be my second try."

"I think I understand," Bixby said.

"Good. This makes us fairly even, right?" Maggie asked.

"I think so," Bixby said, getting up from her seated position. She was glad to have helped Maggie because she would have been completely lost on this puzzle. Bixby made her way over to her items and quickly went to work. She could see Wesley was already taping his paper to the outside of his lantern, and she didn't want to fall any further behind. Marin was already scaling the wall with her lantern, but she slipped on a rock at the beginning of her climb. By the time she was able to catch up, her lantern had smashed into the wall and torn a hole in the side of the paper. It fluttered and crashed to the sand below in a blaze of glory. Marin was then zapped with the usual shock on her arm that contestants got when they didn't get something right.

"For all of this, I may break Cody's nose when I meet him," she said, rubbing her arm.

Wesley's lantern was ready to fly, so he rushed over to the wall, and with the last little bit of candle burning, he lit the cloth. Up it went. It took him no time at all to scale the wall. He gave one little puff to adjust its trajectory, and through the hole in the cavern it went.

"It was fun, Bixby," he shouted down with a wave and a wink. With that snide remark, he was gone.

"I should have let you knock his teeth out," Marin said. "Your sappy, *do-the-right-thing* attitude is rubbing off on me."

Bixby cracked a smile as she began taping the paper to the side of her lantern.

Maggie was finished with her balloon and hurried to the rock wall. "Wish me luck," she said.

The second time was a charm for Maggie. Her lantern didn't need any wind aid, and it went straight up and straight through the hole in the ceiling. "Catch me if you can," Maggie followed with a laugh.

Minutes later, Bixby was putting the final touches on her lantern, and Marin started in on her. "I could crush that right now, and you'd have to wait five minutes to start again."

"Then when your stuff showed up, I would crush yours, and we'd have a pretty vicious cycle," Bixby replied.

"Why are you trying so hard to make friends with everyone, Bixby? Don't you realize that, at one point or another, you're going to have to start worrying about yourself if you plan on winning this thing?"

"I do worry about myself, but I was also taught that to let someone bully someone else without helping is just as bad as being the bully. If I'm going to win this thing, I'm going to win it fairly."

Marin burst out laughing. "Is that why you wear that earpiece?" she said, stopping Bixby in her tracks. "You're not the only one talking with people outside of the puzzle, Bixby. Practically everyone's cheating one way or another."

"How do you know it's not actually for hearing?" Bixby questioned.

"I first saw it when we were eating outside of the limo doors. I thought nothing of it, and when you started talking to yourself at the bridge, really loudly, I was sure that you were part deaf. It wasn't until Wesley stole it from you at the beach that I knew you weren't. He spoke in a whisper in the ear you normally wore it in, and you understood. And then when you stood up, you put it in your pocket and ran off, and that sealed it."

"Well, it must not be cheating if the Riddle doesn't zap you," Bixby replied, half expecting a shock after being so bold. "So, if everyone is cheating, how would you say you're doing it?"

"I watch people," Marin started as Bixby lit her lantern and climbed.

"You snipe answers."

Marin shrugged. "I guess. It's a sound strategy."

"Why are you telling me all of this?" Bixby asked.

"Because you have a huge target on your back, and I don't want a guilty conscience. Don't say I didn't warn you," Marin cautioned as her pieces reappeared in the sand.

As Bixby reached the top, her lantern made its way through the ceiling void with inches on one side to spare. Curious, Bixby stopped and asked one final question.

"You said practically everyone has cheated. Who hasn't?" she asked.

"I'll let you try and figure that out on your own."

With that, the conversation ended, and Bixby disappeared through the open door.

The path was just as dark and dank as before. Bixby started to jog, knowing that Marin was only going to be a few minutes behind her. She cleared her mind and started to think about their conversation; the thought of being out of last place instantly made her happy, but if Marin knew she was talking to the outside world, what else did she know? Wesley had to be cheating to be able to catch up to the group over and over, but neither Greg nor Maggie seemed like they were cheating. But maybe she was wrong. Maybe Wesley, and because he was buddies with Greg, they could be sharing the answers. That would make Greg a cheat, too, right? Maggie was following her breadcrumbs which would then make her a cheater along with Bixby.

There were at least ten scenarios on how people were cheating that flooded Bixby's mind. Her brain was so full of ideas, she almost missed the fact that there was a cliff with a bottomless pit right in front of her. Bixby's feet glided along the dirt floor and slid to a stop only a few inches from the edge. She tried to maintain her balance by making big circles with her hands and arms. Reaching out, she barely caught a root hanging from the wall but managed to pull herself to safety.

"Yikes!" she cried. "That was close."

Bixby looked over the edge and couldn't see the bottom. There were no riddles on the walls, and the other side was almost thirty feet away. Bixby had seen in the movies where the path was invisible. To tell where it led, she had to throw dirt over the cliff, and if it landed on the unseen path, she would know where to step. Unfortunately, this wasn't like the movies, and the dirt simply sailed over the cliff.

"Okay, now what?" she wondered, continuing to clutch the tree root. Slowly, she turned to look at the root she was grasping, following it up to the top of the cave. Every three or four feet there was another shorter root protruding from above.

"Me. Tarzan," Bixby said, then wasted no time climbing up the root, swinging from one vine to the next. As she reached the last vine, she realized that there was no way to climb down safely. She was going to have to swing over to the ledge, let go, and hope she made it far enough to survive. With a big breath, she started to swing as hard as she could on the vine, hoping it wouldn't break. With one last swing, she let go of the rope and, on the edge of the cliff, hit the dirt and tumbled to a stop on her butt.

"*Eshh, ahhh,*" she breathed in and out again in pain, certain she'd broken her tailbone.

"Make that the third time I almost died today," she said aloud, trying to walk off the pain. She could hear footsteps coming and knew Marin would have no trouble with this test since it was a physical one.

Bixby took off running again, a breeze on her face now. If she'd been swinging on tree roots, she couldn't be too far underground. Bixby didn't want another foot race with Marin, so she pushed as hard as she could go. There was sunlight up ahead. Bixby had completed several challenges today, and if today was going to be like the others, the checkpoint had to be up ahead. As she came to the cave's exit, Bixby had to stop momentarily to let her eyes adjust to the light; being in a cave for almost a whole day made it hard to focus in full sunlight. Bixby rubbed her eyes and looked around for the next campfire.

"Nothing," Bixby said.

"Bixby?" a voice shouted in her ear.

"Hucklebee?" Bixby replied.

"Hey, everyone, she can hear us!" Hucklebee shouted so loud it made her ears ring.

"Bixby!" came shouts from all her family.

"Guys, I can hear you. I thought the water wiped this thing out," she said, talking about the earpiece.

"There must be some interference when you go under-ground. We could see you on the Holo-TV, but there was no signal at all to your coin. Coming or going," Tipton said.

"Bixby, are you okay?" Mrs. Timmons screeched.

"Yes, Mom. I got a nasty bump on the head, but I'm okay," Bixby said.

"When you get home, I will fix you right up," Miss Marmalade interjected.

"I heard Grandpa's voice back at the beach. Did you all hear it?" Bixby asked, hoping she wasn't crazy.

"Bixby, Grandpa has been gone for a long time now," Mrs. Timmons said, sounding worried.

"I know you think I'm crazy, but I heard him through the earpiece just before I left the ocean," Bixby said, trying to con-vince the team that she wasn't looney.

"Bixby, you can tell us more about it when you get home, but for now, you need to run!" Harvey shouted, switching topics.

"What do you mean?" Bixby asked.

"You have to go back underground, Bixby, which means we'll probably lose you, and there are no campfires up ahead. The other kids are still running," he filled her in as he searched the other contestant's feeds.

"This could be the last leg of the race, then," Bixby realized aloud.

"It could be," Harvey said.

Bixby searched for another cave entrance, which wasn't hard to spot, as her legs began to churn again.

"I'm sorry about what I said this morning. Everything was happening so fast, and I was scared," Bixby continued in hast knowing the signal was going to drop.

"Bixby, this is the first time we've heard anything from you all day," Mrs. Timmons answered.

Bixby gasped with a bit of joy. Tipton was the only one to hear those terrible things she'd said. Knowing that Tipton would be watching on his Holo-Writer at school, she simply said loud enough for the news feed to hear, "Sorry, T."

"Remember that we're all here for you, Bixby," Mrs. Timmons consoled, despite not knowing what was troubling her. "Your Dad has been called into work every day for extremely long hours. It seems they know that he's helping you. They're trying to make it impossible for him to do so."

The realization that her dad wasn't abandoning her made her heart race.

"Tell him I'm sorry for doubting him," she said as she reached the end of the trail that led into the side of the next mountain.

"He already knows, Bixby. Now go get 'em!" she shouted. A cheer rang in her ear from her family, and Hucklebee shouted a positive thought: "You don't have to outrun the bear! You just have to outrun the person in fifth place!"

Bixby laughed, pausing briefly at the mouth of the cavern. With renewed strength, knowing that her family didn't hate her, she tore off into the opening.

CHAPTER EIGHTEEN
CHEATERS NEVER PROSPER

AT THE BASE of the tunnel, before moving further downward, Bixby stopped to let her eyes adjust to the deep darkness around her. It also allowed her to peek back to see if Marin was closing in on her. Just as she'd thought, Marin was already emerging from the last cave, blinded by the light. Bixby quickly disappeared, in hopes that she didn't see her go in.

There was the distinct sound of water dripping from the stalactites hanging from above and splashing on the floor of the cave. Bixby could hear footsteps pacing along the ground ahead of her. She put her left hand on the wall and began her journey in.

For every step the other person was taking, Bixby tried to take two quiet steps. The sound of the other person's feet splashing through the puddles made it easy for Bixby to tell she was getting closer. Suddenly, the footsteps broke out into a run. Bixby picked up her pace but couldn't see a thing as she tried to keep up with the person in front of her. She was hoping that it wasn't Wesley because he could do some serious damage here in the dark.

Up ahead, there was a glow much different than the orbs back in the last cave. It was greenish blue, and as Bixby drew closer, she could see that there was another massive cave structure up ahead. This must have been where the other footsteps started to run. Bixby followed suit as she burst into what looked like the middle of a hollowed-out mountain. She looked up, and there was a single hole hundreds of feet above, in the very top of the mountain where Bixby envisioned lava would spill out. But there was no lava, only an empty mountain.

"Again, with the heights, Cody," she moaned.

Bixby could see a shadow of Maggie running towards the opposite side of the floor of the cavern. Bixby ran after her. As she went, she could also see the shadows of the boys making their way up the side of the inner wall. To Bixby's surprise, they were not as far up the side of the mountain as she had thought they would be. Greg was about a hundred feet up, and Wesley was only moments behind him. The path to the top encompassed the inside of the mountain's walls many times. Bixby could see the first leg of her climb was a simple path, but it was followed by wall climbs, rope swings, and riddle walls. Bixby's only chance was to zip through the riddle walls and hope to make up enough time to compensate for her lack of physical strength.

Maggie was already climbing up the steep hill as Bixby approached. Marin was hot on their trail as she made her way into the vast expanse of the mountain.

Bixby quickly started her climb. Each time Bixby pushed herself further up the mountain face, loose rocks crashed down below her. Bixby paid close attention to where Maggie was as rocks fell with every step. Bixby was still having trouble recognizing what was giving the mountain its glow, but she was grateful for what little light it gave. Without it, each of Maggie's steps had the potential of sending down a rock to thump her on her already well-beaten head.

It was hard to make out at first, but as Bixby finished scaling the loose rocks, she could see Maggie working on a riddle. Bixby raced to the wall to try and catch up, but Maggie had already dropped her glowing rock and scaled the ladder that lurched from the wall beside her.

Approaching the riddle, Bixby saw that the words on the wall were hard to make out, so she reached down for the glowing stone Maggie had discarded. She expected to grab something rough in texture, but instead it was warm and squishy.

"Glowworms," Maggie said from above her, then laughed at Bixby's grossed out face.

Knowing it was her only option, Bixby quickly went over to the wall with a slime-covered hand and read the riddle:

An airplane crashes on a desert island.
Three people survive: the co-pilot, plane mechanic, and a pregnant woman.

256

There is only enough water for two passengers to survive long enough to fix the plane and fly away.

Who gets the water and why?

"This riddle is kind of dark," Bixby whispered to herself, pondering. "Okay, if I give it to the mechanic and the pilot, then the lady and her baby dies. Which is the obvious answer, so there must be a catch," Bixby reasoned. "But...what if the lady is also the co-pilot?" She decided against it, though, because the riddle specifically listed the lady *and* the co-pilot, separately, even if they considered her baby as a passenger.

Bixby could now hear Marin making her way up the rock wall.

"Think, Bixby! Think!" she said in a muffled shout, aware of more seconds slipping by.

"*Duh!*" she shouted, running over with the slime from the worm and wrote in the empty space below the riddle:

The pregnant woman and the mechanic. The co-pilot is not a passenger.

Rock steps appeared up the side of the mountain, and Bixby dashed towards them. Maggie was nearing the top of the stairs that were sticking out of the side of the wall. They wouldn't be as scary if it weren't for the fact that there was no railing to hold on to; each landing was only a foot wide and hung well over a hundred feet off the ground. Bixby wobbled up the first few, attuning herself to being up so high. Maggie didn't seem to be a big fan of heights, either, as Bixby was able to get within ten steps of her before Maggie reached another platform. As Bixby reached the same landing, Maggie was already putting the finishing touches on another puzzle. It was a slide puzzle just like the one over Bixby's fireplace back at Pinnacle Manor. Maggie climbed the ladder rungs that emerged from the wall to the next landing. Bixby grabbed another gooey worm, made her way to the jumbled slide puzzle, and started to shuffle the tiles into place. Lucky for Bixby, she was able to see the final picture of Maggie's slide puzzle before she finished. Since she knew what the picture was supposed to look like, Bixby made quick work of it.

"Done," she said, slamming the last piece in place. She looked over, waiting for the ladder to appear. On cue, the rungs glided out from the wall, and Bixby raced to the top. Now she could see that not only was she gaining on Maggie, but the boys were not much farther ahead. What came next made Bixby smile.

"This could be fun," Bixby said as she watched Maggie grab a slingshot from a table in the middle of the platform. She was firing stones at several levers that were holding a footbridge in the upright position. Maggie had already struck two of the three of her levers when Bixby got to the table and put her wrist rocket on. Her first shot missed wide right, almost hitting Maggie's last lever.

"Feel free to knock that one over for me," Maggie said in a rushed but joking voice.

"Yeah, I'll pass," Bixby replied, reloading her weapon.

"Huh, look at that," Maggie said as she got her bridge to fall. "Guess I don't need your help after all."

With that, Maggie dashed across.

It took Bixby a total of ten rocks to knock down all of her levers. As she slipped the slingshot from her wrist, she could hear the slide puzzle clacking below her. Marin was right behind her.

The next obstacle seemed easy if it weren't for the fact that she was now hundreds of feet off the ground. All she had to do was sit down in a human-sized slingshot, push it back to the big X on the floor and throw herself across a twenty-foot crevasse. "This obstacle must test our bravery, huh?" Bixby said, unsure if anyone was hearing her. Already beaten and bruised from the moment she'd woken up this morning, Bixby didn't have a place on her body that didn't hurt; what was one more bruise?

Maggie was already on the other side of the void, working on a puzzle. Bixby rushed over to the sling and sat down in it, pushing it back with all her might. She reached the spot where she was standing right over the X.

"Please say I'm right on this one, Grandpa?" Bixby said, just before she picked her feet up off the ground and went flying through the air. She easily cleared the empty space but realized she was about to make a crash landing. Bixby curled up in a ball, closed her eyes, and braced for impact. Much to her surprise, her landing was not painful at all. Instead, the abrupt stop was soft and squishy, like a mat from her gym class. As she opened her eyes, she got a big surprise; it wasn't a mat at all. She had squished at least a thousand glowworms as she skid across the floor; she was now covered in slime.

"The hits just keep on coming," Bixby grumbled.

Knowing that there wasn't much she could do about it now, Bixby made her way over to the puzzle that Maggie was still working on.

"Awe, you crushed out my light," Maggie said, squinting closer to the puzzle.

"Sorry about that," Bixby said instinctively, making her way to the puzzle.

Above them was a series of numbers:

1-12-13-15-19-20 20-8-5-18-5

Thanks to Harvey's suggestion back at the bridge with the robed man, Bixby quickly recognized it to be an actual number cypher. Each number corresponded with a letter of the alphabet. 1=A 2=B 3=C; and so on. She reached down to the back of her leg and scraped off some glowworm goo and started writing letters:

ALMOST THERE

Bixby and Maggie each turned towards each other, and in a panic, raced towards where the ladder rungs slid out from the wall. Maggie reached it first, and Bixby followed right behind.

"Do you think it means almost to the end of this leg of the puzzle, or almost to the end of the level?" Maggie questioned Bixby as they went up.

"I don't know, but I do know we're still ahead of Marin. If it means we're almost to the end of the level, we both still have a chance to finish in the top four," Bixby said, looking up to see how many more rungs were left to climb. Bixby's attention was drawn to the tread on Maggie's boots. The glowworm ooze on Bixby's shirt was now flickering off something shiny. Bixby raced to get as close as she could. As Maggie stopped to step over to the platform, she could see that there was a large chunk of glass wedged into the tread of her shoe. It wasn't the crystal from the beach; that had a mirror quality to it. This was broken glass, like that from a shattered hut window.

Bixby froze. The crunch of the glass that Bixby heard behind her before someone knocked her lights out hadn't been Wesley; it had been *Maggie*.

Eventually, Bixby kicked herself back in gear and reached the platform where Maggie was.

"We've almost caught the boys," Maggie said proudly, pointing to Greg and Wesley, who were both climbing the ladder up to the top of the mountain's lip. Bixby's face had turned from anticipation to anger, and she was sure that Maggie could see it.

Maggie cocked her head. "What's up?"

"Why did you do it?" Bixby asked.

"Do what?"

"It was you who tied me to the bed," Bixby said, tone full of anger. "You wrote the letter that sounded like something Wesley would write, threw the rock through my window, just like I did to Wesley. Then you bashed me in the head, just like Marin did to Wesley on the beach as he accused me of hitting him with the coconut."

"Come on, Bixby, we don't have time for this. The boys are getting away," Maggie urged.

"I stood up for you, Maggie!" Bixby shouted. "The only place you could have gotten the glass jammed in the bottom of your shoe was just before you cracked me over the head!"

Maggie's face went cold, and her tone went almost evil.

"Do you know how hard it was acting like I was your friend, Bixby? I wanted to knock Marin off first, but you kept coming around right when I had the chance to pin her down. I came close twice. The first time was the rock climb; if you weren't so nosey, I could have caught her and yanked her off the side of that mountain. The second time was at the beach. I had the chance to sabotage her boat, but you got your arm burned at the coconut trees and let out a scream. Everyone turned around, and Marin saw that I was following her into the ocean.

Bixby's eyes filled with terror, thinking about how much she had aided Mad Maggie. "I gave you clues to help you catch up to us," Bixby said, frustrated at her stupidity.

"That's why I wanted to go after Marin first, but you kept getting in the way," Maggie said as she drew closer.

"Your plan was to leave someone stranded in each level?" Bixby asked, looking for a way out.

"Wesley was right. You don't belong here," Maggie hissed as she pulled a shard of glass wrapped with part of a towel for a handle from her pocket. "Now then, since you're on to my strategy, you have two choices. You're going to either jump off the edge willingly, or I'm going to force you off."

"Seriously?" Bixby shouted as she quickly glanced over her shoulder at the five hundred foot drop below her.

"Seriously," Maggie growled as she took her first swipe. Bixby jumped back in time to avoid getting gutted, and when Maggie lunged immediately after, Bixby put some of her training to use. She caught Maggie in the face with a fist. The girl's nose crunched, and blood gushed.

Maggie staggered back as she wiped herself clean with the back of her sleeve. "I keep underestimating you, Bixby. I thought for sure you'd jump off the edge for me."

Maggie swiped again and missed. Bixby went to reach for the glass, but with a backhand, Maggie buried the knife into her right arm, knocking Bixby to the ground. Bixby winced as she saw blood start to pool on her sleeve. Maggie pounced on top of Bixby, intent on finishing her off once and for all.

"That hundred million dollars belongs to me. You should have lived out your life on that beach, Bixby," Maggie said, rocking forward to push Bixby over the brink of the cliff.

Thunk.

Maggie's body suddenly went limp and collapsed. The knife slipped from Maggie's hand and fell into the darkness below. The extra weight was more than Bixby could support as she started falling. Maggie's shirt collar tightened around her neck, and Bixby could feel a muscular grip now latched to her left wrist. With a jolt, Bixby was heaved up onto the platform.

"I knew she couldn't be trusted," Marin said, pulling Maggie over to the other side of the platform. "You okay, Bixby?" she asked, untying Maggie's shoestrings in order to use them to tie her hands behind her back.

Bixby's mind was swirling so much that she could hardly see straight, let alone answer. She rushed to look at her arm where the knife had entered her shirt. Normally, a thrust like that would have gone all the way through her arm, but as she looked over her wound, something had stopped it from pushing all the way into her skin. Tugging at her sleeve, she saw the family crest ripped in half and small electronic parts dangling out of it. The knife had found its way through the coin, but the metal had stopped it from ripping into her arm. Bixby sat up and breathed a sigh of relief. "Four times in one day," Bixby muttered. "This is really getting old."

When Marin had finished tying up Maggie, she turned her attention towards Bixby, who was still in a daze from the near-death experience.

"Bixby? You with me?" Marin asked, snapping her fingers in front of Bixby's face.

"Yeah, um, yeah, I'm here," Bixby said, starting to refocus.

"Listen, we can stay here until you're feeling up to moving and finish third and fourth, or we can make a run at those two meatheads," Marin offered.

"What about her?" Bixby asked, pointing towards Maggie in the corner.

"She's out cold, but when she wakes up, she'll eventually make her way out of these knots."

"She tried to kill me, *twice*," Bixby replied, shocked at what she had just said. "She deserves to be left here forever."

"I don't want that on my conscience. Now, you want to stay here and wait until she wakes up, or catch those two pretty boys up ahead? Either way, I'm going."

Bixby gathered her thoughts and nodded. "Alright, let's go."

Helping Bixby to her feet, Marin noticed the broken chip on her sleeve. "Clever girl," she said.

"I get that a lot," Bixby said, reaching into Maggie's pocket for her leaf pouch filled with coconut jelly. She quickly applied it to her fresh wound and wrapped the leaf back up, putting it in her own pocket this time.

"Race ya!" Bixby said with a smirk.

CHAPTER NINETEEN

BRAINS OR BRAWN?

IT WAS A single line. No more. No less.

drop thy Dog or Can?

"What kind of gibberish is this?" Marin asked. "I don't see a dog or a can anywhere," she said, holding a glowworm out to see if she could find anything that resembled the two artifacts.

Bixby and Marin had made their way to the last puzzle in the mountain, and Bixby had a chance to do a little teaching as they went.

"My grandpa used to say that if the riddle was short and made no sense, then it was probably an anagram," Bixby said, starting to silently untwist the letters in her mind.

"Speak English, Timmons," Marin said, making her way back to the riddle wall.

"An anagram is when you take the letters of one phrase and turn it into another while using all the same letters," Bixby instructed, seeing that Marin was still a little confused.

"The words 'Dog' and 'Can' shouldn't be capitalized, grammatically speaking," Bixby said.

"Yeah, so?" Marin questioned.

"So, if this is an anagram, then the 'D' and the 'C' are important clues," Bixby continued.

"Clues to what? A sentence? A phrase? A name?" Marin asked.

"It's definitely a name," Bixby said, scraping the letters C and then D on the wall with a little space in between. "Do we know anyone with the initials 'C.D.'?" Bixby asked, already knowing the answer to her question.

Marin took only a few seconds to think, but then she grabbed some of the glowworm slime off her own shirt, and, separately, they each wrote out:

Cody Dragonthorp

The ladder slid out, and Bixby insisted, "After you." Marin didn't hesitate because they were now in a hurry to catch the boys.

At the peak of the mountain, they could see the entire landscape of Level 1. Below them, the coastline stretched out along the right of the mountain, and to the left was the forest that led to the prairie where Marin and Bixby shared a close footrace.

"I almost beat you," Bixby said, knowing they were looking at the same spot in the distance.

"Never had a chance," Marin replied.

"I guess the overcast sky hid this mountain from us the whole time," Bixby said, looking out at the rest of the level.

"Yep," was the only reply Marin could give, already absorbed in the next challenge.

"What is it?" Bixby asked.

"Did I ever mention that I hate heights?" Marin asked.

"I thought I was the only one," Bixby said, coming to the realization of what they had to do next.

"*Rock, Paper, Scissors* to see who goes first?" Bixby asked.

"I went up the ladder first, so it's your turn," Marin insisted.

Bixby and Marin quickly strapped on the harnesses that were sitting on a table next to a cliff. On the desk was also a note that read:

Use the brake at the bottom or your stop will not be pleasant.

Bixby quickly added zip line to the things that involved heights that she was not a fan of.

Above the table was a wire connected to the side of the mountain, and it zig-zagged all the way down the side of the mountain, over the coastline, and through the treetops of the forest, finally stopping just over the bridge where they'd first started. The boys were almost done with their ride as Bixby clipped in.

"See you at the bottom," Bixby said, lifting her feet up to increase her speed. For the first time in a long time, being a few hundred feet above the ground wasn't so scary. The wind whipped in Bixby's hair as she zipped along. She could see the hole in the top of the cave where the Crystal Lake challenge was. Bixby shuddered at the idea that she'd actually ridden a rocket slide into that cave. Then there was the coastline where she'd started her day off tied to a bed. Other than hearing her Grandpa's voice, it was one part of the adventure she wanted to forget. She flew over the puzzle monument where she got her first arm burn and the only lead of the tournament. The sun had just started to set over the ocean, which was completely calm at this point—the view was spectacular. She took a moment to watch the beautiful colors she hadn't noticed while worrying about solving puzzles.

Minutes later, she was riding through the treetops where her shadow mimicked her for hours. Bixby could see the path wound back and forth a hundred times.

"That's why it took me forever to get from the bridge to the stone door," Bixby mumbled to herself.

"The bridge!" Bixby exclaimed. She quickly looked for the hand brake and started to slow herself down. She could now see the tower where the whole puzzle began. The boys had already dismounted and were almost to the doorway. Bixby decided that the run would be a lot shorter if she unbuckled her vest at the end of the bridge instead of all the way down at the bottom of the hill. She was now ten feet above the ground and still zipping along. It was her only option if she wanted to catch up with the two boys.

Bixby braced herself for a rough landing. With all her might, she pulled on the hand brake, and it shot out sparks as it tried to slow her down. Just over the bridge, she gave the buckle on the front of her vest a tug. Bixby dropped from her harness, and the ground came up on her just as violently as she'd expected. She tumbled and rolled across the dirt until she skidded to a complete stop. Standing up, she could see that Marin was right behind her and getting ready to do the same maneuver.

"Get out of the way!" she screamed as the buckle unclasped.

Bixby jumped as hard as she could sideways, but Marin's legs clipped Bixby's and sent them both cartwheeling through the air. As they both came to rest on the ground, each of them let out a groan.

"You okay, Marin?" Bixby asked.

"Yeah, you?" Marin replied.

"Not your best landing," Bixby said as they both stumbled to their feet.

"I have had better," Marin agreed. "Are you ready to beat those two chumps?"

"Lead the way," Bixby said with a wave of her hand, and she and Marin started to run to the castle.

As they approached the door, they could hear the two boys arguing.

"Dude, the door doesn't work!" Greg shouted.

"It has to. The riddle says enter with the turn of the apex!" Not a moment later, Wesley yelled as the door zapped him.

Bixby and Marin slowly made their way up the spiral staircase. They smirked at the boys as they zapped themselves over and over while trying to open the door that would lead them into the first limo room they'd left not three days ago.

"Look who we caught up to," Bixby snarked.

"I thought for sure you two dopes would already have this figured out," Marin mocked.

"And I thought for sure you'd show up, Marin, but Bixby is definitely a surprise," Wesley said as he stood blocking the door while Greg fiddled with the latch.

"Have you tried *open sesame*?" Bixby heckled a little, seeing that Wesley's arms were now a complete red blister. "You've been rushing through all the possible answers. That's why your arms are raw," Bixby said, finally prodding Wesley about his injuries.

"Bixby, people don't solve puzzles for a living. In the real world, I will have a real job, with real power, and real responsibility. Peons like you will do the work to get me answers that I need. You'll learn that when I become your boss someday," Wesley snarled as Greg continued to fiddle with the door latch.

"You're absolutely right, Wesley. But here you morons are, too dumb to figure it out on your own, so you use the trial and error method," Bixby continued. "The only problem with that approach is that now the peons have the answer, and you don't."

Greg's head popped up from his search, "What do you mean?"

"You're dead, Bixby Timmons!" came a blood-curdling shriek from outside on the zip line.

"Time to bounce," Bixby said, as the girls turned and raced towards the spiral stairs.

In hopes of detaining Bixby and Marin for the final answer, the two boys raced after them. Bixby quickly leapt on the banister and spun down the spiral staircase faster than ever before. Marin followed suit, and by the time the boys could get halfway down the stairs, Maggie burst through the door.

On the back wall, there was a stone that had been moved away from its original position. The girls stood at the threshold, looking up at the boys. Maggie assessed the room and immediately lunged towards Bixby and Marin.

"She's all yours, boys!" Bixby hollered, stepping through the opening, followed by Marin. With a jolt, Maggie smacked into the stone that slammed shut behind the two girls, and a fresh burn appeared on her arm as she crumpled to the ground.

Marin and Bixby recognized the room upon entry—stark white with a table of food in the far corner, surrounded by lounge chairs. Neither wasted any time digging into the feast that lay before them.

"You realize if Maggie comes through that door before the boys, she's going to try to kill each of us as often as possible during the next level?" Marin commented in between her carnivorous devouring of chicken wings.

BRAINS OR BRAWN?

Bixby was busy piling turkey between two pieces of bread as she pondered that thought, "You realize that no matter who comes through that door, you and I are stuck together until the end?"

"I don't follow you, Timmons." Marin said, barbeque sauce dripping down her cheek.

"If Maggie comes through that door, she'll try to team up with whoever comes through with her. If it's Greg, the three of us eliminate her together. If it's Wesley, then it's the crazy kids versus us; and if it's the boys...boys against girls. No matter what, you and I are stuck together for the next level."

"I'm okay with that, Timmons, as long as you put in a little work to get in shape," Marin poked at her.

"As long as you put in a little work with actual puzzle solving," Bixby jabbed right back, but she still put down her sandwich, knowing they were a big reason she was out of shape.

They both slouched down in a lounge chair and waited. Who would come through the door next? The seconds ticked by. Then minutes.

"They can't be that stupid," Marin said, now extremely impatient. She stood up and started pacing the floor.

"The riddle was pretty easy, Marin," said Bixby. "A turn of the Apex basically says turn the crest. It was a play-on-words riddle. There's only one crest in that whole place. In fact, it was the only thing in the entire place you could conceivably turn.

The familiar sounds of steal clanking together started as the wall lock shifted open. Through the door tumbled Wesley.

"Get me away from that crazy chick!" he shouted in terror.

"Whoa, man. What happened to you?" Marin asked, seeing Wesley's face beaten almost to a pulp.

"She went nuts after you went through that door. She started screaming about being set up and framed for a crime she didn't commit. Greg tried to hold her down, but she started swinging at us, saying we were conspiring against her. She packs more of a punch than you think," Wesley said, trying to control his breathing.

"We can tell from your face," Bixby said, smiling.

"This is all because of you, Bixby!" he shouted. "She wanted you. I should throw you back in there with her!"

As he finished his rant, the clanking noise happened again, and the door swung open. Through the archway barreled Greg and Maggie. It was impossible to tell who'd crossed the threshold first, but Maggie didn't stop to find out; she had Bixby lined up in her sights. Bixby had no time to react; Maggie was now airborne. The only thing Bixby could do was turn her body as Maggie's arm caught her around the neck, throwing them both into the food table.

Bixby could feel herself roll through the dessert section as they toppled to the ground. She closed her eyes and braced for impact. Maggie clung to her throat while they tumbled. The floor came with a hard thud on her shoulder as she rolled to a stop. Jumping to her feet, Bixby whirled around and swung in self-defense, but her strike was caught midair, and she crumpled to the ground. Luckily for Bixby, the fight didn't go any further because her shoulder was now in horrendous pain.

"I believe you should calm down now, Miss Timmons, before I allow your family to enter the Launch Room," Arthur said with Bixby's fist tightly grasped in his palm.

She was back at Pinnacle Manor. In her very own Launch Room. Alive.

The door slid open, and her team engulfed her. Mrs. Timmons reached Bixby first with a hug as Mr. Timmons propped her body up. Bixby smiled at the faces of her loved ones, as one by one, they congratulated her on winning Level One. Her body was battered and almost to the point of being completely broken from the last few days of challenges. Miss Marmalade began to work on cleaning up the gash on her head and burns on her arms. Just like they'd seen on the Holo-TV, Bixby had received all the bashing in the Launch Room that she had in the Riddle.

Weak, she rested her head on Mr. Timmons's shoulder as he lifted her up from the cold slab.

"Thank you," she whispered.

"Let's get her to her room," Mr. Timmons said as he carried her wrecked body down the corridor towards the Great Hall. Hucklebee was reciting well wishes about perseverance as Tipton was assessing the damage to the equipment. Her earpiece was barely salvageable, and the prototype of the coin that he'd created was now sliced nearly in half.

As the team entered the Great Hall, Bixby could see Harvey standing in front of the TV watching the live feed. He must have stayed while everyone went to the Launch Room.

"Who moved on?" Bixby asked, raising her head from her father's shoulder. He gingerly set her down upon her request.

"Maggie solved the puzzle first, but somehow Greg must have beaten her through the door by a hair," Harvey said, still focused on the replay of the last two contestants dashing towards the portal. "The angle is a little weird," he explained. Unable to see what Harvey was getting at, Bixby squinted at the replay to catch any subtleties. Before anything stood out, the footage stopped short and cut to a reporter with the words 'Breaking News' rolling at the bottom of the screen.

As Bixby stood beside Harvey, and the rest of the team watched on, the final results flashed up on the Holo-TV: Bixby had a new ally in Marin, and she would need it. Wesley still hated her, and he also still had his alliance with Dragonthorp Estate intact. Mad Maggie's name sat at the bottom of the list with a black line through it. For Bixby, the black line brought a welcomed relief, knowing Mad Maggie wasn't going to be around trying to pummel her next time she entered the puzzle. Bixby did, however, have growing concerns about facing the boys with an ally she barely knew.

At that moment, none of it mattered. Bixby was surrounded by her entire family, and she knew that the people in that room, both new kin and old, were all she needed. Even Harvey was getting a little emotional as he uncharacteristically put his arm around her shoulder.

"We have a lot of work to do to get you ready for the next round of riddles," Harvey said, still staring at the screen.

BRAINS OR BRAWN?

"I could really use a turkey, cheese, and hot sauce sandwich right now," Bixby said, exhausted.

Acknowledgments

This book is for those who seek out the right thing to do, and in so doing, find themselves exploring depths of this life never thought possible. Doing the right thing may have costs, but will never come back void of benefits. Love is always the answer to the puzzle of life.

Love is why we...
    stand up for the weak,
    comfort those who are sad,
    rejoice in other's victories,
    speak for those who are without a voice,
    and befriend those who, like us, have been created unique.

About the Author

Dwight D. Karkan is a man of puzzles, and he loves the challenge of a good riddle! Currently, his favorite puzzles and riddles are being a parent, husband, and youth pastor. Dwight knows we are all designed as a beautiful combination of awesomeness, uniqueness, passion, gifts, and talents, and the only way to get a little closer to discovering the answer of who we are is by engaging each other with love.

In 2019, Dwight's daughter Selah was diagnosed with Leukemia which has been their family's biggest puzzle yet! His hope for Bixby Timmons is not only to bring a light to students who want to do bigger things than they think they are capable, but also to help families who have been through a similar struggle. If you would like to know more about how Bixby is helping those in need, join our team on our Facebook Group "Bixby Timmons Series" or visit his website www.dwightkarkan.com

ABOUT THE PUBLISHER

Tiny Fox Press LLC
5020 Kingsley Road
North Port, FL 34287

www.tinyfoxpress.com